Kal covered her hand.

"In order to make this betrothal really work, there will have to be an obvious attraction between us. It would be best if people assumed we were in love."

"In love?" Cynehild repeated.

"Can you do that? Can you pretend you desire me?"

"Possibly," she said, barely above a whisper.

"Good." He leaned over the table and brushed his lips against hers, then he sat back.

She touched her mouth. "Simply being betrothed doesn't confer the right to kiss or cuddle with impunity."

"In my culture it does. We don't consider cuddling, as you call it, to be anything but pleasurable."

"We follow my rules."

"Rules are meant to be broken, particularly when pleasure is involved."

Her tongue tested her bottom lip. "Was the kiss pleasurable for you?"

"Do you need another demonstration?"

Author Note

I love reading about archaeological discoveries, particularly long-buried treasure hoards, and speculating about the original owners. Some of my musings led to this story about Lady Cynehild, the eldest daughter of Wulfgar of Mercia, and her quest to fulfill her promise to her late husband.

Hopefully you will enjoy the second book in my Vows and Vikings trilogy. The first book is *A Deal with Her Rebel Viking*, but each book can be enjoyed on its own.

As ever, thank you for being one of my readers. If you'd like to get in touch, I love getting comments from readers and can be reached at michelle@michellestyles.co.uk or through my publisher or Facebook or Twitter, @michellelstyles.

MICHELLE STYLES

Betrothed to the Enemy Viking

HARLEQUIN®
HISTORICAL™

Recycling programs
for this product may
not exist in your area.

ISBN-13: 978-1-335-50609-2

Betrothed to the Enemy Viking

This edition published by arrangement with Harlequin Books S.A.

For questions and comments about the quality of this book,
please contact us at CustomerService@Harlequin.com.

Harlequin Enterprises ULC
22 Adelaide St. West, 40th Floor
Toronto, Ontario M5H 4E3, Canada
www.Harlequin.com

Printed in U.S.A.

Born and raised near San Francisco, California, **Michelle Styles** currently lives near Hadrian's Wall with her husband and a menagerie of pets in an Edwardian bungalow with a large and somewhat overgrown garden. An avid reader, she became hooked on historical romances after discovering Georgette Heyer, Anya Seton and Victoria Holt. Her website is michellestyles.co.uk and she's on Twitter and Facebook.

Books by Michelle Styles

Harlequin Historical

Return of the Viking Warrior
Saved by the Viking Warrior
Taming His Viking Woman
Summer of the Viking
Sold to the Viking Warrior
The Warrior's Viking Bride
Sent as the Viking's Bride

Vows and Vikings

A Deal with Her Rebel Viking
Betrothed to the Enemy Viking

Sons of Sigurd

Conveniently Wed to the Viking

Visit the Author Profile page
at Harlequin.com for more titles.

Chapter One

Early March 875, Hangra Hill in the Five
Boroughs, Danelaw, formerly East Mercia
Modern-day Thyngehowe, Sherwood Forest,
Nottinghamshire

The spring sunshine shone through the catkins of the
willow, highlighting the first shoots of new grass and the
flowers which carpeted the woodland glade. Jaarl Kal
Randrson, more commonly called Icebeard, since he'd
singlehandedly held the shield wall of the Great Army of
the Danes at Basceng, adjusted the crossbow he carried
to a more comfortable fit over his shoulder and surveyed
the dales, fields and valleys of his holdings.

His worn-out lands back across the sea in Denmark,
with their harvests of squelching mud, stunted wheat and
starving livestock, seemed a lifetime ago. His belly was
full, and his reputation as an effective warrior ensured
none tried to wrest these lands from him. All boded well
for achieving the oath he'd sworn on the graves of his
wife and young son. Except an undercurrent of bitter
cold still clung to the spring-warmed air—a reflection

of the unease he'd experienced in his chamber earlier, which had sent him out to this overlook.

Lady Cynehild, the widow of the Mercian warlord who had once called these lands his own, was due to lay her husband's sword at the altar of the ruined church any day. She claimed it was to honour his dying wish, but what did she truly require? The rumours of a buried hoard of gold had swirled about the lands when he'd first built his new hall on the ruins of the old one, but despite his extensively searching for it, he'd discovered nothing.

'Good luck with trying to steal anything from under my nose,' he muttered. 'What is mine, I hold.'

Lady Cynehild would be like all the other Mercian ladies he'd encountered in his time on these shores—overly proud, officious and utterly certain of her own desirability, particularly to an unmarried *jaarl*. For the sake of peace with his fellow *jaarls* she'd be allowed to lay the sword, but she'd depart with nothing.

'Show yourself.' He notched an arrow into the crossbow.

A shaft of sunlight hit a stag's many-pronged antlers as he led his herd of pregnant does into the clearing. When Kal lifted his bow and aimed for the stag's heart, the animal turned his head towards him and pawed the earth, as if he could sense his presence. He shook his head. The sound of his roar filled the glen. One antler loosened and fell to the ground, swiftly followed by the other.

Kal lowered the bow and saluted the stag and his herd. 'Thank you for your gift on this spring morning. Go and guard your herd. Until our next meeting, when your antlers have returned.'

The stag blew out a huff of air. No doubt when Kal re-

turned to the hall his cousin Alff would laugh at his fancy
in sparing the stag's life in exchange for a pair of antlers.
But these days Alff seldom had a good word to say about
anything. Kal blamed his cousin's new wife, Toka. However, Alff refused to hear a word against her, claiming
Kal suffered from unreasonable prejudice against the
woman who'd been Kal's late wife's sister.

'I've the measure of that woman. The scales will drop
from his eyes soon, eh, Stag?'

The stag's nostrils quivered, sensing something in
the wind, and he turned and vanished with his herd into
the undergrowth. The glade settled as if the deer had
never been there.

Somewhere a lark began a trilling song, reminding
Kal that he was needed elsewhere, to ensure his lands
continued to prosper.

He reached to pick up the nearest discarded antler.
He'd take the stag's unexpected gift as a sign that he
should follow the stag's lead. When he returned to the
hall he would do what he'd been avoiding—take a wife.
But one he could cherish—not someone like his cousin's
new wife or the mysterious Lady Cynehild. He would get
more sons and ensure these lands belonged to his family for evermore. Today was the day his ghosts ceased
walking beside him.

'Thus shall all tyrants fall, Icebeard!'

The whispered words from behind him allowed him
no more than a heartbeat of warning. He reacted instinctively, thrusting the antler forward. Something large and
heavy hit his head and Kal Randrson—the mountain who
had kept the Great Army's shield wall from buckling by
planting his feet at Basceng, the restorer of prosperity for
his new people through his purchase of cows and sheep,

the great Deniscan *jaarl* of Ecgmundton, with a war band which numbered more than a hundred warriors—fell to his knees as the world went black.

Lady Cynehild of Baelle Heale struggled to climb Hangra Hill. If she reached the top she'd spy the lands her husband had lost years ago, when the Great Heathen Horde had first swarmed over Mercia and the warriors' courage had failed.

All around her she could see the emerging signs of spring, with new grass and tiny flowers, but the old fern fronds kept catching on her gown. Despite it being early March, the day held more than a promise of warmth, with a hint of the land returning to growth after its long winter slumber.

Cynehild wiped the sweat from her brow with the back of her arm.

'Get the gold and silver I buried when we fled, Cyn, for Wulfgar, for our son's future,' her husband had whispered in those quiet few moments before his death eighteen months ago. *'Ensure our son is looked after. Keep my secret even from your sisters and your father.'*

The woods had grown in the time since she'd been away, becoming denser and more closed, but she reckoned that from the crest of the hill she could find her way to the cave where he'd hidden part of the treasure.

Somewhere over her head a raven flapped its wings and called out its mournful cry. She paid it no mind. She stepped over a fallen beech and narrowly missed outstretched fingers—a human hand connected to a human body. Giving a muffled scream, she scrambled backwards, dislodging some stones.

On the ground before her lay a man—not just any

man, but one of the largest she'd ever seen. If he'd been standing upright, he'd have towered over her. Blood seeped from his head wound, soaking the ground. His dark brown eyes snapped open and appeared to stare deep into her soul, seeing everything she wished to keep hidden. Then, seemingly satisfied with what he had seen, he grunted and his eyelids fluttered shut.

Alive, not dead.

There was something noble about his strong features—high cheekbones, dark blond hair flowing over his shoulders. The golden brooch which fastened his cloak was clearly Northern in style. However, she could see no weapons lying beside him, and nor was anyone else in the moss-hung clearing.

Had there been a fight? Was he the loser, left there to die? Or some sort of strange sacrifice? A warning to any unwary person who climbed up this hill?

'Why are you in this place?' Cynehild whispered. 'What has happened to you? Where are your companions? Who are you?'

He groaned slightly and seemed to mouth words— *Help me, please.*

The wood wore a complete hush…even the raven had vanished!

'Palni! Brother Palni!'

'My lady, have you encountered trouble in your toilette?' Once a Northern warrior, but now a Christian monk, Brother Palni shouted back to her.

Cynehild gritted her teeth and wished she'd given him a different excuse about her need to be alone in the woods.

'Come up here. At once.'

She awkwardly placed a hand on the injured man's

shoulder. At her touch, his eyes blinked open again. A faint worrying film covered them. Was he dying?

'Keep breathing. Help is coming.'

His lips turned up into a smile which transformed his face. 'Good.'

Then a gurgle escaped his throat and his body went rigid.

'Brother Palni! I need you now. Not tomorrow morning!'

Brother Palni appeared a few breaths later, wiping the sweat from his face with one corner of his monk's robe. 'Now, what is all this here fuss about, my lady? What has startled you? Another raven? Or was it a magpie this time?'

Cynehild tugged at the victim's massive shoulders, trying to raise his head up and get a better look at his wound. 'This man is injured…possibly from hitting his head on a rock.'

Severe lines settled on Brother Palni's normally placid face as he glanced at the body on the ground. 'He won't be alive for long, my lady. Even now death seeks to claim him.' Brother Palni crossed himself. 'I'm sorry. Shall I pray for him?'

Pray for him. Brother Palni sounded more like the priest back home every day.

Cynehild made a disgusted noise in the back of her throat. 'He spoke to me. And his chest moves. Watch.' She rocked back on her heels. 'People can recover from a head wound.'

Brother Palni came and knelt beside her. He put his hand on the man's chest. 'What do you want to do, my lady?'

'Save his life, Brother Palni.'

The monk took his hand away, pursed his lips as if he'd encountered a sour apple and stood up. 'Your men wait for your order to continue towards the church at Ecgmundton, my lady. Go to them. I will wait for the inevitable and then catch up with you. It shouldn't take long.'

Cynehild balled her fists. *She* led this expedition. Surely Brother Palni had to see the value in what she wished to do. 'I may lack skill at trepanning, but I can nurse a simple concussion. I've tended enough over the years.'

'My lady? I am afraid this goes beyond a simple head injury.'

'We keep him quiet and warm. Should the worst happen, then he'll die in comfort—not on the cold ground.'

'He is a Deniscan, my lady. Examine his brooches if you doubt my assessment.'

Cynehild wrapped her arms about her middle. A Deniscan. A Dane. Possibly someone to do with Jaarl Icebeard, the man she was going to rob—or rather from whom she would liberate the gold which rightfully belonged to her—the man she had to consider her most dangerous enemy.

'But what sort? Where does he hail from?'

'There is only one sort, in my experience—the worst sort. Your late husband would agree with me, my lady.' Brother Palni bowed low, as if his invocation of Leofwine settled the matter.

'My husband never sought the death of an innocent. The Danish warlord who caused his death breathes no more, thanks to my sister and her new husband. I seek no more revenge for that killing.' Cynehild gestured towards the man. 'Have a proper look. Take your time and see if you can discern anything. Do you know him?'

Brother Palni shook his head. 'No, Lady Cynehild, but the Great Army was a vast one. I've not yet met the Deniscan who controls these lands either—the Jaarl Icebeard—but I know his fearsome reputation. He is more ruthless in many ways than the man who caused your husband's death. Mark my words: his hand will be in this. Walk away while you can.'

It would be easy to follow Brother Palni's advice and comfort her conscience that this man's fate had been sealed long before she'd stumbled upon him. But she knew she wouldn't. She'd given the man her word—she would help him, and she would do everything she could to save his life.

She tilted her chin upwards and allowed righteous indignation to fill her. Mercians did things differently from the Great Heathen Horde. 'The killing must cease at some point, Brother Palni. How can we be at peace if we keep taking sides and being at each other's throats? This man is someone's friend, son, and possibly a father. He deserves better than to die like this. You must know the parable of the Good Samaritan now that you are a monk instead of a warrior from the North. It is one of Father Oswald's favourites.'

'And if he turns out to be someone who would be better off dead? What will you do then?'

Cynehild firmed her mouth. If she left now, the expression in the man's brown eyes would haunt her for ever. That brief glimpse had been like looking into the mirror of her soul. But explaining that to Brother Palni would simply result in him tutting and finding yet more reasons why they should turn back without encountering Jaarl Icebeard. She strongly suspected the monk had only agreed to accompany her on this journey because he had mistakenly believed she'd give up long before now.

'It is up to God to decide whether or not a person lives or dies, not me,' she said.

'Let God take care of him. Death will gather him to her bosom and there is little to be done about that.'

She rose and jabbed a finger at the monk. 'What if God has guided my footsteps, Brother Palni? You should consider these things now that you've become a monk, instead of being like a heathen warrior, prattling on about Death's bosom.'

'Where do you propose taking him, my lady?' Brother Palni lifted his palm upwards. 'We are in a strange wood. And the ordinary people in Danelaw country have been less than friendly. That farmer tried to set his dog on me this morning.'

'I seem to recall there is a dry cave near here. My husband and I sheltered there once.' She was proud of the way her voice remained steady. She forced a smile. 'It will serve our needs.'

'A cave?'

'It should be big enough to accommodate all of us. Two men can guard the covered cart if you think it necessary.'

Brother Palni lifted a brow. 'I thought you were determined to press onwards towards your old lands at Ecgmundton, regardless of the weather.'

'Plans can be altered,' she replied.

'This is the first time in the entire journey that you have admitted that.'

Cynehild toyed with the belt fastened about her waist. The scissors she wore made a metallic noise when they hit the tweezers next to them. 'I didn't expect to discover an injured man in need of our assistance. The cave is some distance from the track.'

'It must be well off the beaten track. We could carry him to the covered cart instead, my lady. Stay there.'

'Another damp night in that covered cart will make me ill, and if I become ill we will have to delay our journey.' She forced a sneeze. 'There—you see?'

'My lady, how are we going to find this here cave? You sent us in circles yesterday, looking for a stream just so that you could wash.'

Behind Brother Palni's head, Cynehild spotted the forked oak she'd been searching for and wondered how she'd missed it before. She could make out the faint pathway off to its left, which she knew led to the cave.

'I know where the cave is.'

Again, a raised brow from Brother Palni. 'You appear very certain that this cave will revive him.'

'Once there, we can examine him further, to see if there is truly nothing which can be done.' She gestured up to the darkening clouds. 'A hard rain approaches, Brother Palni. I can feel it in the air. My covered cart cannot accommodate all of us, and it does leak something dreadful.'

'You're right about the hard rain. My scar has started aching.'

Brother Palni absently rubbed his calf muscle in a reminder of how he'd come to be injured and how he'd first entered her life, as a member of a raiding party on her home who had been repelled by the brave actions of her sister Ansithe.

'You'll not want to hear my views, my lady, as you

are stubborn when your mind is made up, but I beg you to listen to me all the same.'

'Explain the problems to me later.' Cynehild pointed towards where the man lay. 'First, help save this man's life.'

Palni pressed his hands together and made a low bow—almost a perfect mimic of Father Oswald. 'I exist to serve, my lady. I'll tell the men to prepare for trouble... deep trouble.'

'I sincerely doubt whoever did this will return. Why should they?'

'I know what the Deniscan are like.'

At her sharp intake of breath, Palni bowed again.

'Pardon an old warrior for speaking bluntly. I have little practice yet with being a monk. The good Father is constantly exasperated with me over it.' He ran his hand through newly tonsured hair. 'Oddity and the Deniscan rarely augur well for anyone else.'

'It seems fairly straightforward to me—the man was attacked, robbed and left for dead.'

Palni pointed towards the man's cloak. 'Whatever happened here, robbery was not the intention. He wears far too much gold, but has no sword or weapon of any kind.'

Cynehild peered more closely at the man. His cloak was fastened with two large gold brooches and he wore a torc about his neck and several arm rings. His clothes were fashioned of fine wool and his cloak was a thick soft pelt.

'I gave my word to him that help was coming and Mercians do keep true to their word—unlike others I could mention.'

The man groaned slightly and mumbled a few words

which sounded like a name and another plea for help. His fingers scrabbled at the moss.

Cynehild went to him and caught his hand. 'You're safe now. I will ensure it.'

'So cold. Stay with me.' His fingers tightened about hers, becoming almost painful in their grip. 'I beg you. I need you. Always.'

Cynehild was unclear if he was speaking to her or to someone he saw in his fevered imaginings.

'I've little intention of leaving you. You'll be safe once we've moved you to the cave.'

His lips turned upwards. 'Believe you.'

She gave a triumphant glance over her shoulder towards where Brother Palni stood, with an increasingly gloomy look on his face.

'Does he seem like a man who is about to die? Help me to bind his head so that he will be comfortable during the short journey to the cave. That is an order, Brother Palni.'

The monk departed and returned with linen strips and several of the men, who were able to fasten together a makeshift stretcher. Cynehild carefully bound the stranger's head so it wouldn't begin bleeding again on the journey.

'I just hope you don't have cause to regret your actions, my lady.'

The driving rain trickled down Cynehild's neck. She lifted her hood and concentrated on getting inside the dry warmth of the cave. After showing Brother Palni that the cave existed, she had accompanied him back to the covered cart, so she could ensure the right selection of herbs and bandages were procured before her men carried the patient to his new resting spot.

'We will be safe here for a little while. Water is nearby and we now have a dry roof over our head,' she said with satisfaction.

Brother Palni moved the vines at the cave's entrance to one side. 'How long are you reckoning on staying, my lady? I'm willing to wager that man will not last the night, but if I'm wrong he will need several days before he can move. Can we afford that time? In and out, you said. Jaarl Icebeard is ever likely to change his mind about agreeing to allow you to honour your husband.'

Cynehild allowed the words to roll over her. All Palni's negative predictions did was increase her determination that the man would live.

'There are plenty of provisions, and we have Lord Icebeard's solemn promise of safe passage to the church so I can finally fulfil my oath to Leofwine and lay his sword at his ancestors' feet. Icebeard will hardly wish to make an enemy of my brother-in-law by reneging.'

Cynehild crossed her fingers. The angels had smiled on her so far. Bringing the injured man here solved everything. She could find the jar with the silver and gold coins that Leofwine had buried in this cave and look after the stranger at the same time, without having to answer awkward questions. If Brother Palni knew about the true nature of her quest, he would turn the party around and head straight back to Baelle Heale.

Brother Palni tapped a finger against his mouth. 'This cave bothers me. Something in my water tells me trouble is coming. It is the way I used to feel before I went into battle.'

'At the first sign of trouble the guards will race up here to help with our defence.'

'Bury the sword on your old lands without confronting Icebeard and be done with it, my lady. Your late lord would never know.'

'I swore before Almighty God that I would deliver that sword to his ancestors.' Cynehild gave Brother Palni a hard stare—the sort which usually sent her son scurrying for his nurse when he'd been misbehaving. 'Would you have me break that vow?'

'I'm sworn to the church and to you, my lady.'

'I could hardly have planned to encounter this man and his injuries,' she said, going over to where one of the men had piled wood for the fire.

She spotted one of her favourite spindle whorls lying in the dirt beside a flat stone.

Cynehild gasped and bent to pick it up. Surely its presence here was an omen? She must have dropped it when she had last been in the cave. She'd hunted for it ages ago, when they had first arrived at Baelle Heale. Her sisters and Leofwine had been less than understanding about its loss.

She squinted in the dim light. The pile of stones at the back of the cave appeared undisturbed. The time to search for the jar of coins would be after everyone was asleep.

'I'll take one of the night watches,' she said, quickly fashioning a makeshift pallet for the injured man out of dried fern fronds and her second-best cloak. 'I'm used to being awake in the night. Many times when my son was small I'd simply sit, watching his cradle and listening to his soft breathing.'

'As my lady commands.'

After the man had been brought in and deposited on his new bed, Brother Palni rapidly lit a fire in the mouth of the cave, just under the overhang so that the space remained clear of smoke.

Cynehild put her heaviest cloak over the injured man. The trembling of his limbs settled as the warmth from the cloak combined with the fire seeped into his bones. His breathing eased and became much gentler and steadier. Within a little time, the man's skin ceased to be quite as deathly pale and his lips recovered to a rosier hue.

'See, Brother Palni, he still lives.'

'Did you find what you were looking for? I saw you pick something up,' the monk said in a low voice. 'I mean no disrespect, my lady. I merely seek to understand. I am certain you came to this cave for some other purpose than to save this man's life. I've been a warrior far too long not to know an excuse when I hear one.'

Cynehild curled her fingers about the spindle whorl. *'Trust no one—particularly not a Northman or a Deniscan.'* Leofwine's final warning held true both for Brother Palni and for her new patient.

'I found a spindle whorl I lost many years ago, that is all. It is a sign that our journey will be a fruitful one. I look forward to your apology in due course.'

Chapter Two

Kal struggled against the thick, all-pervasive darkness which clawed at his soul. His head felt as if it had been gnawed by Fenrir the Wolf, or worse. The heaviness of his limbs meant he could barely lift his arms. It was as if he'd fought long battles back to back, holding both an axe and a sword.

His fingers instinctively searched for his sword, but encountered a woollen cloak instead of the more familiar scabbard which he always wore into battle.

He cautiously opened one eye, then the other. The embers of a small fire cast shadows on rough-hewn stone walls. If he craned his neck, he could just make out the inky darkness of the night sky beyond the fire. Night. He was certain it had been morning when he'd last opened his eyes. Worse, he had no memory of where he'd been, how he'd arrived here or who his companions were.

How had he come to be in this place?

He rolled onto his side and wished he hadn't as a searing pain washed over him. His body jerked upwards. The dark wall which had invaded his mind threatened to send him into the deep abyss again.

'Keep still. Hold your tongue if you can.'

A woman's voice, low and gentle, but one which held the note of command. Her accent was not Norse, but something more pleasing to his ear.

'Others sleep in this place.'

'Who?' he whispered around the dryness in his throat, moving his aching head towards the voice.

A woman with golden hair silhouetted against the firelight appeared on the other side of the flames. She bent down, retrieved something and put it on the fire, sending up a cloud of sparks which flickered and then died. The fire highlighted her ample curves. She could be a Valkyrie—or maybe an angel such as the Christian priests spoke about. Until he'd encountered this woman he'd had his doubts about their existence, but no longer. He would be prepared to swear that such creatures were beyond beautiful.

'Who are you? Am I even alive?'

She came over and smoothed the rough wool cloak which covered him. 'One who wishes you well. Lie back. Gather your strength. All will soon become clear but, yes, you are alive.'

He struggled to think what this woman meant to him. Nothing. No woman could mean anything to him now that his wife and their child were dead. The grief of their passing still clogged his throat.

He frowned. Surely he'd only left her grave this morning. How had he arrived in this place?

The memory of his last sight of those freshly dug graves suddenly swamped him and a lump formed in his throat, but no tears came. He had been unable to cry at the graveside either.

Toka had screamed like a harridan at him, saying

her sister's death had been his fault for failing to provide the food she'd needed. She had held out the body of his child, a boy who had lived no more than two days, and demanded he bury it instead of being useless, before turning on her heel and leading her nearly grown stepson away.

He'd dug the small grave with his own hands and then left, vowing to be the successful warrior his wife Ranka had always said he could be if he simply tried. The farm he'd loved had yielded only a bitter harvest.

Did this angel woman on the other side of the fire know about his wife and child and his unwitting part in their deaths? Was that why she'd watched him earlier, with an uncertain expression marring her lovely face? Did she know how the rains had come late, becoming unceasing? How the crops had all failed, and how he'd argued that he should stay with his wife instead of going to Ribe to sell the remaining cow and her calf? How he'd come back to find her insensible and burning with fever after giving birth, the newborn baby lying by her side, crying? How he'd tried to give him something to eat? How he'd begged her sister to save the child?

'Where am I?' he whispered, instead of asking for forgiveness. The words came like a groan.

The angel woman put a hand on his shoulder. 'Remain still or you'll do further injury to your head. Do you have a name?'

She spoke Saxon, not any of the languages from the North. An escaped captive? He'd learned the language years ago, from the captive his father had bought to assist in the house when his mother had died.

'A name? What should I call you?' She spoke again,

this time in something which was more akin to the language of his childhood.

'Who are you? Should I know? Why am I here?' he asked.

She rocked back on her heels. 'I…we found you lying on the ground, having taken a blow to your head. You requested my help. Brother Palni predicted you'd never wake again, but you must have a hard skull.'

'I requested help?'

He shut one eye. Palni was a name from the North—from the lands now controlled by Harald Finehair rather than by the Deniscan. But she called him brother, as if he was one of the Christian monks. A Northman as a monk? He was tempted to call this a strange dream, except his body ached far too much for it to be one.

'Death would have stalked you if you'd spent the night in the bone-chilling rain.' She held out an unadorned hand. 'Lady Cynehild, daughter of Ealdorman Wulfgar of Baelle Heale in West Mercia. We're in the Five Boroughs controlled by the Northmen—what used to be the eastern edge of Mercia.'

He turned her words over in his mind. No jolt of recognition. Either from her name or the location. Nothing but a void.

'Lady Cynehild…'

A distinct prickling went down his spine. Her name suddenly seemed to have some meaning, but it slipped away like water draining through a sieve.

He concentrated, willing his brain to furnish him with his own name to give her in return. For three heartbeats there was nothing but suffocating blackness. Then the knowledge rose with certainty from the depths of his being.

He lifted his hand towards her. 'Kal, son of Randr, from the homestead near Ribe in the land of the Danes, my lady. How far are we from Ribe? Less than a day's march, by my reckoning.'

She shook her head. 'We are far from Baelle Heale's boundaries today. Travelling towards where I once lived. And a long way from your home in Ribe. Across an ocean, in fact.'

He released a breath of air. One less thing to concern his mind. This Lady Cynehild was a stranger to him. But that meant he'd have to solve the mystery of why he was here, wherever 'here' was, without assistance, in whatever Danelaw country was. Across the ocean from Ribe? He didn't remember sailing.

'Where is my cousin? Where is Alff, son of Alfuir the Long-Legged?'

'You were alone when I discovered you.'

He tried to concentrate and think, rather than panic at his growing bewilderment. He knew he dealt in certainties like the heft of a sword, the weight of a shield or the feel of an oar under his palm, rather than in the niceties of navigation. He was the shield who refused to bend. A man with ice in his veins in the face of the enemy.

'I've never heard of any of these places you say,' he confessed. 'Perhaps I was journeying to Northumbria when I hit my head. I've no notion why my comrades abandoned me. My cousin Alff and I swore a blood bond never to leave the other on the battlefield. Is he alive?'

Lady Cynehild did not suck her teeth or make a cutting observation about his inability to command loyalty, as Toka would have done. Instead she tucked the cloak tighter about him, putting her cool hand on his brow before rocking back on her heels.

'I came upon you in the woods, near the large stones. Absolutely alone. You suffered a fierce blow to your head. Such a blow can cause your mind to play tricks. Your cousin may be elsewhere for a reason you can't remember.'

Her words were soft and soothing, helping to keep the darkness from invading. Kal knew he could listen to her gentle voice for days and not be bored.

'I know I want to live,' he whispered between parched lips. 'I'm a warrior, not a sacrifice to the gods.'

'A human sacrifice to the gods?' She shuddered. 'The Deniscan have odd practices.'

'Some believe it appeases them.'

He didn't add that he'd stopped believing in the gods when his wife had died. He'd raged and sworn that never again would he trust anything but his own two hands. But those were private thoughts, and this lady travelled with a monk.

'Then it is settled. You will live. You'll be able to travel to Northumbria to meet your sworn king once you're healed.'

Her face turned away from him, revealing the length and slenderness of her neck in the firelight. He followed her gaze to the flickering shadows on the cave walls.

'This land has seen more than its fair share of death. It's long past time to celebrate the living,' she said.

'I owe you a life debt, Lady Cynehild,' he said into the silence.

'You are not in my debt.'

She turned back towards him, looking straight at him for the first time. She was not the young maiden he had first thought, but a woman who had gone past the first flush of maidenhood and emerged even better-looking for it. She moved with an air of authority. A managing woman.

Kal grimaced. Normally he avoided such women, but right now he would follow her to the ends of the earth. She was mistaken—he did owe her a life debt...one he'd struggle to repay.

'The pain in my head prevents me from knowing many things about my recent past, but my gut instinct tells me you are kind. And I know my instinct has kept me alive many more times than I care to count.'

Lady Cynehild's soft laugh resembled the brook which bubbled over the rocks at the back of the longhouse where he'd grown up.

'Even though you can't remember them?'

'I trust my instinct.'

He felt better for admitting his ignorance to her about the entire situation. He knew deep down that he normally never admitted such things, but right now he needed answers, rather than to prove his strength and independence, or try to bluff his way through. And he marvelled at how the words came out of his mouth in her own language so easily, without him having to think about it.

'My younger sisters might disagree with you about my kindness. They chafe under my guidance.'

'Do your sisters travel with you?'

'Ansithe is with her husband, but the youngest, Elene, remains with my father, and we are many days' journey from both.'

'Where am I, then?'

'A cave. I had you moved here after we discovered you lying on Hangra Hill. You must have fallen, hit your head and then wandered disorientated before collapsing.'

It was on the tip of his tongue to say that someone

had struck him on the head. *'Tyrant. Fall.'* The words reverberated again and again in his mind. How could that be him?

He hated the sluggish way his brain was working—like three-day-old porridge which had been kept in an iron pot and sliced, as his grandmother would have said. He knew he actively disliked porridge. That was a start, at least.

'I don't remember why I was in that place.'

His fingers began plucking at the threads of the cloak, as if through simple touch the answer would come to him. The harder he sought the answer, the quicker his fingers moved, until he was trying to pull tufts of wool from it.

Her gentle touch on his shoulder made his hands still. 'Brother Palni predicted that if you woke you might not remember, or perhaps wouldn't want to remember. He has seen many injuries like this before.'

'Palni? That is the name of a man from the North. My father distrusted them, but that is because a man from Viken once cheated his father out of a farm.' He swallowed a gulp of air and fought to calm his racing heart. 'Not a battle, my lady, we were at peace. The Northman warrior lies.'

'Slowly.'

She placed a hand on his chest. He covered it with one of his.

'A breath in and then out. Like this.'

He tried to match his timing with the rise and fall of her chest. The world righted. She gently withdrew her fingers and his hand curved about the air where they had been, trying to recapture their warmth.

'Brother Palni travels with me now as a monk—

having dedicated his life to God and our saviour Lord Jesus after the Great Army conquered these lands. He provides protection…' Her full lips quirked upwards. 'And counsel, even if I rarely take it. He is a good and trustworthy man.'

'I doubt we conquered you…not really,' he said, when her smile came and lit up his corner of the cave.

'My forefathers were on these lands long before you and we will still be here long after you depart. You and the rest of your Heathen Horde. It may not happen in my lifetime but some day it will.' She nodded. 'Rest. We're at peace. You've nothing to fear from me or my men.'

His sworn enemy had saved him. She knew what the Great Army had done to her people, and still she'd saved his life. Would his late wife have been that kind?

He redoubled his concentration, trying to reach into the black wall of pain and remember how he came to be in this place. Faint flashes of memory flickered—of crossing a windswept sea, of battles and watching men die, of knowing he'd won a victory and that afterwards men had lauded him as their leader, calling him something…but not his given name. He could remember lifting his sword aloft and kissing the ring of the Danish warlord, Ivar the Boneless, and then the ring of Ivar's brother Halfdan. He had helped to conquer these lands…

The memories suddenly faded, like the smoke rising from the fire. All that was left was a taste inside his mouth as if he'd swallowed spiders' webs.

'Comrades died.'

He concentrated on the embers. Those men might have gone to a better life in Valhalla, but he knew their passing had ripped a hole in his soul.

'I can't tell you their names. I should know their names. I'm not a tyrant, I tell you. There is good in me.'

She moved the cloak up to his chin. 'Did I call you a tyrant?'

'Someone did. I know it. But I'm not. I want to be good.'

'I'm sure there is good in you. You miss your fallen comrades and your family. Someone out there cares for you. Don't worry.'

Her words soothed the swirling blackness. He would give anything not to have to worry about who he was, what he'd become and who he'd caused to die. He very much feared the answers, but this Lady saw some good in him, and he clung to that like a man who had been washed overboard clung to an outstretched oar.

'Do you believe in me?'

'Yes. I believe anyone can choose to be good, no matter their past.'

Cynehild firmed her mouth. It had to be true, or else she had made a terrible mistake in saving his life. Her whole life seemed to be an exercise in making mistakes and desperately trying to recover from them.

She placed a hand on her patient's forehead. It remained cool to the touch. An excellent sign. He might yet avoid a fever and fully recover.

The jar filled with coins which her husband had hidden three years ago in this cave weighed heavily in the pouch she wore about her waist. She'd finally located it a short while ago, but Kal Randrson's awakening had prevented her from counting it. Provided the gold Leofwine had hidden in the Ecgmundton church remained undisturbed until she could retrieve it, some of her troubles would be over. Although her father had already indicated his price for any assistance she wanted in raising Wulfgar—she would have to marry a man of his choosing… something she refused to do.

'My lady, your hand feels good. Keep it there.'

'No fever,' she said, pushing away all thoughts of finding the correct warrior to train Wulfgar while avoiding her father's machinations and focusing instead on the injured man in front of her.

One task at a time rather than be scattered, like she'd been as a young bride, driving her husband to distraction.

The man raised himself up on his elbow. His face was etched with pain. 'Are these my men? Or yours?'

'Mine.'

She eased him down again. Leofwine had been like this in his last hours, not knowing where he was or who she was, and always questioning. When she had kept him quiet there had been moments of lucidness, such as when he had given her this quest for the buried treasure.

'You were alone and without weapons of any sort when we found you—not even an eating knife.'

'Not even my eating knife?' His hands started flailing. 'I can't have lost that. I wear it always. It is all I have left of my father.'

'I presume you were attacked and your weapons were taken.'

His hands curled about the golden torc he wore about his neck. 'If they took my weapons, why did they leave my torc? Why am I even wearing one? I know all I have to my name is my sword and shield, yet I wear a king's ransom in gold beyond my wildest imaginings. What sort of witchcraft is this?' His brows drew together and he banged his fists on the pallet. 'Why must I endure this? Why is my head full of shadows and no answers?'

She retreated several steps from where Kal lay, curled on his side, with gold about his neck and arms. He definitely had more than a sword and shield. His clothes were finer than she had ever seen.

'Are you hungry?' she asked, forcing a note of calmness into her voice.

A solitary tear escaped Kal Randrson's eye.

Practical. She had to be practical and control the anxiety which clawed at her. She could fix things like hunger, even sometimes a broken head. She had no idea how to fix a broken mind.

'Is that why you require an eating knife?'

'No—which is odd. My belly ached with hunger when I lived in Ribe. Always.'

She forced a light laugh. 'You ached with hunger but you wear gold like a great *jaarl*? We have had too many mysteries for one night; concentrate instead on something else.'

There was a long pause, and she'd just begun to hope that he'd fallen asleep when he spoke.

'My wife gave birth and then she died. My son swiftly followed her into the grave. He never felt the sun on his face or had a gentle breeze ruffle his hair. My world became black and I vowed that I would make their shades proud of me. Have I done that?' he asked.

'You are wearing gold and I presume it is yours.' A cold shiver went down her back. 'Perhaps my crashing through the undergrowth disturbed your attackers and they ran off before they were able to rob you? I don't know. All I know for certain is that I found you like this.'

'My wife would have found a use for this gold.' His lips turned up. 'Do you have any children?'

She released a breath. A question she could answer— even if a sudden longing to hold her son tight swamped her. 'A boy of nearly four. He grows very sturdy. Wulfgar used to cling to my skirts and cry whenever I went out of the room, but now he tells me as often as he can that he is a big boy and is able to do things on his own. He doesn't require his mother. He wants to be a warrior.'

Kal Randrson sat bolt upright and looked about wildly, before sinking back to the pallet, causing the cloak to slither to the floor. 'Is he here? Or is he with your husband elsewhere, my lady?'

She leant over and gave the fire a stir rather than answering straight away. Sparks flew into the air with a crackle. One of the men snored loudly. Simple noises. Night-time noises which reminded her of her duty to others. As intimate as this night seemed, Kal Randrson remained a Deniscan without a recent past, and he was clearly a warrior who had greatly prospered from the invasion which had ruined her late husband.

'Why do you think my husband is elsewhere?'

'You wouldn't be awake and watching over me if he were here. A beauty such as you would be kept far away from one like me.'

A beauty? Kal's tongue had obviously been dipped in honey. From her increasingly ample curves to the ever-deepening shadows under her eyes, her looks had never recovered in her grief over Leofwine's death. She didn't need to look in a still millpond to know that simple truth.

'My husband died. Wulfgar remains with my father and my youngest sister in West Mercia.'

She concentrated on the fire and thought of Wulfgar's

angelic smile, and the way he held his wooden sword in his chubby fist. How tall would he be when she returned? Would he still hold his tongue between his teeth when he concentrated?

'I look forward to seeing how much he has grown when I return home.'

She replaced the cloak about Kal's body and wrenched her mind away from the solid mass of longing to see her son.

Kal's fingers captured her hand. 'Does it get any easier? My being still aches for my lost wife and newborn son.'

Cynehild watched the embers flicker and allowed her hand to remain in his tight grip. She knew that she wanted to answer his question truthfully, rather than give the polite lie about feeling fine and coping admirably— the answer that she normally gave when anyone asked.

'After my husband died my world turned grey. For many months I went through the motions of living. I got up, washed myself, did my appointed tasks...but the world held no joy. Then one day I heard my son laugh at something silly my youngest sister had done, and suddenly my heart was easier. I knew there were places I could still find light and happiness.'

'A place of light and happiness? I've been searching for that for a long time but haven't found it yet.'

His hand relaxed its grip on hers. She gave it an awkward pat before letting go.

One of her men stirred. The strange intimacy between her and this Deniscan vanished.

She forced a brisk smile and stood up, twitching the pleats of her gown into place. The warm imprint of his fingers lingered on her palm—a far from unpleasant sensation. She pretended an interest in the cave's roof. She was a widow, immune from such considerations as a man's sensual touch. Her heart remained encased in ice and devoted to her late husband.

'You must have lived through it. Your heart did heal, even if it remains scarred. You prospered. Cling to that thought.'

He frowned. 'I *will* remember what I did last time to live through it—won't I, Lady of the Light?'

Her teeth worried her bottom lip. What sort of answer did he require to keep him calm? In the morning she'd work out what to say to Brother Palni in order to find a way through this self-inflicted tangle.

'You know your name, and you know you once had a family you loved.'

'Did they love me?' he asked forlornly.

'Your grief wouldn't be as great if they hadn't.'

She put her hand around the pouch which contained Leofwine's jar—his gift to the son he'd never properly know. Some good had come from this journey. The tightness in her neck eased.

'You speak wisely, Lady Cynehild. I could listen to your voice for a lifetime.' His eyelids fluttered and his yawn bounced off the walls of the cave. 'My wife's sister cursed me. Said I was always to be a wanderer and would die without anyone caring about me.'

'Then she lied.'

He rubbed a hand against his temple. 'How can you say that for a certainty?'

'I found you, and now you're safe. You are not out on a hillside with your life ebbing away from you. You know your name. We'll find who you belong to. I promise.'

'Let me chase away your shadows...' His words were

slurred with sleep. 'Sweet. Kind. Lady. With the beautiful smile…'

That is something no one can do. She held the words back with difficulty.

'Sleep. The watch changes now.'

Cynehild woke with an aching back and neck as the first rose tints of dawn entered the cave. Her sleep had come in snatches after one of her men had relieved her watch. Every time she had dozed, her old dream—the one about being chased, seeking a safe haven and being unable to find it—had returned to haunt her. And her dilemma about how she was going to locate the second store of gold remained unresolved.

It was far worse than a game of *tafl*, and that particular game of strategy had always managed to confuse her whenever she'd attempted to play it as a young woman.

When Leofwine had suggested a few months into their marriage that she stop trying to learn a man's game and leave such things to him, concentrate instead on a woman's sphere of making cloth, she'd readily agreed. Only now she wished she'd persisted in learning. A widow with a young child had to use her wits to survive, and more importantly to carry out her husband's final wishes in enemy territory.

She needed to concentrate on remembering the precise instructions regarding the gold in the church that Leofwine had whispered on his deathbed—not worry about one of the enemy who had lost his memory. Kal was a Deniscan—one of the people responsible for turning her secure world upside down when they'd invaded, regardless of how safe her hand had felt in his.

And she wasn't soft-hearted. A hard shell of ice had

encased her when Leofwine died. Her father often found reason to remark on the change—normally when she refused to allow him to have his own way in some domestic matter.

She needed to acquire the pragmatic logic of a war leader. If she had to use this man as a counter, in order to secure Leofwine's gold, she would do so and have no regrets. Ensuring Wulfgar's future was paramount.

She rose from where she'd lain and checked the sleeping Kal Randrson again. The Deniscan warrior appeared to be resting comfortably, oblivious to the turmoil he'd caused her. His face held a certain fragile peace. She wondered if he truly had forgotten the last few years, or if he simply wanted to forget them and the horrible things he had done. When he woke, would he even remember their intimate conversation and the way they'd held hands?

The sudden awareness of him as a man jolted her. She had assumed that everything inside her of that nature had been buried with Leofwine.

'Your Deniscan survived the night. The man's head is harder than I considered,' Brother Palni said, coming to stand beside her. His simple robe sparkled with raindrops. He'd obviously been outside to say his morning prayers. 'You were right—he has been spared. But for the life of me, I've no idea why.'

Cynehild pulled him away from where Kal lay. *Her Deniscan*. 'He's not mine, even in jest, Brother Palni,' she said in a low voice, so as not to wake the others.

'You were the one to find him and insist on saving his life. Whose is he supposed to be, if not yours?' the monk asked. 'Are you having regrets? Perhaps we should have spoken earlier... But I like to greet my God first thing in the morning. I speak with him about my failings, including being less than charitable towards my fellow man.'

'Regrets about what, Brother Palni? I've no regrets about saving a life.'

Merely about what I might have to do afterwards, she added silently. *Whom I might betray.*

'The pinched look about your mouth tells another story, my lady. However, there is no need for you to become crone-like through lack of sleep. You have a good few years left in you before the inevitable withering happens.'

How to condemn her looks in very few words… A withered crone, indeed. Had he not noticed her hips? Nothing withered there. In fact, she was far too plump, in her own estimation.

She pressed her lips tight. What was wrong with her? Her looks had ceased to matter when Leofwine died. Widowhood brought other responsibilities. Fussing about her figure or her face was for women like her sister Elene, who had yet to marry. There again, men buzzed about Elene like flies around a honeypot—something which had never happened to her. Leofwine had been one of few men to compliment her figure.

'The warrior woke in the night. We had quite a conversation. His sleep appears less restless this morning.'

'You spoke?' the monk asked curiously.

Cynehild briefly explained the gist of their conversation.

'He has no idea how he came to be on that hillside? How convenient.' Brother Palni tucked his hands into the sleeves of his robe. 'God preserve me from the treacherous Deniscan. He does not want you to know—or, worse, he wishes to forget all his misdeeds.'

'Do you know the name? Kal, son of Randr, is not one I recall hearing.'

Brother Palni pretended an interest in straightening his monk's robes. 'Randr is a common enough name among both the Northmen and the Danes—as is Kal. But I can't recall any Kal who is a son of Randr that I have heard of specifically.'

Cynehild almost sighed aloud. She knew that tone of voice. It meant she must not enquire too closely. 'You are being overly precise in your words, Brother Palni. This isn't one of your theological debates with Father Oswald. What are you keeping from me? I'm not some child who is frightened of the dark.'

'I will meditate on it, my lady. I feel I should know the name…' He screwed up his face for a long breath and then exhaled. 'No, nothing. Moir used to claim that the only reason I remembered my *own* name was because I heard it so often, and that I ought to make more of an effort.'

'My brother-in-law may have a point.'

'Maybe his name was changed when he arrived on these shores. Maybe he created a new identity. Does he have a nickname? I'm always better with nicknames. For example, the man who holds your old lands is called Icebeard. I don't recall his proper name or heritage. Everyone mentions his exploits in hushed tones—he is a warrior capable of physical feats beyond those of most ordinary men. His actions at Basceng live in legend. No one should have been able to withstand what he underwent that day and live. Without him standing firm, the conquest would have failed before it ever properly began.

They named him after one of the legendary frost giants because of the ice in his veins.'

A shiver went down Cynehild's spine. She hated to think about Icebeard's fearsome exploits, his legendary ability with tactics and his responsibility for the Great Army's winning. She knew she would loathe the man when she encountered him, but she'd control her temper and she wouldn't do anything stupid—like spitting in his face or telling her people to rise up and drive him from these lands.

Early on in her marriage she'd learnt the wisdom of controlling her temper, instead of flying into what Leofwine had used to call 'an ungovernable rage'.

'The last thing I wish to do is to tweak Jaarl Icebeard's nose,' she said.

Brother Palni put his hands together. 'Sense from you at last.'

'I like to think I always speak sense,' she said indignantly.

'My lady, you're too tender-hearted. Father Oswald has often remarked on it. But sometimes the secular world requires flint-like nerves to protect the weak.' Brother Palni drew himself up to his full height. 'We will go where we intended—to the church to deliver that blasted sword—then home again, without asking Icebeard to investigate who this man is or even mentioning his existence.'

'What are you saying?'

'Leave this Deniscan to his fate in this cave. With food and water, naturally. He'll be safe enough, I reckon. Your charitable duty ends here, my lady. Your life is destined to follow a different path from this man's.'

'You think Jaarl Icebeard had a hand in what happened to him?'

Cynehild glanced towards where Kal lay. His body had gone completely still, as if he was trying to listen to the whispered conversation. Brother Palni was right, and a more sensible person—the sort of person who was good at *tafl*, like Ansithe or Leofwine—would hold his words close to their heart and heed them. Except she couldn't.

'The Deniscan know their own,' Brother Palni said, and then barked at the men to get moving as the day was wasting.

Cynehild clapped her hands and everyone froze. 'Some of the villagers remained when my husband and I left—including my former maid Luba. We will try Luba first…see if she knows who this man is. She always seems to know everything almost before it happens.'

'What if it turns out Jaarl Icebeard is searching for him because he has done something objectionable? Or he simply wishes to rid himself of an irritant? What will you do? Return him here, even if your former maid knows who he is? How will that help anyone? You will put everyone in danger. Whoever this man is, he's far from tame or benign.'

Cynehild stared again at where the man lay, peaceful for now. It was impossible to put into words the connection she had felt with this man when he'd touched her hand. Something long slumbering inside her had woken, and for a little time she had felt less alone. She hadn't realised until that moment just how much she'd missed feeling part of something. She was not going to abandon him to his fate.

'This Kal Randrson is a good man, Brother Palni. I will work out a way to keep him alive if it comes to it.'

'How do you know that if he can't remember himself what he has or has not done?'

'My instinct tells me. Deep within me, I know I must do more to help him.'

Chapter Three

After Brother Palni had directed the men to pack up, Cynehild went over to where Kal lay and gently shook his shoulder. There was no response.

She leant down and shook harder. 'Wake up. You need to wake up. Please wake up, Kal. I'm not going to leave you behind, but you must wake up.'

His hand shot out and grabbed her arm in a strong grip. She gave a strangled cry. The fingers relaxed and let her go so she stumbled backwards.

'Kal? What is going on?'

'I feared you were someone else, but just who that was has vanished from my mind.' He put his hands together and made a vague semblance of a nod with his head. 'Deepest apologies, my lady. I must have thought the enemy who did this to me had returned to finish the job. I keep dreaming of the voice that called me a tyrant. I know it must be connected to what happened, but I don't know how.'

Cynehild rubbed her arm. Brother Palni's warning rang in her ears. Kal was a Deniscan warrior and had a warrior's instincts. 'I woke you suddenly from a restless sleep. Always a dangerous thing to do to any warrior, my late husband used to say. I bear part of the responsibility.'

He pressed his hands to his eyes. 'You offer a feeble excuse on my behalf, but it must serve. I thank you for your understanding, Lady Cynehild of Baelle Heale, and humbly beg your pardon. I hope to prove worthy of it.'

'You remember my name?'

'And our conversation.' A smile tugged at his full lips. 'Did you hope I would forget? Forget such a lovely-looking woman who gave me the secret to healing my broken heart? Already this morning my grief feels like a dull throb rather than the usual sharp pain.'

Cynehild gave a careful shrug. He didn't think she was a crone and he had remembered their conversation. Maybe he was just an accomplished liar. She hoped she had not confessed anything untoward, and that he had not noticed her reaction to his touch last night. She needed to remember that, even though she'd promised to help him, he was still dangerous.

'Do you fear being attacked while you sleep? Have you been attacked before?'

'As a warrior, battle is my life.'

'But we're at peace now.'

'Peace always requires vigilance.'

'You sound like Brother Palni.'

'I'm far better than any Northman.'

He struggled to rise and waved away her steadying hand. He eventually stood, swaying from the effort. He was even taller than she had imagined, his chest far broader, and his legs resembled tree trunks. In the morning light she could see the network of fine scars which he wore like battle honours on his face and hands. Ev-

erything about him screamed of a competent and fearsome warrior.

'I'm upright now and intend to remain so.' His cheeks
had an unhealthy pallor, and his mouth was pinched, but
there was a determined set to his jaw. 'How much danger are we in? I pledge you my sword arm, Lady Cynehild, to keep you from harm for as long as you need it.'

Cynehild forced a smile. The last thing she wanted
was Kal fighting for her in this state when she might require him to be a sacrifice to Icebeard, if Brother Palni
was to be believed.

Would he do that for her? Her stomach twisted. She
hated it that she'd even *thought* about sacrificing another
human being. Did that make her as bad as her enemy,
Icebeard?

'You remain injured and your sword is missing. You
might already have a sworn liege lord. Save the pledge
until your memory recovers.'

His slow smile in return warmed her through.

'Wise. Sensible. Beautiful. The Fates were indeed
kind to me when they made our paths cross. I'm better
than yesterday, though not as good as tomorrow.'

'You speak my lady's language better than most,
Deniscan,' Brother Palni said suspiciously, coming to
stand beside her. He bounced on the balls of his feet, as
if he longed to punch Kal on the nose, even though the
warrior was taller than him by several inches.

Kal gave a half shrug and examined his cloak, as if
he were searching for clues. 'For a time my father had a
Saxon captive. I believe I learned it from him. He used
to say I had a flair for languages. However it happened,
the words flow easy and I'm grateful for it.'

'What do you know of Jaarl Icebeard?' Brother Palni jabbed his forefinger towards Kal's chest.

'Jaarl Icebeard?' The colour drained from Kal's face.

Cynehild caught her breath.

'You see, my lady—' Brother Palni began.

'The name means nothing to me—I swear it,' Kal said, far too quickly. 'Who is this person Jaarl Icebeard? Why should I have heard of him? The only Icebeard I know is from a child's tale my mother used to tell me, and he scared me half to death. Is he your enemy? Do I need to be your champion? Because this monk will refuse, my lady.'

Cynehild ignored Brother Palni's scowl and the drawing of a threatening finger across his throat.

'Icebeard is the name of the Danish lord in these parts, that is all. Perhaps he adopted it because he knew the story and wanted to be feared.'

'You think this Jaarl Icebeard has something to do with my injury? That we quarrelled in some fashion?' His brow knitted. 'Beyond his fearsome name, what is his reputation? Is he likely to attack a man and leave him covered in gold, waiting to be robbed? Is this what passes for justice here?'

His words had unerringly hit on a weak point in their speculations. Cynehild had no real idea what Jaarl Icebeard was truly like, except that—like most of the Great Army—he had a love of gold. Why would he leave such a wealthy-looking man to be robbed by any passing stranger if he could have done so himself?

'My lady is on her way to discover his true nature. On reflection, it is better we continue our journey while you remain in this cave.' Brother Palni bowed low. 'You will heal, and we will leave supplies for a few days.' He turned to Cynehild. 'He will be able to use his gold to purchase what he needs once he reaches the next village. Although perhaps he will want to head away from Ice-beard's holdings instead of towards them.'

Cynehild clenched her hands. Brother Palni was supposed to be her advisor, not her guard. He wouldn't treat either of her sisters like this.

'You refuse to allow me the option of travelling with you?' Kal sat down and put his head in his hands before she could say anything. 'I've pledged my sword arm to your lady until the danger you face has passed. And I know in my heart that Lady Cynehild is facing danger. She barely slept last night.'

Brother Palni tilted his head to one side. 'Even though you have no idea if your sword is yours to pledge?'

'You discovered me on my own. If I had a lord or lady I would have been with others. Clearly my people have turned their backs on me.'

Brother Palni scratched his cheek. 'Perhaps they had just cause to do so.'

'My friends would not abandon me—just as I would not abandon them in a crisis.'

'How do you know that if you have no memory?'

'Flashes of scenes…but they slip away before I can fully understand what they mean.'

'Treat Kal Randrson with courtesy, Brother Palni,' Cynehild said in her firmest voice, seizing control of the conversation.

The warrior-turned-monk sometimes resembled a mother hen with an errant chick, rather than show any understanding that she could make her own decisions about her welfare.

'I have one condition, Kal. Will you tell me if you remember anything about your relationship with Icebeard before we arrive at the hall?'

Kal held out his hands and grasped hers. 'With pleasure, my lady.'

Brother Palni rolled his eyes. 'May the Good Lord give me strength.'

'I want my memories to return more than you do.' Kal's glance flickered over Brother Palni in an insulting fashion. 'Can a Northman even be a monk? My father used to tell me that you should only trust a Northman as far as you could throw him, and the best place to throw him was straight into a lake.'

'Brother Palni is a trusted friend,' Cynehild said, before the quarrel between the two men broke out in earnest. They were behaving as if they were even younger than Wulfgar. 'We are fulfilling *my* promise to my late husband. This is *my* expedition.'

Both men stared at her open-mouthed.

Palni grasped Cynehild's elbow after Kal had been helped into the covered cart. 'Before we leave, you *must* hear me.'

She tried hard to suppress her sigh.

'I distrust him more than ever,' he continued in a low voice. 'Far too smooth for my liking. He knows more than he lets on, and he only required one arm to make it into this cart, so he is clearly stronger than he appears. My duty is towards you—not some adventurer.'

'Going to Luba to see what she might know is the best solution for now,' she said. 'Hopefully his memory will be jogged along the way. It is quite possible Luba will know nothing and your concern will be unwarranted.'

Cynehild willed Brother Palni to understand.

'I'll not abandon an injured man simply because it seems expedient. How could I ever look my son in the eye again? How can I instruct him to be true to his heritage and the best sort of Mercian, honourable and decent, if I leave someone to die when I could save him? Explain that to me, Brother Palni, for I'm certain this simple woman cannot work it out.'

Palni bowed his head and gave his long-suffering sigh. 'My lady, I used to think your sister Ansithe was the most determined of you, but now I see my mistake.'

The swaying motion of the cart made the pain in Kal's head worse than ever. The journey to the cart had been excruciating, but he'd forced his body to do it. After taking the first few steps, all he'd wanted to do was collapse down onto the ground, but he knew the monk would have found a reason to leave him there.

Lady Cynehild remained his only hope of getting through this alive.

The cart hit a deep rut and swung wildly. Kal put out a hand to steady himself.

'Carts take some getting used to,' Lady Cynehild said, breaking the awkward silence which had sprung up between them since she'd sat down. 'Everyone thinks they are the easy option, but they can be hard on the bones. Pay attention to what I do, and you will soon acquire the knack.'

'I can see you have it.' He gave what he hoped was a winning smile, but suspected was more of a grimace. 'I doubt I will get used to the motion.'

'Normally I avoid carts wherever possible.'

'Why travel in one this time?'

'I want to demonstrate to the Jaarl Icebeard that I retain some standing in this world.' Lady Cynehild sat up straighter, keeping her body carefully away from his. Her eyes shone with barely suppressed hazel fire. 'I do it to honour my husband, Lord Leofwine, who once ruled these lands.'

Lord Leofwine. The words sent another pulse of uneasy cold coursing down Kal's spine. He should know the name. His instinct told him that Lady Cynehild travelled towards danger. However, given the fierceness of her expression, he knew better than to voice his concerns. He flexed his hands. When danger came, he would have to be strong enough to defend her, as he did not consider any of her men capable of doing so.

The cart lurched again. Lady Cynehild overbalanced and gave a sudden cry of alarm. Kal put out his hands to keep her from tumbling to the floor. Her breasts accidentally brushed his arm, making him aware of their inherent softness as well as the curve of her mouth.

He set her back on the bench and tore his mind away from such thoughts. 'You must heed your own advice, my lady.'

She bent her head and carefully rearranged the folds of her gown. 'I rarely fall like that.'

'The road's fault.' He shrugged. He pointed towards the fine sword which had fallen into the footwell. 'Yours?'

'My late husband's.' She gathered it up and placed it behind the bench. 'His dying wish was to have it returned to the church where his forebears are buried. Despite the danger which everyone keeps telling me about, I organised this expedition in his honour. I think my father thought I'd return before I had been gone three days, but my goal is in sight and I won't give up now.'

Kal pinched the bridge of his nose. It occurred to him that Lady Cynehild's journey had something to do with why he'd been out on that hill. But as quickly as the thought arrived, it vanished again into the dark abyss.

'Impressive,' he said.

'What is? The fact that I am able to organise my men properly? That I am willing to take responsibility for you? Or that I am aware I'm taking a chance on your peaceful intentions?' She tapped the bench with an impatient finger. 'Out with it, Kal. Why exactly am I impressive?'

He laced his fingers about his knee. 'It is impressive that you control your men so well. And that you venture into enemy territory to honour your husband's dying wish despite the obvious risks.'

'Why do men continually think women are fragile flowers, incapable of coherent thought and their own defence?'

Lady Cynehild leant towards him. The neck of her dark blue gown gaped open, affording him an intimate view of her chest.

'Widows like me very quickly discover that batting your lashes and hoping for a man to rescue you is fruitless. Why would I want to depend on a man for my rescue, in any case?'

'Because they are more likely to have been trained in using a sword. There is more to it than picking it up and swinging it,' he said, to redirect his thoughts from her lush curves.

'I know all about the need for proper training. I gave a promise to my late husband that I will raise our son, Wulfgar, to honourable manhood. He is going to be the sort of warrior his father would have been proud of—

dedicated, decent, and above all honourable. The very epitome of what a Mercian warrior should be. As his father was.'

He wondered if she knew how she stole the breath from his lungs when she banged her fists together like that. Such passion for her son's future. He'd be willing to wager that she'd accomplish it successfully, and a thousand other things besides.

He silently cursed. He had nothing. What business did he have hankering after a capable lady like Cynehild— particularly one with a son? Despite his child only living for a short breath of time, he knew he'd loved him with his whole heart and that he'd failed him as a father.

'I've always found wilting fragile flowers to be more trouble than they are worth,' he said. 'Would I even be alive if you were prone to fainting or hysterics?'

Cynehild's distinct sniff bounced off the walls, but the corners of her mouth twitched upwards.

The renewed jolting of the cart as it hit another bump in the road sent him careening into her. This time his chest hit hers, her soft curves a welcome cushion against his hard muscle. He watched the bow-like curve of her mouth like a hawk as her tongue came out and moistened her bottom lip. Their breath interlaced and time slowed to a standstill.

The temptation to taste the sweetness of her lips swamped him. He moved forward, his mouth hovering over hers, but his last remaining sense of what was right and proper stopped him.

Drawing on all his reserves, he levered himself off her and moved as far away from her as he could get. His whole body thrummed from their brief encounter.

If anything, his increasing desire for her showed him

that she'd been wrong about him—his goodness did *not* extend to propriety towards ladies of high birth and knowing his place in the world. But he longed to demonstrate to her that he could be the sort of warrior she'd described—honourable, courageous and decent. For Lady Cynehild's regard, he was willing to try.

'My balance remains the tiniest bit unsteady,' he said into the uncomfortable silence. 'Forgive me.'

She bent her head and fiddled with her belt, but her cheeks had turned the colour of a spring dawn. 'Brace your feet and you will find it easier to maintain your balance.'

'An excellent suggestion.'

Kal forced his gaze out through the narrow slit of a window. A stone wall and a great oak with branches like curved longboats waiting to go to sea sent a surge of recognition through him. They were passing through his lands. *His.* Not anyone else's, but his.

His mouth went dry. But if these lands belonged to him, then *he* was Jaarl Icebeard, the ruthless warrior who had taken Lady Cynehild's land. And if he was that man, the very last thing he was, was honourable and decent.

The voice that had come to him once he'd regained consciousness resounded once again in his mind, this time uttering a fuller sentence—*'Thus shall all tyrants fall, Icebeard!'*

He put his hand over his ears. *Impossible.* He would surely know if he was a great lord who had abandoned all notions of honour. He was simply Kal, son of Randr, from a forgettable homestead near Ribe, a long way from home, slow to anger and very much attracted to a woman who was far above him in station. His heart told him that he was a better man than any tyrant who ruled these lands with a sharp sword and an even quicker temper.

'Such a serious expression, Kal. You don't need to cling on to the bench as if it is your one hope of life.'

He couldn't confess his growing suspicion to Cynehild. He wanted her to look at him with kindness for a little while longer.

Truly, his one hope was that this woman they sought would put his fears to rest.

He swallowed hard and sought to regain some sort of control. 'My head aches something fierce, my lady.'

Sometimes in her dreams, when she was back at Baelle Heale, with Wulfgar snuggled up close to her and all was still, Cynehild would be coming down the Fosse Way towards the old hall, banners flying, triumphant, with everyone pleased to see her return because she brought peace and prosperity to a war-torn land.

Now that they were nearing Jaarl Icebeard's new hall there was no denying that the woods, with their stands of freshly coppiced trees and the scent of charcoal-making hanging in the air, were being worked, rather than being allowed to grow unchecked as they had done when she lived here. And the fields were full of livestock rather than left fallow and gorse-strewn as she'd last seen them.

To her slight disappointment, after their most recent collision, Kal had discovered his balance and not jostled her again. The ease between them had vanished as if it had never been.

For several heartbeats, she'd thought he might use the unsteadiness of the cart deliberately, to give him another opportunity to kiss her, but he seemed to have dozed off.

Much to her chagrin, she'd spent most of the journey

wondering what his lips would feel like against hers. She still wondered now—and she wasn't sure what sort of widow, whose heart had supposedly been buried with her husband, that made her.

They shuddered to a halt. She angled her head so that she could peer out through the narrow slit of the window better. A curl of smoke filtered lazily up through the thatched roof of a cottage which was set some way away from the others. Occupied, certainly, but by whom?

Luba, she hoped.

Her former maid had refused to go with them, even though Cynehild had attempted to cajole her. Luba had said that the land was in her family's blood and neither she nor her husband wanted to run like scared hares.

'Breathe, Lady Cynehild. All will be well,' Kal said.

'You sound awfully sure for a man who has little memory.'

His eyes crinkled at the corners, making her want to tumble into their smile. 'Who could resist your plea for help?'

'Are you trying to calm my nerves with easy words, Kal? Or are you like this with all the ladies?'

'I prefer to speak the truth as I see it. It saves having to remember the lies.' He lowered his voice. 'I have faith in your ability to persuade. Shall we?'

He held out his hand. In the unforgiving early spring light, the battle scars on his hands shone silver. She ignored the outstretched fingers and busied herself with straightening her *couvre-chef*. Kal had seen through her bravado and sought to reassure her. She struggled to remember when Leofwine or her sisters had ever done that.

'Wait in the cart until we know what is happening.

Caution above everything,' she said, giving him a severe look.

'I wouldn't want you to be without protection,' he said, with a youthful half-smile.

However, there was nothing about his muscular body that was remotely immature. Whatever he had done before the accident, she knew he had not sat around nor allowed himself to run to fat.

'Brother Palni will be sufficient, I promise.'

A dimple winked at the corner of his mouth. 'I keep forgetting the esteemed Brother Palni. Call me if you need a warrior who is well used to battle instead of one who is used to prayer.'

With Brother Palni at her side, muttering about the impertinence of Deniscan warriors, she knocked on the cottage door. An elderly woman peeped out, spied the visitors' identity, and rapidly started to close the door. Cynehild stuck her foot in the doorway.

'Luba? Is that any way to greet an old friend?' Cynehild said with forced cheerfulness. 'I know I'm fuller of figure than the last time we met—my clothes inform me of that fact—but surely I'm not that greatly altered?'

'My lady? After all this time and looking so well...' The woman opened the door a touch wider and made the barest of curtsies. 'We heard about your late husband, my lady. Over a year ago, if I'm remembering rightly. My condolences. I never expected to see you here again, what with the peace treaty and all. We are content under the Danelaw. Our lands prosper.'

Cynehild pressed her hands together. Once Luba would have been fawning over her, inviting her to eat, drink and gossip, but now she practically seemed to be shooing her away with her hands, as if her former mistress were an unwelcome memory rather than an old friend.

'The Jaarl Icebeard has granted me permission to return Lord Leofwine's sword to his ancestors' crypt,' said Cynehild, ignoring Luba's disapproving expression. 'Lord Leofwine asked me to do it with his dying breath. He held these lands and the people on them ever dear in his heart.'

'We are well-settled under the Danes,' said Luba. 'My daughter has just married one of them—a good provider and well connected. Jaarl Icebeard himself favoured the match.' She came out into the yard, slamming the door behind her before speaking in a low whisper. 'You'd have been better to remain far away from here, Lady Cynehild. You *and* Lord Leofwine's sword. You are stirring up things which are best left to lie, if you understand my meaning.'

Cynehild blinked rapidly. Luba had it wrong. The last thing she wanted was a revolt or unrest. There was no way she could command an army. She wanted only to get Leofwine's gold from the church and leave. Return to Baelle Heale and her life. Unfortunately, the unvarnished truth was one thing which had to remain hidden.

'What is the harm in greeting an old friend?' she asked.

The woman's hands gripped each other until her knuckles shone white. 'You are not intending on staying and causing trouble, my lady? This land has seen far too much already. The fields burned and the rivers ran red with blood during the war.'

Cynehild tilted her head to one side, trying to fathom Luba's mood. 'We're well-settled at Baelle Heale with my father. My son, Wulfgar, grows strong, but remains a young boy. We respect the peace treaty and have no plans to challenge it.'

'It is good to know that you and the bonny lad are happy there.'

'My invitation remains—there is room for you and your family at Baelle Heale should you require it. And Jaarl Icebeard has promised safe passage for me and all of my party.'

'I said it before you left and I'll say it again—the only way out of this cottage for me is in a box. But thank you kindly all the same, Lady Cynehild.' The woman flicked her tongue over her lips and made another perfunctory curtsy. 'Our business ended years ago, my lady.'

She reached for the door.

'I refuse to believe you wish us harm, Luba,' Cynehild said, before the woman vanished inside. 'My men and I plan to go to the church today and lay Leofwine's sword. Are we walking into a trap? Is that what you are trying to warn me of, without saying it directly?'

The woman let out a huge sigh. 'Things are in a to-do, my lady. A right to-do. Mind you keep out of trouble. I did love that little boy of yours as a tiny baby... But best to leave that there sword elsewhere, if you get my meaning. In fact, stay away from people if you can. Best for all concerned. And don't mention this visit, for all our sakes.'

'I only arrived in these lands yesterday, after being away for three years. How can I have done anything wrong?'

Luba put a hand to the side of her mouth and whispered, 'The Jaarl Icebeard has gone missing. He went out hunting on his own yesterday morning and has not been seen since. Vanished into thin air. Some whisper that he has been murdered. Others claim that it is witchcraft, and he has been enchanted at some fairy feast. Even now they are searching the lands for him, but no one holds out much hope.'

A sliver of ice went down Cynehild's spine. She didn't dare look at Brother Palni, but his warning about becoming involved in peculiar Deniscan affairs resonated in her mind. Between Kal's appearance and Icebeard's disappearance, *odd* was the most polite word to describe things.

'Do you know that he is dead?'

'If he has been murdered or harmed it will go ill for us.' The woman twisted her apron. 'Things were settling down, what with his reputation and all, and the raiders left us in peace. I do not know what this world is coming to... If it is all the same to you, my lady, I don't wish to stand here and chat—particularly not to the lady of my old lord, who is going to plant a sword on the very day after my new lord has vanished without a trace. Surely even you must see that?'

Cynehild understood what the woman was saying. If this Icebeard's body was discovered, and it was found that he had been murdered, the temptation to look no further than the old lord's lady, who had chosen that very day to appear, waving her late husband's sword, would be overwhelming.

'I'm innocent in this,' she said.

'Do you really think that will matter?' Luba asked. 'Go, my lady. Consider yourself fortunate that you learned of the peril before you blundered into it. Lord

Leofwine would have insisted you remain safe. He never wanted a warrior for a wife.'

She went back in the cottage and started to pull the door shut.

Cynehild put her hand up. 'Please—please. Wait. Listen to me… I discovered an injured Dane yesterday, called Kal Randrson. His memory has gone. Kal Randrson, come out of the cart! Immediately!'

Kal slowly unfolded his bulk from the cart. In his hand he carried Leofwine's sword. A slight breeze blew his dark blond hair from his face.

Luba peered around Cynehild and then crossed herself. 'By all the saints!'

'Do you know him, Luba? Tell me the truth—what sort of Dane is he?'

'That is no ordinary Dane,' the woman whispered. 'That is Icebeard himself. Or someone who is his exact double. But Jaarl Icebeard never wore that expression on his face. He normally scowled instead of smiling. What in the name of all that is holy has happened to him? What game are you playing, Lady Cynehild?'

Cynehild's stomach roiled at the enormity of it— someone had attacked Icebeard and left him for dead on that hillside, and it seemed likely they had intended that she, or rather her visit, would get blamed for the action.

'Kal Randrson is the Jaarl Icebeard? Are you certain of it? For goodness' sake, Luba, do not play me false on this.'

'I'm certain, my lady.' Luba raised her voice. 'I know my new lord, don't I? Jaarl Icebeard visited this very cottage not eight weeks ago, to insist my daughter marry the man who is now her husband.'

* * *

A rushing roar filled Kal's ears. His growing fear had been confirmed.

The elderly woman continued to speak and to call him Icebeard, getting more and more agitated. He struggled to place the woman standing before him, but she was simply another Saxon face. She appeared adamant in her claim, coming over to him and tugging on his arm until he wanted to call out.

The pain in his head had increased to unbearable levels. He wasn't a tyrant. He knew he cared about people.

He took her hand from his forearm. 'You know me, woman? Can you tell me my recent history?'

'My daughter serves at your hall, my lord.' The woman swept into a very low curtsy. 'You gave a farm to my son-in-law as a wedding present. You are Lord of the lands of Ecgmundton, which used to belong to this lady's husband until he fled them in a blind panic rather than staying to defend them. I may be old, but I'm not daft, Lord Icebeard.'

Kal shook his head. Her words were like annoying bees, swarming about him, piercing the pain in his head. Echoing through the agony, he heard the name *Icebeard* being shouted over and over, and knew deep down that he despised it, even though he must have claimed it.

He had no true idea what Icebeard represented—what he had done or how he'd gone from nothing to being the *jaarl* of these lands—and it frightened him. He knew how other men had behaved to gain land and wealth, and how he had once pledged to be different. He feared that in the testing time of battle he had been worse than they could ever be.

His stomach roiled. *Tyrant.* Maybe he had deserved

death at his attacker's hands, but instead Lady Cynehild had given him life.

Lady Cynehild and the others in her party regarded him as if he'd sprouted two heads and a curling tail. He held out his hands and tried to make light of it, but deep in his heart it hurt—they had already judged him.

'The name Icebeard is not one I care for. How did I get it?' He rubbed his hand along his jawline and felt the rough stubble. 'I sport no beard.'

The old woman gave a grunt which might mean anything. Shadows crossed over Lady Cynehild's countenance, and Brother Palni gave him a black look. No smiles of understanding or wry humour there. His heart sank.

'I discovered him bleeding and hit on the head.' Lady Cynehild's voice was far too high-pitched, her nostrils flared.

His arms ached to gather her to him. He wanted to whisper that she had done the right thing in saving his life, and he wanted the chance to prove her instinct correct—there *was* goodness in him.

'He took quite a blow. Now you are telling my lady there are rumours that Lord Icebeard has been murdered, possibly by a Mercian.' Brother Palni's face turned thunderous. 'What else, woman? Quick about it.'

'Aye, but you know what rumours are like,' the woman protested. 'They crowd out the truth before the sun rises oft-times.'

'But the truth will come out,' Kal argued. 'Once I return.'

'They will say Lady Cynehild bewitched you,' Brother Palni pointed out.

'Someone clearly wants to discredit me. Do they seek

to destroy me?' Lady Cynehild hunched her shoulders and pointedly refused to look at him. 'I found him in the woods at the top of Hangra Hill, barely conscious and weaponless. Far from wishing him ill, my men and I saved his life. Tell Luba what happened, Kal.'

'My name is Kal, son of Randr. I come from a homestead near Ribe. I know I intended on joining the Great Army after my wife and child perished.' Kal told the truth with a heavy heart. 'That is all I can recall clearly, until I woke in the cave with Lady Cynehild looking after me.'

The elderly woman's cheek paled. 'Jaarl Icebeard, you've been bewitched. A mighty fearsome witch indeed has cast a spell like that one.'

'No witchcraft, but merely a blunt object. Lady Cynehild has saved me.'

The woman sniffed. 'My lady swore vengeance on the people who took these lands. Many will remember her words, and the way she shook her fist at them. My daughter spoke of them just this morning to her husband, wondering if indeed Lady Cynehild's curse had come home to roost.'

Kal took a step forward and stumbled to his knees as the world blackened at the edges. 'Please. No more nonsense about witchcraft or Lady Cynehild's curse. Why would she bring me back here if she sought to kill me? The simplest thing would have been for her to abandon me on that hillside.'

The woman's face contorted. 'I will take my time about believing you. It still smells like an enchantment to me.'

The black darkness swirled about Kal and whispered that he was destined to be all alone, because all tyrants must fall. 'Help me… Don't leave me here, Lady Cynehild…'

Lady Cynehild was instantly there, supporting his arm. He gave in to instinct and leant on her, drinking in her faint floral scent and drawing strength from her warmth.

'Can we get him inside the cottage? Whoever did this will not know where he is. It is to our advantage if we keep it that way. Surely you must see, Luba, that his head wound was no accident? And it was certainly not I nor any of my men who inflicted the blow, whatever these false rumours claim. For all our sakes, *help* us, Luba. Your *jaarl* will reward such loyalty, I'm certain of it.'

A pulse of warmth went through Kal. He was far from alone. Cynehild had decided that she was on his side. She saw the good in him. He clung to that thought above all others. He wanted to show her that he was capable of being a better man than he greatly feared he had been. He wanted to show her that he was not her enemy…at least not any longer.

'A reward?'

'A substantial reward—particularly if we discover the true culprits.'

The woman kicked the door open. 'My daughter and her new husband are away with the searchers. Something odd is afoot here, and nobility's strange goings-on rarely benefit us common folk. But I reckon you can enter for a short time, if there is a reward in the offing.'

The buzzing pain receded and Kal began to think like the warrior he knew he was. He cast an eye over Cynehild's small band of men. If they tried to take the hall while others were out searching, it would be doomed to failure.

'Can I count on you?' he asked Cynehild.

'Yes.' Lady Cynehild put her hand under his elbow, steadying him. 'My men and I will assist you in regaining your place.'

'I will try to keep you safe.'

Lady Cynehild gave a crooked smile. 'Danger doesn't frighten me.'

'It should, my lady. But you are a lady of rare courage.' Kal ignored Brother Palni's increasingly thunderous countenance. 'We will prevail.'

Chapter Four

Luba's tiny cottage showed some alterations since the last time Cynehild had visited, but its essence remained the same. The pattern on the half-finished cloth on the loom was very different, but the pot of pottage still bubbled over the open hearth, the rough-hewn table remained under the open window and drying herbs hung from the eaves.

In the corner by the hearth a wide variety of sticks, antlers and half-carved pieces of wood stood, as if someone in the household spent most of their time carving. She focused on them, doing her best to breathe normally and trying not to think about the man standing next to her and what he represented.

'Are you truly Icebeard and not some strange double?' she asked Kal, unable to decide if she was appalled by the revelation of his true identity or not.

She had saved her enemy's life. Or if not her enemy, a man her late husband would certainly have considered *his* deadly enemy.

'I've no reason to doubt your maid's words.' He sank down heavily on the wooden bench beside the table and buried his face in his hands. 'I've little idea how I received the nickname, or what I did to deserve these lands, but it wasn't my fault you left them. My gut tells me that I have not been here long.'

Her stomach twisted. His gut and her knowledge. Like her brother-in-law, Icebeard had only acquired these lands after the peace treaty had been agreed. The lack of a lord had been one of the reasons her expedition had faced delays until now. Her brother-in-law and her father had refused to allow her to travel across such unsettled lands.

She'd fled these lands because of the Great Heathen Horde rather than because of one man. Her entire being trembled. She lifted her chin and tried to ignore the fact that he had been part of that army. She'd known that last night. Why should it be different now?

Except somehow it was.

Her own stubbornness in wanting to save Kal's life had brought her to this. She carefully avoided Brother Palni's eye. He'd have his chance to crow later.

'How did the attacker know I was expected here?' she asked, around the ash which seemed to have formed in her mouth.

'We were all aware that you planned on visiting, my lady,' Luba said, moving the pot into the glowing embers. She stirred it, releasing the sweet scent of soup into the room. 'I'd hoped to see you until the disappearance. Then I hoped you wouldn't arrive until after this was all sorted. I wish you no ill will, my lady.'

'Is this the work of someone who wants to see Lord Icebeard gone and is attempting to blame it on me?' Cynehild tried not to glance at Kal.

Luba concentrated on what she was doing before answering. 'Are you asking me to guess, my lady? If so, I'd prefer it to be witchcraft. Better for everyone if it were a witch or an enchantress and be done with it.'

Kal removed his hands from his face. 'My unseen enemy is flesh and blood.'

'I never asked anyone to attack you on my behalf,' said Cynehild. 'We—all my family—have respected the peace treaty. We did not harm you, Kal... Jaarl Icebeard. Someone else d-did.' Cynehild hated how her voice trembled on the last word. 'You offered me safe passage here. My husband's final request is all I seek to honour.'

Kal got up, laid down the sword at her feet and then backed away. 'We share an enemy, my lady. Someone has gone to considerable effort to ensure you would bear the blame, but they have made an error—you saved my life. I owe you and your men a life debt which I shall struggle to repay.'

'You do?' The tension in her shoulders relaxed. He still intended to honour that life debt. She might get out of this alive after all. However, Brother Palni would insist that they abandon all plans to lay Leofwine's sword in the church and leave immediately. He would argue that Luba could do it for them, and then any hope of finding the remaining treasure her husband had secreted away would be gone for ever.

So close, only to fail—but her mind refused to yield any ideas of how she should proceed. If she didn't come up with a workable scheme in the next few breaths her only child would be denied his opportunity to become a warrior, as she'd promised Leofwine. The jar of coins she'd already recovered would not be enough.

Brother Palni cleared his throat. 'My lady? After careful consideration...'

Cynehild examined the knot in the table as the monk began to explain his views. The glimmerings of a plan were appearing. Provided she presented it properly, Brother Palni would be left with few options except to agree.

'May I speak?' Kal thundered, interrupting the other man's ramblings. 'Someone is trying to take advantage of your visit to stir up trouble. More than that, I need you to help me regain my rightful place,' he continued in a quieter voice. 'Whoever did this to me will not rest until the deed is completed. I need to find them first. To do that I require your help, Lady Cynehild, even though I have little right to ask for it.'

'We already know that whoever did this seeks to blame you, my lady,' Brother Palni said before she could speak, his robes quivering with indignation and self-importance. 'We must return to your father immediately. Leave the Deniscan to solve his problems alone. With your former maid, he is among friends and allies.'

Cynehild lifted her chin and met his gaze. 'I made a promise to my late husband that I would deliver his sword to his ancestors' crypt. He asked it with his dying breath. My husband would not have wanted to bring more suffering to this land. Maybe as he lay dying he had some sort of fantasy that people would rise up if they saw his sword, but that was before the treaty. I am not interested in raising a rebellion; I value peace far more than I value these lands.'

She firmed her mouth. Brother Palni sought to wrap her up in freshly carded wool and keep her safe. And she was grateful for his concern, but she knew he would have never dared speak to her sisters in that fashion.

'We are left with the conclusion that it is someone

close to you, Kal, who seeks to use my intended visit as an excuse to cover his tracks, rather than someone close to me. You will be in danger if you return to your hall in this weakened state.'

Kal tapped a finger against his mouth. Since learning of his identity he seemed to be far sterner…colder, somehow. 'Agreed. It leaves them free to strike again, and the next time you might not be here to help me.'

'Lady Cynehild definitely won't be. Because she will be leaving,' Brother Palni said.

'Do you think you should return to your hall even with little memory? Let the people know that you remain alive despite the rumours? Or is there another way to deal with this?' Cynehild asked, ignoring Brother Palni.

Kal reached out and captured her hand. A warm pulse travelled up her arm. She tugged gently and he let go.

'Who can I trust in that hall? Who will keep me safe? I beg you, Lady Cynehild, have mercy on me.'

'I have already promised to aid you, and I vow to you again now that I will remain with you until the true culprit is unmasked,' Cynehild said firmly, ignoring Brother Palni's bleating about doom and being cautious. 'But we must first consider if you are fit to travel.'

The dark lights in Kal's eyes deepened. 'If at all possible, my head wound must heal. I want time to remember properly, and to ponder on who might have done this to me. We can then proceed with a plan to bring them to justice and discover how I can regain my hall.'

'As a general rule of thumb, the culprit is normally the person who will benefit most,' Brother Palni said with a raised eyebrow. 'But what can a mere man of the cloth know about such things?'

'Who *does* benefit most from doing this to you?'

Cynehild asked, trying to contain her excitement. 'Who stands to inherit if you die, Kal?'

Kal shrugged and shook his head. 'Do you know, Luba?'

Luba bustled self-importantly. 'Icebeard's cousin Alff—but he has been ill since just after my daughter's wedding. That man is no leader of men, from what my new son-in-law has confided.' Luba pursed her lips. 'There may be others who want your lands, though. You are unmarried, my lord. True enough. And you've no children. People have remarked on this. You were even overheard at my daughter's wedding saying that finding a wife was a task which must be achieved soon. The wagers certainly flew at the feast about the possible identity of your bride.'

A dimple flashed in the corner of Kal's cheek. 'Wagering on the identity of my bride? Did you do so?'

Luba's cheeks turned crimson. 'I wouldn't like to say, my lord... You merely laughed and shook your head when questioned as to who she might be.'

'Excellent,' Cynehild said, striking her hands together. 'My scheme will work even better than I'd anticipated.'

Brother Palni cleared his throat dramatically. 'My lady, you're wearing that troublesome expression again. Think before you act, I beg you. Your sisters would beg you on bended knee. Return to your young son.'

Cynehild planted her feet more firmly on the ground. Ansithe seldom paused for consultation. She simply acted. And Elene did likewise.

She knew a pretend betrothal between her and Kal was the perfect solution to both their problems.

Her mind raced at the possibilities. If the treasure's hiding place was not immediately obvious she would be able to spend time praying alone in the church, under the guise of being his betrothed. She would be buying time to find it and then, once she had, she'd confess to Kal, who would be so grateful that she had saved his lands that she'd be able to depart with the gold which rightfully belonged to Wulfgar.

If looked at properly, Kal being Icebeard was an opportunity—a sign that she was being correct in adhering to her pledge to help him. And it wasn't as if they were really going to marry, or were even attracted to each other in that way—it was merely a tale which would serve them both well.

Liar, a place deep inside her whispered. He'd awakened something she considered long dead, but she wasn't about to explore that. He could have his pick of young beautiful women, while she knew well that her waist was no longer less than a double handspan and that her hair had become a dull straw mass instead of spun gold.

'We will use our betrothal to explain Kal's sudden absence.'

At everyone's perplexed expression, she smiled and pretended that Kal's open-mouthed shock failed to sting.

'We will say that he and I have reached a prior understanding about marriage, but wanted to meet face to face before announcing it to anyone else. It will explain why he laughed at the wagers, as no one could have guessed who I was. Very simple. I've decided to be a peace-weaver between the new lord and my old people.'

Brother Palni muttered various curses which a monk surely should have forgotten under his breath. 'Now I wonder whose head has been injured! My lady, think about what you are saying. You're volunteering to marry a Deniscan—not just anyone, but the man who holds your late husband's lands. Leofwine will be spinning in his grave. Icebeard's reputation is one of great fierceness. What he has, he holds. No quarter given.'

'It is as well you have such a high opinion of me, monk,' Kal interjected fiercely.

'It is as well that you're injured and I am a man of God or we would meet in combat, Deniscan.'

'I look forward to that time.'

'Please… Quarrelling only benefits our mutual enemy.' Cynehild stretched out her arms and waited for silence to fall. 'Be calm, Brother Palni. I do not intend *actually* to marry him. We simply need to be betrothed for the little time it will take to uncover our mutual enemy. We will set a trap to capture him when Kal is well enough to return.'

'But what do you gain from this, my lady?' Palni tapped his temples. 'I am trying to get my thick skull around the idea. You are going to be betrothed without any intention of marrying. Without your father's leave, I might add.'

'I gain justice.'

'For a Deniscan? I will hold my tongue and pray for divine intervention.'

'No, Brother Palni. I gain by not being falsely accused of trying to start a war, for one thing. For another, I will be able to finish the task my husband gave me. If I go into the church now to lay the sword someone will accuse me of engineering Kal's disappearance. Or blame me for Kal's injuries if he goes with me.'

Brother Palni scowled. 'Your father would not approve.'

'Under Mercian law, as a widow, I'm my own person and can make binding contracts myself. My father's views on the subject are therefore unimportant.'

Brother Palni bowed his head. 'Return to Baelle Heale. You have almost accomplished what Leofwine demanded of you. Allow this woman to place the sword on your behalf. Go back to your son. Be the sort of mother he needs—a living one.'

'My promise to Icebeard binds me.'

Kal lifted his head. 'Your man is right—you will be putting yourself in grave danger for a stranger.'

'I trust you to protect me. You pledged your sword to me earlier. Does that pledge still hold?'

'Obviously.' He stood and held out his hands. 'I'm honoured by your faith in me. I accept your unorthodox proposal. Shall we seal it with a kiss?'

'A kiss?' Cynehild retreated several steps. 'It is a betrothal of convenience—that is all.'

A shadowy dimple appeared at the corner of his mouth. 'If anyone asks, I must be able to say I have kissed my betrothed. Keeping to the truth as much as possible is best in these situations.'

'A wise precaution.'

She strode to where he stood and rose up on her toes, intending to give him a quick peck on the cheek. His arms came about her and brought her against his chest. He lowered his mouth to hers and claimed her lips. The searing kiss which lasted no more than a heartbeat infused her with heat from the top of her head to the bottom of her feet.

His arms fell away. He nodded. 'That is how I kiss my future bride, in case you are interested.'

Cynehild tested her lips with her tongue. They ached for more than just the briefest of touches. She was tempted to return to Brother Palni's side, but her legs had turned to water.

She forced her knees to lock before stepping stiffly backwards, increasing the distance between them as quickly as she dared. 'Our betrothal begins.' Her voice sounded far too breathless for her liking.

'You and the Jaarl Icebeard are betrothed?' Luba fanned herself. 'Oh, my... Nobody will have anticipated this. I wonder if the wagering remains open.'

Kal took off one of his golden brooches and pressed it into the woman's hand. 'Keep my secret and you will have another of these when all this is completed.'

Luba retreated. 'If someone finds me with it they will think I had something to do with your disappearance.'

'Keep it hidden until this is over,' Cynehild said. 'And tell no one about Kal's injury.'

'Not even my family?'

'Especially not them.' Cynehild took a deep breath. 'They work in the hall, and we want to keep this our secret.'

'I'd best be putting this away, then,' Luba said, and left the room.

Kal watched Cynehild closely. 'What happens after we discover who did this to me and bring them to justice?'

'We go our separate ways.' She pressed her palm against her belt. The tweezers dug into her flesh. 'Return to our old lives. My desire to remain a widow is well established. Before I left Baelle Heale I made this fact known to my father.' She gave a pointed cough. 'Nothing that has occurred since has altered my views.'

'I will abide by your conditions.' He bowed, captured her hand and raised it to his lips. 'Our betrothal lasts until it no longer suits our purpose.'

The soft touch of his mouth on her skin sent another pulse of heat racing up her arm. She gently tugged and he released her hand. 'A second kiss?' she asked.

He bowed. 'The second agreement required one, my lady. May we find many things to agree to in the future.'

Cynehild ignored the renewed aching in her mouth. She was not about to fall into his arms. Her heart belonged to Leofwine, but she could not deny that the ice which had encased it for so long had started to melt.

'There will be little need for a third agreement, I think,' she said.

'But I shall continue to live in hope.'

'What do you want me to do, my lady?' Brother Palni asked, elbowing his way between them, breaking the spell. 'Someone is sure to notice your men milling about this place and ask awkward questions. Not wanting to pour cold water on your scheme, but I can see grave flaws in it. You should have discussed this sensibly before making an agreement.'

'Return to Baelle Heale. Acquire a larger contingent of men. We may have need of them.' Cynehild ticked off the points on her fingers. 'Without my covered cart you will go much faster.'

'It would be better if I went to Moir, even if the journey there is less straightforward.' Palni frowned. 'You should come with me, but I doubt you will do that. You are too stubborn for your own good.'

'Can you visit both—Moir and Baelle Heale? We will be safe here,' Cynehild said.

A great longing to see her son's face swept over her. She wanted to cradle him to her bosom and drink in his little-boy scent. Wulfgar would squirm and protest, as he always did these days. But she was doing this for him, she reminded herself.

'I've a message I want to send to my son, Wulfgar, Brother Palni—one I want you to deliver personally. And Father Oswald may have remedies which assist in recovering memories.'

Brother Palni appeared unhappier than ever. 'We don't have time to waste, my lady. I want to go to Moir and—'

'No, you must go to Father Oswald and Wulfgar first. Promise me. That way you won't get lost, trying to go across country.'

The monk gave an unhappy nod. 'Where will you wait for me? Back at the cave?'

'Is the charcoal burner's cottage still empty?' Cynehild turned towards Luba, who had returned from secreting the brooch. 'The one in the middle of the woods?'

'Imagine you remembering that place, my lady. I haven't thought about it since the cankerous old man died. Far too fond of his own company for my liking.' Luba was suddenly all smiles. 'It remains empty as far as I know. You are wonderfully clever, my lady, to remember that tumbled-down hut.'

'We will stay there, waiting for your return, Brother Palni. Far more sensible than returning to the cave. I reckon we will be fine for some days there.'

The monk made a few more clucking noises but promised.

Kal inclined his head. 'My fortune changed when I encountered you, Lady Cynehild. But I think another long journey in that covered cart would have been the death of me.'

Luba promised to get all the information she could, as well as providing provisions for them, and began to bustle about the cottage, pulling out the various herbs Cynehild requested while Brother Palni and his men piled food and bedding into the cart.

'My lady,' she whispered as she handed the herbs to Cynehild. 'It would not be a bad thing if you became his wife in truth, now that I turn my mind to it. He is a fine figure of a man and he would treat you well. I saw how he kissed you. And I know a love potion or three.'

Cynehild watched how the afternoon sunshine played on Kal's face, highlighting his cheekbones and the network of silver scars on his skin as he attempted to help Brother Palni by carrying a feather pillow, rather than remain seated in the cart. This man was her enemy, who had ultimately taken away her son's birthright. She was engaging in this play-acting to prevent a blight falling on this slowly recovering land, rather than because she harboured any notions about marriage or anything else with him.

She ignored the small place in her which instead of whispering now screamed, *Liar!* 'That will never happen,' she said.

Kal regarded the small cottage which had once belonged to the charcoal burner with a dispassionate eye. His childhood home had not been much bigger than this. It was marginally better than the cave for comfort, but he agreed with Lady Cynehild that it would be easier to supply and there was even a half-ruined outbuilding where the covered cart could be stored.

Lady Cynehild had put herself in danger for him, but he wasn't quite certain of the reason why. He was grateful, but he didn't flatter himself that she secretly wished to be his wife or was seeking power. There was something important about her visit, something she wanted to keep hidden from him, but the precise knowledge hovered just on the edge of his memory, tantalising him with its nearness. He would have to discover another way to get her to reveal her secret.

The memory of how her mouth had trembled under his and how it had left him longing for more filled him. He wanted her, but their coming together had to be her decision, even if he would be delighted to assist in the making of that decision.

'Does it suit?' Cynehild asked, coming up to stand beside him.

Her gold-blond hair had slipped from its confines, and a dirty smudge had taken up residence by the side of her nose, but what he really noticed was the brilliance of her expression.

'Despite it not being used for a few years, the roof is not in a bad state of repair,' she said. 'Tomorrow my men will begin working on making it even more secure.'

Kal forced his gaze upwards. A few small holes showed in the thatch. 'This cottage will have to be put to good use after we go. It is hard to believe I was unaware of it.'

'How do you know you were unaware?'

'Because I know what good shelter can mean to a person.'

He pushed away the memory of his father's hovel. A place like this would have once meant so much to his family and he'd allowed it to decay. What sort of leader had he become?

'Are you willing to do all this simply to deliver a sword?' he asked.

Her hands trembled as she began to sort through the

herbs, separating them into piles. 'I haven't travelled all this way to give up now.'

'Then I'm grateful.'

She handed him several pillows. 'Put those on the pile of ferns over there. You'll need to rest and regain your strength.'

Before he could ask more, she hurried off, shouting orders to her men. Lady Cynehild was one of those managing women Kal normally avoided, but he stood for a heartbeat longer, watching how her skirts swayed about her full hips, revealing the slenderness of her calves.

'Lady Cynehild was an excellent lady to my former lord,' Luba said, sidling up to him with a further pile of bedding. 'You could do far worse than to get her for a wife. Her figure is fuller than it used to be, but still pleasing, yes?'

Kal took the furs from her. The pain of losing Ranka and their son had diminished steadily since he'd left the cave. But he knew he did not require another relationship like the one he'd once had—one of passionate fights and even more passionate coming together at the beginning, and one in which he'd feared coming home to Ranka's uncertain temper and her scorn at his lack of ambition near the end. He wanted a partner to share confidences with, to grow old with, to spend time with.

'Are you trying to be a matchmaker? I've no need for one. I will get a wife of my own choosing—those are words which I have probably repeated over and over throughout the years.'

Luba rushed over to the ferns and rapidly made up a bed. 'At my daughter's wedding you admitted that you would have to marry soon as you required sons. Alff shouted out that you must ensure any wife you chose was capable of bearing live children. You agreed. Lady Cynehild has had a child.'

'You heard the lady—our relationship will end when my enemy is unmasked.'

'It is something to think on, my lord.' The woman patted the bedding meaningfully. 'Ponder how your destiny lies, if you get my meaning.'

Kal's heart plummeted. He greatly suspected the woman had made a similar remark to Cynehild. No wonder she'd appeared more nervous than an unbroken horse earlier.

'Nothing can be settled until I regain my lordship and the person who did this to me is punished.' He pointed towards the door. 'I need time to heal, with Lady Cynehild as my nurse. Time to plan my next move.'

Luba curtsied. 'I understand, my lord. You can count on me and my family.'

'Excellent. Return to your cottage and get about your business, before people start questioning you on your whereabouts, and you will have yet more gold.'

The woman hurried off. He watched her retreating figure and hoped that he was doing the right thing in allowing her to go. She appeared loyal, but appearances could be deceptive. Kal resisted the temptation to touch his aching head. In his gut, he knew Cynehild and her men had not caused the injury, even though he strongly suspected they would be blamed for it unless he could find the true culprit. He couldn't do enough to keep her safe.

Cynehild stormed into the cottage, hands on her hips, nostrils flaring. 'That woman! She seeks to matchmake! Despite her promises to say nothing, I am certain she will find a way to place a wager on us marrying.'

Kal tried not to smile. 'I take it you overheard the conversation?'

Her feet skittered to a stop. 'Luba spoke out of turn to me earlier. She has always had a romantic streak, but this is beyond ridiculous—she put herbs for ensuring my womb won't quicken amongst the ones I require to make a salve for your head. I want you to know I've no intention of marrying you, lying with you or anything else Luba might have suggested.'

Her tongue moistened her bottom lip, turning it the colour of a newly budded rose. Kal fought against the urge to grab her hand and pull her down to the bed with him.

'Our relationship is purely for show,' she went on. 'I must insist on it being strictly platonic.'

Platonic. The word fell like a hammer blow. The hand which had almost reached for her stayed at his side. His task was going to be harder than either he or Luba anticipated, but he wanted to show Cynehild just how good it could be between them. Her earlier response to his kiss had already proved the existence of a strong attraction between them.

'We will find an excuse which suits when the times comes,' he said.

Her hands toyed with her belt, clinking the scissors and tweezers together. 'I just wanted to make sure you understood.'

'There needs to be a spark of affection between us if we are to convince people we have agreed to meet face to face to discuss a betrothal.'

'There wasn't between my husband and I to begin with. It was all my father's doing. He sought to increase his power at court with our marriage.' Her gaze dropped to the rushes. 'Affection and desire came later, but when it arrived I knew I never wanted another husband.'

A surge of jealousy coursed through him. Familiarity had certainly bred contempt in his marriage on Ranka's side. But Lady Cynehild had genuinely loved her husband. He was going to be fighting a powerful ghost if he enticed her into his bed. But before their time here ended, he hoped Cynehild would reveal that her entire heart hadn't been buried with Leofwine.

'Your devotion to your husband continues beyond the grave?'

'I've a son to raise. He needs to be the sort of warrior his father would have admired.'

'Yet you're here without your son. You entrust his care to another.'

Her hands clenched. 'Travelling can be dangerous. His safety is my paramount concern. Keeping him tied to my skirts would have been a poor idea. He'll need to start his proper training soon. But I miss him with every breath I take.'

Her explanation was almost too pat and easy, as if she'd rehearsed it. Was she expecting trouble when she laid Leofwine's sword? Or did she simply want to ensure Kal did not make the wrong assumption about her?

He balled his fists and concentrated, trying to remember why he'd permitted her journey here in the first place. What had he wanted from her? Why had he invited the widow of his enemy onto his lands? He pressed his fist into his forehead.

'You've gone pale. You've done far too much today.' She pointed towards the bed. 'If you won't go willingly, my men will force you.'

He raised an eyebrow. 'You'll find me more willing

to obey if you lace your orders with honey, rather than coat them in vinegar. A promise. An inducement. *Go to bed, Kal, and I will tuck you in.*'

'You're older than four.'

'I still like being tucked in. What say you, Lady Cynehild—shall we get to bed?'

Her cheeks turned bright pink. 'Distractions won't work. My son constantly tries them as well.'

He bent towards a chair, but the world tilted and then righted itself. He sat down heavily. 'The spring sun on my face warms me. I'll rest here for now and save bed for when you are in a more indulgent mood.' He deliberately crossed his arms and closed his eyes.

'Until the cart is unloaded, then. But don't try my patience. You will lose.' Her heels clicked against the stones as she strode away.

'Deniscan! I know you are awake!' Brother Palni said, setting something down on the floor with an almighty crash.

Kal opened one eye and quickly shut it again.

'You might have fooled her with soft words and an appreciative look or three, but I know what your kind are like. Anything happens to her—anything at all—and I will come looking for you. Then you will really wish you'd died out there on the hill. My skills with a knife are renowned.'

Kal sat up straighter. Should anything dire happen to Lady Cynehild, Brother Palni would not have to do anything, because Kal himself would ensure her attacker didn't live. But he refused to give Brother Palni the satisfaction of knowing that.

'Christian monks take a vow of peace and charity towards all, don't they?'

Brother Palni stuck his nose closer to Kal's. 'Sometimes I have trouble with my vows.'

'I'll carry your words in my heart and ponder them at regular intervals.'

The monk gave a large huff and stalked away, his robes twitching in disapproval.

'I'm going to try one last time to convince you to leave, my lady,' Brother Palni said, standing beside his horse, his weathered face creased with concern.

Cynehild hugged her arms about her waist. The missing gold represented so much more to her than precious metal—it was Leofwine's final gift to his son, proving that in his final breaths he'd understood the necessity of ensuring Wulfgar's future and trusted her to give their son that future. He'd finally shown that he believed she could do more than simply keep house, and she didn't want to betray that faith in her. If she left now, she betrayed everything.

'I gave Kal my oath to look after him before God, Brother Palni. I know you consider the promise unwise, but I refuse to abandon him for expediency's sake.' She touched the monk's arm.

'But why can't someone else place the sword?' he asked.

'It wouldn't be the same and you know it.'

'Kal Randrson lied to you earlier—he omitted to tell you that he was Jaarl Icebeard. No one, my lady, becomes as great as Icebeard without being ruthless. He seeks to play games with you. Why keep a promise to one like him?'

'I will let Moir know you think so highly of men who become *jaarls*.'

'There were circumstances for Moir acquiring power, as you well know.' Brother Palni jabbed his finger towards her. 'But Jaarl Icebeard!'

'He prefers Kal. Icebeard was the name of a frost giant who used to frighten him as a child.'

'Kal the Icebeard wants more from you than you are prepared to give. I saw how he watched your hips move.'

'First you tell me I'm a withered crone, unlikely to tempt a man, and now you say he is overcome with barely controlled lust. Do make up your mind.' Cynehild rubbed the back of her neck. More than she was prepared to give? Was this Brother Palni's mealy-mouthed way of saying Kal desired her? 'I'm old enough not to have my head turned by a handsome face.'

'That remains to be seen.'

'Knowing who he is, is not the question; what's more important is what we are going to do with that knowledge?'

Brother Palni played with his rosary and muttered about the follies of women playing politics.

Cynehild fought against the urge to scream. She'd experienced too much of that attitude from Leofwine as a young bride. In the interests of marital harmony she'd learned to swallow her opinions, but no one was going to silence her on this expedition.

'Please remember who is in charge, and also that I possess a functioning brain.'

'What are you hoping for with this, my lady? Was that woman right—do you want an actual betrothal with the Jaarl? Do you seek to become mistress of these lands again? Is that why you were so insistent that we travel here without your son? I know you were reputed to be a beauty, but that was some years ago.'

'A betrothal to Kal was the last thing on my mind until it became clear that we needed an excuse to be together,' Cynehild said. The betrothal had been a sudden inspiration, not part of some long-planned scheme. Surely Brother Palni of all people understood that. 'Why do people persist in thinking that I have plans to remarry? Why should I want another husband? Why can't I be trusted to make my own decisions?'

'You haven't entered the church.' He shrugged. 'Most women who wish to remain widows devote their lives to God, the church and good works. Father Oswald has spoken to me of this conundrum on several occasions.'

'I've a young son who needs looking after, and I've little vocation in any case.' She tried to repress a shudder. She had found Mass comforting when Leofwine was captured, but she knew the endless hours of kneeling, enforced silences and other rigours that nuns endured were not for her. 'Allow me the privilege of choosing my own future.'

Brother Palni shook his head. 'Even with the Deniscan at your side, you risk being blamed. This could yet end in your tears.'

Cynehild started, and quickly schooled her features. Brother Palni remained in ignorance about the true nature of her quest.

'Must you always be pessimistic, Brother Palni? We could be gaining a new ally.' She held out the pouch containing the coins she'd emptied out of the stone jar she'd discovered in the cave. 'Give this to Elene to hide. Wulfgar may have need of it before long.'

'The Deniscan take it ill if someone parts them from their gold.'

'I seek to fulfil my promise to my late husband and

I took precautions in case I had to…to bribe anyone,' Cynehild finished brightly. Inwardly she winced at the lie, and steeled herself for more questions.

'A healthy dose of scepticism has saved my hide more times than I like to count, but I will do as you say and ask you no questions on where you obtained these coins.' Brother Palni pocketed the pouch before jerking his head towards the cottage. 'I will return, my lady. Be prepared to depart when I do. Your business must be completed with no prevarication. And keep away from that hall.'

'My "business", as you term it, will be completed when I say it is.' Cynehild kept her head held high and refused to show the hurt Brother Palni's lack of faith in her had caused. 'Go, before your presence here is discovered and our plans unravel.'

Brother Palni nodded. 'Then you refuse to change your course?'

'I gave my word.' She lifted a brow as he continued to stand there. 'The sooner you go, the sooner you can return.'

Chapter Five

Going back into the hut after Brother Palni and the bulk of her men had departed, Cynehild felt the enormity of what she'd done hit her and make the breath go from her lungs. She shook her head. Giving in to fears was what she had done before the Heathen Horde had arrived at Baelle Heale and she, along with her sisters, had defeated them.

Kal lay on the fern bed, staring up at the wooden beams. His cheeks were paler than she liked, but he was awake, and she had to hope coherent.

'What other secrets are you hoarding?' she mused out loud.

'Secrets, my lady? I wish I knew myself.' He raised himself up on one elbow. 'What lies has that Northman been spreading? Ask me anything and I will give the best answer my memory affords.'

His voice sounded so eminently reasonable that Cynehild wanted to believe his sincerity. 'What have you remembered? Surely you must know how you came to lead your war band.'

'I held up the shield wall at Basceng. My entire being

ached, but I planted my feet and started to inch forward. They broke and we overran them. After that they started to call me a giant, and I chose the name Icebeard because I wanted my enemies to be frightened of me.'

'That is far too simple.'

'It is the truth. People made up stories about me, but there was seldom any truth in them. When you are my size, few care to tangle with you.'

Kal turned his head. In the dim light his expression was inscrutable.

'Did you require something else from me, my lady, or have I told you enough?'

'Why did you keep your identity hidden from me? Why didn't you warn me of the possibility of who you might be?'

'I didn't intend on deceiving you, whatever Brother Palni says. He does not possess the ability to read a man's heart, for all his supposed piety.'

Kal held out his hand towards her, his dark eyes beseeching her to believe his words. She hated it that a significant part of her wanted to believe in him, even though he was her enemy.

'You must see that,' he said. 'It would have served no purpose to keep my saviour in the dark. And I needed to be sure. What if I had told you what I feared and you had insisted on us travelling to the hall? What if I had been wrong? From what you said of Jaarl Icebeard, I assumed him to be unforgiving of anyone claiming dominion over his lands.'

'And are you unforgiving?'

'I have to hope any action I take will be tempered with mercy, particularly when my saviour angel is involved.'

Saviour angel? That was a blatant appeal to her better nature. A lock of dark blond hair tumbled over his forehead, making him appear like a young boy rather than a warrior who enjoyed a fearsome reputation. And his tale was of exactly the sort of thing she would want Wulfgar to do—use a strong reputation so he didn't have to fight or risk his men.

Her fingers itched to smooth the lock of hair away, as she would to Wulfgar—except her feelings towards Kal were anything but maternal. Cynehild firmed her mouth. Both Luba and Brother Palni had put ideas in her head which had no place being there, particularly after she had so grandly informed Kal of her complete lack of interest in him.

She clenched her fingers about her belt and did not move closer into the room. She was a widow, not some giddy maiden inclined to forgive a pair of darkly fringed eyes any manner of transgression. Those sorts of feelings had gone into the grave with her husband.

Her love for Leofwine was undying. She'd sworn the same thing every morning since she'd first recognised her feelings for what they were. It bothered her that she'd forgotten to do that this morning, because she'd been too busy getting the covered cart ready. She immediately repeated the words of undying love to Leofwine in her mind. However, to her dismay, they seemed more like the mouthing of mere words rather than a deep and meaningful utterance.

'Just remember I'm on your side,' Cynehild said, and busied herself with carefully sorting through the dried herbs once again—self-heal, rosemary, raspberry leaf and mandrake root.

Her cheeks heated. Luba had not paid any attention to Cynehild's claim of not being attracted to Kal and had included the raspberry leaf as a simple precaution against pregnancy. Her fingers hovered over the leaves before she swept them into a small pouch on her belt, intending to return them to Luba.

'Is something wrong with the herbs?' Kal asked.

'Luba has made a mistake and I didn't want to do something in error. Stop trying to change the subject.'

'How can I change the past? What I planned to do before we met has no bearing now.'

'Brother Palni swears you will find a reason for me to go to your hall. He thinks it would be a grave error.'

'My hall contains my unseen enemy and is no place for either of us until your men return.' He smiled. 'Perhaps the monk is not the meddling fool I considered him.'

'You're incorrigible.'

His shoulders shook with silent laughter. 'I hope you mean that in a good way.'

'Brother Palni thinks you're one of those men who twist women about your little finger. He's heard your sort of blandishments many times before.'

'I'd like to meet the man who can twist *you* about his finger. You are far too strong-minded.'

Cynehild pleated her gown between her fingers. 'You don't know me at all.'

'I know you better than you think.'

His gaze travelled from the crown of her head to the tips of her boots, which just peeped out from under her gown, pausing on the curve of her chest and where the gown flowed out over her ample hips.

Did he think her lacking in common sense or incapable of logical thought as he gave her that sort of look? Leofwine had. Often. She'd loathed it when Leofwine had done it.

Cynehild gripped the table until her knuckles shone white. What was wrong with her? Forgetting to swear her oath of undying devotion that morning... Questioning Leofwine's long-ago pronouncements and behaviour... That sort of thinking had caused arguments early in their marriage. But she'd soon learned to curb her tongue, and her reward had been a loving and attentive husband. She could not have wished for a better man than Leofwine when they were fleeing the Great Heathen Horde.

She forced three calming breaths and made her hands relax. When she had her emotions under control, she turned back to where Kal lay, cocooned in a variety of furs and with his head on a feather pillow. He was watching her intently, waiting to see if she had accepted his easy reassurance.

'Tell me this—do you already know who your enemy is, Jaarl Icebeard?' She tapped her foot against the rushes and kept her arms tightly crossed. 'Do you want to mock me or play with me for your own purposes? Or worse? For pity's sake, I've a young son. He needs me, Icebeard.'

'To you, my name is Kal. It is true I was once Icebeard, but I wish to be Kal again—particularly to you and your men,' he said, with a soothing note in his voice, as though he spoke to an overly nervous horse. 'You were the one to suggest we play at being betrothed. My future wife would call me by my actual name.'

'Point taken, Kal.'

'I've been lying here thinking about our betrothal and I'm convinced there is more to it than you are telling me. Why were you so willing to do this for me once you knew who I was? What is it that you want on my lands? Why is it necessary for you to bring that sword to the church? What did you expect to happen there when you did? I've not asked these questions of you before because I trust you and your sincerity, even though you don't wear a wedding ring.'

Cynehild regarded her bare hands. 'I'm honouring my husband, no more, no less, and my ring remains at Baelle Heale for safekeeping.'

'You saved my life, Lady Cynehild. I owe you a great debt in return. I do pay my debts. Some day I hope you will trust me enough to tell me the true reason for your journey.'

Cynehild ground her teeth. She hated being patronised in that fashion. Leofwine had— She stopped. She normally struggled to think about any time she had criticised Leofwine since his death, and yet now she had nearly done it twice in as many breaths.

She forced her body to relax. It was coming back to these lands—that was the problem. These lands reminded her of the headstrong girl she'd used to be before she became Wulfgar's mother and Leofwine's wife. But she didn't miss that impetuous person who'd constantly quarrelled with her husband. A harmonious household led to a contented life.

Brother Palni had tried to warn her about what coming here might do to her nerves. Bless him. Being unsettled had always caused her to make unwise decisions. Forgetting that simple fact had led to her current predicament.

'My marriage has nothing to do with you, Kal. Consider the matter closed.'

'I hope to show you that I'm worthy of your trust,' he said into the silence. 'Your brain and your forthright manner are two things I like about you. I suspect you are a formidable *tafl* player.'

'Only two things?'

'Are you fishing for compliments? Shall I mention how the colour of your dress makes your eyes shine or how it flows so delightfully over your curves?'

'That you respect my brain is enough. But I don't play *tafl*.'

'Pity…'

She concentrated on sorting out the grains to make porridge. She saw Luba had thoughtfully put in a distaff, spindle and some wool at the bottom of the basket. Despite what her family thought about her obsession with cloth-making, Cynehild actually hated the process of making cloth—from the careful carding of the wool, the loading of the distaff and setting the spindle whirling, the balling of the thread, the twining of the thread into workable wool ready for washing, the dyeing and most of all the weaving. What she loved was the satisfaction of creating something practical from nothing, and the way feeling the thread develop between her fingers calmed her thoughts. She put the wool aside for later.

It would be easy to send one of the men to recall Brother Palni, she thought. She suspected he was loitering on the road, waiting for such an eventuality. She could almost hear his voice, telling Moir and Ansithe the tale of how Cynehild had managed to become entangled with a Deniscan and that he'd had to come to the rescue. They could leave Kal here and Luba would find him when she called in the morning—if she called.

'My lady, you fall silent. Have I offended you? I like hearing your voice.'

'I don't understand anything about what the Deniscan aim to do now that they control so much of what used to be Mercia, or what political games they are playing. I'm a widow who rarely goes to court. This pretend betrothal was an impulsive suggestion—something I'm not known for.'

'You already regret making me the offer?'

'Alas, regret is not in my nature. Pig-headedly stubborn, my younger sister calls it.'

'Your stubbornness means I live.' He reached out a hand. 'I'm asking you to continue saving my life. Like your former servant, Luba, you'll be well rewarded if gold is what motivates you.'

The walls of the hut pressed in on her. She required Leofwine's gold, not Kal's. It was his parting gift to their son, the child he'd had very little time for. It would be something tangible for Wulfgar from his father. She wished she could explain the difference to Kal, but the words stuck in her throat.

'We need to regain your hall before you start speaking of rewards. My being able to fulfil my promise to Leofwine and return to my son will be reward enough.'

'Women are a mystery to me—they always have been. My mother died when I was young. But they do have their uses.'

He shrugged his shoulders. Typically male...dismissing her concerns as if they were inconsequential, just like—

Cynehild winced. What was wrong with her? She'd spent every moment since she'd learnt of his capture refusing to think ill of Leofwine. Except he had been human and not a saint, a little voice reminded her.

'I won't be used like some counter in a political game.' Cynehild struggled to keep her voice from shaking with rage. 'My father did that when he married me off to Leofwine and arranged my younger sister's first marriage. He seeks to do it to my youngest sister too, but I will find a way to prevent it.'

Kal turned towards the wall. 'You told me before that your marriage was an arrangement of convenience— and yet you fell in love with him. It makes me feel quite jealous.'

'The arrangement worked for us. Leofwine and I were happy together.' She reached for the spindle and felt its familiar calming weight in her hands. 'Why should you be jealous? You and I are strangers.'

He turned back. His dark gaze caught hers, enticing her to tumble into its velvety depths.

'Because I've seen the devotion you give his memory. My late wife would never have done the same for me.'

Cynehild rolled the distaff between her fingers. Kal was only jealous of the devotion she showed Leofwine, rather than the fact that he'd been married to her. Something else entirely. A tiny pang went through her. When would she learn that she was an overlooked widow now, rather than a vibrant woman to be pursued romantically?

'That's pure speculation,' she said.

'It's the truth. Ranka and her older sister Toka were two peas in a pod. Beautiful to look at, but dark ambition lurked in their souls.'

'You knew her. I did not. Perhaps you have misjudged her. When you woke, you were undone with grief for her.'

'It was guilt I felt. When I left her to go to market Ranka told me that she knew I would fail to return in time, that our child would die. She was right. Our child lived only a short while after I came back, and I lost my wife as well. I vowed on their graves that if I ever acquired land I'd ensure it would prosper before I took another wife.'

'Is that why the fields here are so well-worked?'

'I never want another to suffer as I suffered. It is now in my power to make things happen.'

'All this because of guilt?'

'I suspect so. Don't think better of me than you should—or worse of me either. I know I've never killed a man except in battle.'

'Don't worry, I won't...' Cynehild paused, aware that her voice had grown overly loud. Her remaining men could probably hear her, up at the barn. She filled her lungs with air and hastily set the distaff down. 'I had luck in saving your life, but one day my luck will run out.'

'We don't need luck, you and I. We only need my strength and my sword arm alongside your brains.'

He threw off the covers and rose bare-chested to his feet. He swayed slightly, as if he remained uncertain about his balance. In the faint light his chest gleamed golden with a network of silvery scars interlaced with a dusting of hair which pointed down to his trousers.

Cynehild rapidly developed an interest in her wool and tried to rid her brain of the image of him partially naked. She was supposed to be beyond noticing such things. Except she had noticed. And parts of her she'd considered long dead now showed they were most definitely alive.

Unable to resist, she looked up at him again. He remained standing, arms at his sides, head tilted as he assessed her closely. Her mouth went dry. Against all reason, she desired his touch.

She quickly grabbed his discarded tunic from beside the pallet and thrust it towards him. 'Put this on. Immediately.'

A tiny smile played on his lips. 'We need to discuss things.'

'I will leave and not come back unless you obey me.'
She retreated five steps.

He pointed towards the door. 'Go. Go with your monk
and your men. If you take the horses you will be able
to catch him quickly enough. Keep safe. I will manage.
Abandon me.'

Cynehild shifted uncomfortably. Manage? How? He
could barely stand up straight.

'"Abandon" is a harsh word,' she said, forcing her lips
upwards. 'I merely object to your nakedness.'

'Why do you object?'

'You are seeking to distract me.' She raised a brow.
'I see through your ploy. My sister used to do that when
she was losing at *tafl*.'

A faint smile played on his full lips. 'So you *do* play
tafl, after all. Excellent. I look forward to pitting my
wits against you. It has been a long time since I had a
worthy opponent.'

'You misunderstand. I loathed the game as a girl. Ansithe was determined to win at all costs. I was delighted
to give it up when Leofwine declared that women had
no business trying to play it.'

Kal slipped his tunic over his head, hiding his magnificent chest. 'You really know nothing of the game?'

Fury consumed her. He was about to mock her for not
knowing how to play like a warrior. She'd had enough
of that when she was a bride.

'Enough to know how counters are considered expendable when one is protecting the king. I refuse to be
expendable. I matter. My child's life matters.' She pulled
the door open with a loud crash. 'I will return once my
temper calms. If you want to speak to me, keep your
tunic on and treat me like the equal that I am.'

She fled into the yard, put her hands on her knees and took life-giving gulps of air. When the trembling had stopped, she straightened. She'd nearly walked into his arms and laid her head against his chest. There were any number of reasons why that was not one of her wiser ideas.

Keeping busy until her feelings passed was the best way. Then she'd return—serene, resolute and very much the widow whose heart remained with her late husband.

Kal eyed the firmly slammed door.

'Come back, please,' he muttered. 'You misunderstood me.'

Silence. His heart clenched.

The sound of Cynehild's voice speaking to her men floated back to him. She had every reason to be annoyed with him. He should have realised that Mercian women were fastidious about seeing a man's naked body. He should have obeyed her immediately, rather than enjoying the way her pupils had dilated as she'd stared at him and her tongue had run over her mouth.

He'd behaved appallingly.

He pressed his hands to his temples. He understood Lady Cynehild's unspoken rules now.

He slowly sank to his knees and pleaded with any god who might be listening to help him become a better man—one who might be worthy of her regard, if not her friendship. He knew he'd worked hard to achieve what he had enjoyed, but without Cynehild he was in danger of losing it all.

Outside, all had gone quiet. Kal pressed his lips together. Going out and checking would be no good…he'd have to wait for her to return.

'Forgive me,' he whispered. 'I've sworn to protect you. Believe in me, please. Return. Let me explain.'

The shadows stretched three-quarters of the way across the floor when Cynehild ran out of tasks to do in the barn. She was back on an even footing now. She was impervious to the tug of attraction, the crinkle of a pair of masculine eyes and a charming smile, even the allure of a naked chest. She'd simply been starved of affection, and had been attracted to the first man who treated her like a woman instead a crone.

'The fire has nearly gone out,' she said crossly, going back into the darkened cottage.

It held a distinct chill, but Kal lay on top of the pallet, fully dressed. Just like Leofwine would have—or worse, her father, someone who expected to be waited on hand and foot.

'Why is it that men can never do anything in the house?'

Kal stared at a point over her shoulder, his lips pressed together in a thin white line. 'You came back. I was beginning to fear you wouldn't. There seemed little point in a fire if it was simply me—waiting for whatever the Nourns had in store.'

There was a new, humbler note to his voice.

'There were things I had to do.'

Cynehild gave the embers a stir and the fire flared into life. She put several more pieces of wood on it and soon the hut basked in warmth. She moved the pot of grain she'd set to soak earlier closer to the fire, so it could bubble away.

'My responsibilities stretch beyond you and your little games.'

'I apologise for whatever I did that made you upset. Why shouldn't you play *tafl*? I've known expert players who are women. I've known warriors who are women—far better warriors than I could ever hope to be. I fear that perhaps I tried to drive you away before you abandoned me.'

Cynehild picked up her discarded spindle and distaff and set the spindle to twirling. She'd been too quick to judge him. 'Apology accepted.'

'I have also been thinking that whoever did this to me is very skilled. They have taken no chances,' he said, starting to rise. She motioned for him to stay where he was. 'I've no idea who knew you were coming here, or why I went up that hill. I only know the outcome. Your monk is correct—I have put you in danger. I did know a version of the truth of who I was and I kept it hidden while we were in the cart. I should have trusted you to do the right thing. Forgive me? I do genuinely need your help, Lady Cynehild—as an equal and not as some expendable counter.'

Kal wanted her to be his equal in this? Cynehild gave the spindle an extra hard turn and the thread broke. It went bouncing across the floor, stopping beside where he lay.

He picked it up and held it out to her. 'Yours.'

She hastily retrieved it, avoiding touching his outstretched palm, but her cheeks heated. No man had ever told her that she could be his equal before.

'I can't remember when that last happened. Dropping the spindle, I mean.'

'My memory remains hazy, my lady. Since you left earlier, I've been concentrating hard. Yet my thoughts slip away like water through a sieve.' He put his hand to his forehead. 'I may be *jaarl* of these lands, but I've no memory of who my closest allies are. Do you wish me to knock on the door of the hall and ask? Should I give away the one advantage I have?'

'Luba may know more,' she said, to cover her awkwardness. 'She used to have all the gossip at her fingertips. People confide in her when they go to her for various potions and salves.'

'Whoever did this made their plans very carefully. They used your imminent arrival as a cover.'

'Were you with anyone when you went up that hill?'

Kal clenched his fist. 'I only have the memory of a voice saying, "Thus shall all tyrants fall, Icebeard!"'

'Was it a Mercian voice?'

'I don't know. I can't even say if it was a man's or woman's voice. They expected me to die, but you happened along.'

'I didn't see anyone.'

'They might have seen you, though. That could explain the rumours swirling about my death. You could be in grave danger.' His lips turned upwards. 'I'm treating you as an equal and confiding all my thoughts to you, as requested.'

Cynehild gulped hard. Part of her wished she'd remained in ignorance, but a stronger part was pleased she knew. 'We may have need of your sword arm sooner rather than later. Who knows who Luba will tell?'

'Her countenance shines with greed. She will keep her mouth shut. She wants more gold.'

'Perhaps. Or is it even that she owes you a debt for getting her daughter married?'

'My instinct is that greed is what motivates her.' His

shrewd gaze swept her features. 'And your motivation has to be more than a promise to your late husband.'

A bead of sweat trickled down her back. The need to confess grew within her but she swallowed it. Once she had the gold safe, then she'd explain the entire story to Kal. More than anything, she wanted her son to grow up to be the sort of honourable warrior she knew he could be.

'Simple humanity plays a role.'

'It is a rare thing indeed to encounter someone who doesn't require riches, Lady Cynehild.'

She reached for some more wool. 'You are a cynic, Kal.'

He gave a genuine laugh then, which filled the room and warmed her all the way down to her toes.

'I'm a terrible patient. I dislike being in bed.' He started to rise. 'I should be up, practising with my sword, ensuring I can swing it properly as I fear we both will have need of it, rather than lazing about. Someone wants to kill me, my lady.'

'You will have little choice but to do as I say.' She forced a smile and pointed back towards the bed. 'Who else but me could lend you a sword? And I doubt very much you could lift Leofwine's right now. My father always said that it was far too heavy a sword for anyone except a fully-grown man.'

He flexed his arms in mock indignation, making the muscles bulge. 'Am I some beardless boy?'

'Given your injury, I doubt you could even lift the lightest sword for any length of time. Your balance is off.'

'I could use a stick.' He leant down, but stopped abruptly. He slowly straightened. All colour had drained from his face. 'The world has started spinning…'

Cynehild put her hand under his elbow, helping him to balance. Slowly she led him back to the bed. 'You need to rest.'

'I would rest better if I had some companionship.' He clasped a hand to his head. 'That came out all wrong, my lady. I apologise. I seem to spend all my time apologising to you.'

'I've no intention of taking you up on the offer, regardless. You sleep alone.'

'You aren't angry with me?' His fingers caught hers and held on tight. 'I don't think I could bear it if you were angry with me again, my lady.'

'You are unwell.' She eased him back onto the bed. 'You must remain there, on your side. Your bandages should be changed and then I want you to rest.'

His fingers caught hers again as she started to unwrap the bandage. 'My lady... Cynehild... I won't forget again, will I?'

'I hope not.'

'I'll always remember you. In your debt for ever. Whatever you ask, if it is in my power, it is yours.'

A lump formed in Cynehild's throat. Kal had no idea what he was saying or what he was offering. It was on the tip of her tongue to tell him about her quest, what her promise to Leofwine entailed and her hopes for Wulfgar's future. Once again she swallowed the words. Far too risky. It was one thing to return a sword, but quite another to rob a church or a man who was becoming a friend—even if the money morally belonged to her son.

'I will hold you to that,' she told him gently.

Chapter Six

A deep darkness shrouded the room when Kal next woke, briefly disorientated and wondering where he was. Embers burnt low in the hearth, casting a faint warm glow. His body relaxed as the details of what he'd recently experienced swept over him. He knew where he was and why. His memory continued to function, even if significant gaps remained.

A tiny movement glimpsed out of the corner of his eye made him turn his head.

Cynehild sat holding a distaff piled high with sheep's wool in one hand while she set a spindle twisting, expertly making thread. The amount of thread on the spindle had increased considerably. As he watched, she broke the thread and without a pause wrapped it into a ball, placing it beside three others on the table. She then took two of the balls and placed them on the distaff.

The glow highlighted the sweep of her neck and made her blond hair gleam gold. The entire scene was one of peace and harmony. A wave of nostalgia for when he was young and watching his mother perform the same sort of ritual washed over him. He'd forgotten how safe it made him feel until he'd experienced it again.

'Why do demons trouble your sleep?' he asked, to keep his thoughts from straying towards areas which were best left unexplored. His past belonged in the past. It was something not to be remarked on or mentioned, because he was too busy trying to live in the present.

'Who says they do?' She put the spindle and distaff down on the table with a distinct thump. One of the balls rolled across the table before falling to the floor.

'It's the second night I've discovered you awake.'

She reached down and retrieved the ball of wool, balancing it on her palm. A line developed between the perfect arches of her brows. 'It is a habit I formed when my son was a baby. The night is the best time for uninterrupted thinking—just me and my thoughts.'

'When was the last time you slept properly? Tell me truthfully, instead of giving me an easy answer.'

Cynehild rose and stirred the fire. A great arc of sparks rose before quickly winking out. 'Tonight I do two things—keep watch over you and ensure the wool will be ready for weaving.'

Kal raised his body further and allowed the change of subject. 'What will you do with the balls of wool? Weave them together in a cloth? I remember the clackety-clack of my mother's loom.'

Her face cleared. 'If I tried weaving with those, then the thread would break and kink. This is merely the first stage—they are the ply.' She put two more balls on the distaff and twisted the threads together before fastening them to the spindle and setting it in motion. 'Because they are equal, once they are twisted together they create a much stronger thread. Later Luba will wash and dye it before putting it on a shuttle to be woven into cloth.'

She handed him two different balls—the one he'd watched her wrapping from the spindle and the other, where two ply were twisted together.

'See which one is easier to break.'

Kal broke the first easily, but the second proved harder. 'Do the ply have to be of the same strength?' he asked.

'It helps to make sure the cloth is long-lasting.'

'A ready answer.'

'My son always asks the same question.' Her voice hitched slightly, as it always did when she spoke of her son. 'When he can't sleep, he watches me spin and asks me to tell him tales of brave warriors, and very occasionally about the cloth I make.'

Kal tightened his fist about the ball of yarn. Had his mother loved him as much Cynehild clearly loved her son? 'But he is older now and must sleep through the night, or you wouldn't have left him.'

Cynehild got up and gave the fire another stir. This time the sparks were less vibrant. 'The habit of not sleeping has come back to me on this journey. I must be a poor traveller. I've taken to reviewing the day and seeing how I can improve tomorrow. Spinning is almost as good as sleeping for relaxing me.'

He nodded, knowing it was a slight stretching of the truth, although her eyes were far from sunken. She might have stopped sleeping, but Kal suspected that it had only started when she'd discovered him on the hill.

'Sleep makes things better,' he said.

She shook her head before moving a pot closer to the fire. 'I will bear that in mind. I had intended on sleeping once I'd finished the remainder of the wool.' She raised a pointed eyebrow. 'Alone.'

Kal inclined his head but kept his gaze trained on Cynehild, trying to discern precisely what was in her mind. Another wave of unaccustomed jealousy towards her late husband swept through him, surprising him with its intensity. 'Whatever that monk told you about me and my intentions towards you—he is wrong.'

'You slept for a long time.' She gave the pot a stir, lit a reed and came over to him. She laid a cool hand on his forehead while she held up the spluttering light from the reed. 'No fever, and your wound looks to be healing well. There's no fresh blood.' She pinched the reed out, sending them back into the shadowy light from the hearth. 'All is as it should be.'

He wanted to put his hand over hers and keep it against his forehead. Her touch made his thinking become far clearer. But he allowed her to move away from him and back towards where the pot bubbled and spat.

'I've always healed quickly,' he said. 'This time I will have to heal even quicker than usual.'

She turned from the pot. 'Why?'

'Our time will be limited, despite your brave predictions. Now that I can think with more ease, it is very clear to me what will happen—they will search for me and finally someone will declare me dead. Returning from the dead can be hard.'

'I believe only one man has done it in the history of mankind.'

'I've no idea how loyal my men will be.'

He clenched his fingers about his thumb. *Tyrant.* Was his assailant one man or many? In the shadows or out in the open?

'I'd rather not put their loyalty to the test.'

She pursed her mouth. 'So you've decided that you want to return before they make any such declaration? Even if you won't have the men to hold the hall should your men choose to be disloyal. Even though Brother Palni forbade it.'

'Circumstances may alter before that monk can return with your men. I need to know what is happening inside my hall.'

'What do you want me to do?'

'See Luba and ask her. See if her son-in-law knows anything.'

She gave a wry smile. 'Luba is a survivor.'

'Luba belongs to the land.'

Kal drew his top lip down over his teeth. There was something important about Luba, but he couldn't remember what it was and why he'd allowed his man to marry her daughter.

'There is a risk. She may see a better opportunity elsewhere, or her son-in-law may be unable to resist gossiping. Men are far worse than women. It is why we have to get our story straight tonight rather than waiting until morning. Something to do while you spin.'

She stilled. 'Our story?'

'Whoever did this will know full well that I was not betrothed when I left the hall. Any number of people will know. But we can keep the story as much as possible to the truth. I will say I kept the news close to my chest until I saw that we would suit.'

'Is there someone else who expects you to make her an offer? If there was a wagering, names must have been mentioned.'

'If there is one, matters have not gone that far.' He

swallowed the choking fear. He knew deep within his soul that no woman waited for him or expected a serious offer. 'But blank places do remain in my memory.'

'Whatever we do, we shall have to ensure that no one guesses about those blank spots,' she said with a decided nod, and expertly balled some wool before reaching for more to begin the process again. 'I agree that we need to stick as close to the truth as possible.'

'The blank spaces terrify me,' he said, and waited for the mockery to start.

She merely lifted a brow.

'What sort of man was I? Did I deserve my reputation?'

'Ask instead what sort of man do you want to be?'

'That is not an answer.'

'Would I have stayed with you if I had found you terrifying? Icebeard, the creature who crawled from nightmares, is not you—not now.'

His fingers relaxed at her words. His lady believed in his goodness even if he was uncertain, and that was enough for him.

His lady?

His stomach rumbled, interrupting his train of thought. At the sound, Cynehild went immediately to the pot and scooped out a bowl of porridge.

'I've been keeping this warm for you. Nourishing food to assist in your healing. A far better way to occupy your mouth than speaking about what you might or might not have done.'

He wrinkled his nose. 'Porridge. Is that my only choice?'

'Is there something wrong with porridge? My son loves it.'

Kal stared at the glowing embers. Cynehild had a life beyond these walls. She'd agreed to play at being his betrothed for reasons of her own—reasons which were likely tied up with her son and husband.

His temple throbbed. He struggled to remember if he had ever felt as comfortable with his wife as he did with Cynehild. Theirs had not been the easiest of relationships; he had failed her in the worst way possible. It was in part that knowledge of his failure which had kept him from committing to another woman. He wanted to be sure that he could provide for her and any children properly. As he'd told his cousin Alff, until he could prove his worth, he'd keep his dalliances short.

'Porridge is not one of my favourite foods.' He attempted a smile and pushed away the unsettling thoughts of how he'd failed to protect those closest to him. Even the taste of porridge was preferable to that. 'But I will eat it unless there is something else. Even a hunk of that dried bread and hard cheese you gave me when I first woke in the cave.'

She continued to ladle the cooked grains into an earthenware bowl. 'Pity I'm not in the mood to make you anything else.'

'I thought you'd agreed to be my nurse?'

'Your memory is faulty and you've been thoroughly spoilt.' She shook the ladle at him, but he caught the twinkle in her eye. 'Ordering food as if you are a king.'

'Requesting. I know better than to order you about.'

She brought the bowl over to him. 'You may eat it in bed then.'

'Are you going to feed me?'

She handed him a spoon. 'I trust you will be able to handle this if you believe you can swing a sword.'

'Spoons before swords—very wise.' He balanced the bowl on his knees and stared at its steaming contents. The dark pain in his head receded to a dull ache. Dull aches he could handle. 'I don't have time to be ill. My enemy gains in strength. The next time I may be far more unlucky.'

His enemy would surely also hurt Cynehild if the truth about his location was known. Kal vowed again that he would die before he allowed her to be hurt.

She returned to her spinning. For a few moments they both watched the spindle twirling and the thread lengthening.

'Brother Palni will return with more men,' she said eventually. 'Maybe even my sister Ansithe, whose skill with a bow is renowned.'

'You will have to tell me the tale.'

'I'll tell you while you eat…let's see you have a first bite and then I'll begin.'

Kal studied the porridge and picked up the first spoonful. It was more difficult than he had considered to navigate the spoon to his mouth. He had to concentrate hard…harder than he ever had before. But the effort was worth it. Her porridge tasted far better than he remembered the stuff tasting. Ranka's porridge had always had a distinct acrid taste, as if she'd burnt it and then put too much salt in it.

'Obviously there is something wrong with my memory. This porridge is excellent.'

Cynehild began to tell him about her sister, and how she'd conquered an invading party of Northmen. She made it sound like an adventure, but he knew the women at Baelle Heale must have been terrified. Ansithe sounded formidable.

Kal ate several more bites while he considered his response. With each bite it became easier to get the spoon to his mouth. He noticed how Cynehild watched him intently but did not take the spoon from him. For that, gratitude swelled in his breast. He hated being fussed over—always had.

His spoon scraped the bottom of the bowl. To his amazement he'd finished the porridge. His stomach still growled.

'That was quick for someone who dislikes porridge,' Cynehild said, handing him a cloth and pointing to the corner of his mouth.

'Between the story and the taste, it slipped down very easily. I was wrong about porridge—or rather *your* porridge. You are a good cook.'

She bent her head. 'Making porridge is easy.'

He reached over and covered her hand with his. Her hand trembled but she allowed it to stay within his for a long heartbeat. 'You shouldn't dismiss a compliment so easily.'

'I'm a widow with a young son. Compliments are for my youngest sister, Elene. What looks I had vanished years ago, under the strain of giving birth and losing my husband.'

Whoever had whispered such poison in her ears deserved to swallow their words. In the firelight Lady Cynehild possessed an inner beauty which illuminated her face. He knew he could study it for an age and not grow bored. But he sensed she'd actively dislike compliments about her looks right now—especially from him.

'Why?'

She withdrew her hand from his. 'Elene will need a

husband soon. My father has ambitions to ensure the family prospers.'

'For you as well?'

'I've no plans to remarry. Ever. When my son is old enough, I suspect I'll join a convent. Several of my aunts and cousins have done that.' A sad smile trembled on her lips. 'A fulfilling life, by all accounts, for withered crones like me.'

'There is nothing withered about you.'

Kal tried to think of what Cynehild would be like as a nun. He failed because the curve of her bottom lip distracted him.

'I take it you are in no hurry to join them?'

'No. My son needs me and I have little inclination for the role.' She sighed and gave the porridge pot a strong stir. 'When the time arrives I'll have to trust my vocation will be stronger. Look at Brother Palni—he was a pagan warrior and now he finds solace as a Christian monk.'

'My mind is clearer after the rest and the food,' he said, instead of making a comment about the irksome monk. 'You've a real skill at nursing.'

'A compliment I accept.'

'Deeds, not words—I'll remember that when praising you.'

She placed another bowl of porridge in front of him. 'Tell me what you remember about these lands instead.'

Kal closed his eyes. There were wisps of a memory— his kneeling before one of the great Danish *jaarls* and swearing, quickly followed by his own private ceremony in which he'd plunged his hands into the fertile soil while people, both Danes and Saxons, looked on.

'I swore to the people that I would give my everything for them and I meant it. No one should starve as my family starved.' He reeled off several of the improvements he'd made.

'Your memory begins to return?'

'Porridge appears to be the best medicine.' His stomach growled again. 'Just don't ask me the names of the other *jaarls*.'

'Concentrate on eating. See if we can quieten that beast in your stomach.'

Kal held out his bowl when he'd finished. Their fingers briefly touched when she reached for it. The tiny touch sent a thrill of warmth coursing through him.

'I can say without a shadow of doubt that this is the best porridge I can ever remember tasting. Another compliment based on your ability.'

Cynehild gave him one of her smiles, the sort that made him feel nothing too terrible in the world could happen. It amazed him that in a little over a day he'd started to watch for her smiles, and wanted to discover ways he could touch her.

One day she might become a nun, but today was not that day.

The thought gave him comfort. There still remained time to change her mind.

The rose tint of dawn streamed through the doorway when Kal next woke. Cynehild crouched beside the embers of the fire, using a stick to draw in the ash. He coughed. She rapidly destroyed whatever she was doing with a sweep of her stick.

'Am I interrupting?' he asked.

'Bad habit. I was trying to get my thoughts straight.' A smudge of ash shone on her cheek. 'Shall we see if you have a fever?'

Her hand was warm against his forehead. He reached up and wiped the smudge away. 'Ash.'

'My nurse used to tell me off for drawing in it.' She backed away. 'Your fever has vanished. More porridge?'

'We need to plan what we will do when your men arrive,' he said. Some day he vowed she'd reveal her secrets to him. 'We have no idea how long we have, although my head continues to clear.'

'Eat first,' she said, putting another large helping of porridge in front of him.

Between mouthfuls, Kal rapidly sketched out his concerns, including the fact that his enemy might be using this time to gain in strength.

'We need intelligence from my hall. Has anyone tried to take my place? Which men are loyal? What are the theories behind my disappearance?'

Her mouth became a thin white line. 'Brother Palni was very specific about our remaining far away from the hall and your people. Luba always knows all the gossip. I will visit her.'

'Your face is drawn,' he said. 'You should have let one of your men watch over me so you could sleep.'

She shook her head and pretended an interest in the balls of yarn which were now piled on the table. 'It is a waste to have them watching over you when sleep is far from my mind and we may need their sword arms.'

'I would prefer that other people do not know how badly I was injured,' he said, thinking aloud. 'I want them to think that I went to fetch my bride. It will put my attacker on the wrong foot. When we return to the hall, I want these bandages gone.'

'The person who attacked you will know, with or without a bandage,' she pointed out, with a frown appearing between her arched brows. 'Could it be that we arranged to meet on the top of Hangra Hill and I discovered that you'd been attacked. Then I insisted on ensuring you recovered before returning.'

'But that risks the true culprit blaming you, putting it out that you enchanted me. Or that you attacked me.'

'Why would I attack a man and then seek to save him?'

'Everyone knows the ways of the Saxons are odd.' He held out his hand, but she ignored it in favour of removing the pot from the embers. 'I've sworn to protect you, Lady Cynehild.'

'Yet you intend to use me as bait.'

'I fully intend to keep you safe.'

He heard that word *tyrant* inside his head once again. How many of his men truly thought that of him? What sort of leader had he become?

The pain throbbed anew at his temples. He concentrated on breathing steadily and the pain receded.

'My sisters say I worry overmuch. Forget it,' she said, pushing a strand of hair back behind her ear. 'I am not even sure my initial idea was a good one. Might it be better to tell the full truth instead?'

'You are overthinking it.' Kal grasped the spoon until his knuckles shone white. 'The betrothal will force my adversary's hand. It was a master stroke on your part. Why the nerves now?'

'You are going to use me to force your enemy out into the open.'

A sudden image of Cynehild's broken body clouded his vision. Would his enemy attempt to strike at him through Cynehild if he learned of his growing regard for her?

Kal blew out a long breath. 'When the time comes, my arm will be strong enough. Why are you doubting your idea when it is such a good one?'

Cynehild sat up straighter. Her gown tightened, revealing the curve of her ample breasts. Kal forced his gaze northwards. It was a pretend betrothal, not a real one, and she led a full life far away from him—even if a piece of him kept saying over and over that this alliance between them was exactly what he needed to secure his lands.

'I know about keeping a house, and woman's work, but my late husband used to tell me to keep out of high politics and men's business as it would overtax my brain. Maybe he had a point.'

Kal loathed her late husband. She might have loved him, but from what she said he'd taken pleasure in belittling her. 'Never allow anyone to say that about your brain. I've known women who are better warriors than most men. And far superior strategic thinkers. Your idea buys me that most precious of commodities—time.'

'But how did we meet?' she asked. 'When? Why did you keep this betrothal a secret? We are bound to be asked those questions, regardless of keeping your injury hidden. I've racked my brain all night and each reason I came up with seems more outlandish than the last. This betrothal idea leaks more than my grandmother's sieve.'

'Peace-weaving remains a noble tradition. We will say that in my search to ensure these lands remain prosperous I contacted your brother-in-law to discuss an alliance. The laying of your husband's sword was the excuse you needed to meet me, should anyone question our alliance.'

She nodded. 'It makes sense to keep it simple. We can

say we both wanted to ensure we were compatible before finalising the deal.'

'I travelled without my men because I desired to meet you on my terms. I had no wish to expose you or your good name to any ridicule or innuendo. Sometimes men make extravagant claims about their sisters-in-law.'

Her hazel eyes danced. 'Sometimes men also make extravagant claims.'

He inclined his head. 'True enough.'

'I've been married once and I'm in no hurry to take on a second husband. My heart remains buried with Leof-wine. He was the perfect man for me—our spheres divided equally.'

A surge of renewed hatred for her husband flooded through him. His rival was a ghost who could do no wrong. She remained blind to the way she'd been treated by him. He silently vowed to show her that he valued her counsel.

He covered her hand. This time she allowed it to stay there. Progress. 'In order to make this work there will have to be an obvious attraction between us. It would be best if people assume we are in love.'

'In love?'

He watched her mouth. A spark from the fire flew up and highlighted the shadowy curve beneath her bottom lip. 'Can you do that?' he asked. 'Can you pretend you desire me?'

She bent her head, examining the table but allowing her hand to stay in his. He knew if she refused he would not attempt to persuade her any more, but if she agreed it would be hugely enjoyable for them both.

Just when he had started to give up hope, she lifted her gaze to meet his. He was struck by the depths in her hazel eyes. He watched her mouth, red and bow-shaped, and the urge to kiss her nearly overwhelmed him.

'Possibly,' she said, barely above a whisper.

'Good.'

He leant over the table and brushed his lips against hers. He had intended only a butterfly brushing of mouths, but the pulse of heat ricocheting through him at the contact caused him to linger. His tongue traced the opening of her mouth but she kept her lips softly pressed together. He sat back, released her hand and watched her, scarcely daring to breathe.

Her hand explored her mouth. 'What was that for? You have already kissed me once for the betrothal. We're alone now.'

The reasons were far more complicated than he wanted to say. He had thought a simple touch would put an end to his urges, but instead it had inflamed them.

He forced his body to rise and carried the bowl over to where a bucket of water stood. 'A thank-you for the porridge. What else could it be for?'

'Porridge? You claimed to hate it.'

'Now I love it. That should be enough reason for a man to kiss a woman—particularly his wife-to-be.'

'Simply being betrothed doesn't confer upon a couple the right to kiss or cuddle with impunity.'

'In my culture it does. We don't consider "cuddling", as you call it, to be anything but pleasurable.'

She tucked her chin into her chest. 'We follow my rules.'

'Rules are meant to be broken…particularly when pleasure is involved.'

Her tongue tested her bottom lip. 'Was the kiss pleasurable for you?'

'Do you need another demonstration?'

She glanced upwards and her cheeks coloured delightfully. 'I mean for my rules to be kept, Kal. You need to understand that I've no intention of going to your bed. I buried my heart with my husband.'

'Bedding and husbands don't always go together.'

'With me, they must.'

He rose and gave a pretend yawn, which turned into the real thing as a wave of tiredness hit him. Her rules? He would keep to them…but he would also give her reason to break them. Her late husband should never have made that last request of her, to take his sword into enemy territory. Some day, Kal vowed, and some day soon, she would begin to see that life was for living rather than clinging to the memory of imagined perfection.

She folded her hands in her lap. 'We will continue our conversation in full daylight.'

'My people will need to believe our betrothal is real, Cyn.'

'Nobody calls me Cyn.'

'Why not?'

A frown developed between her brows. 'My mother disliked nicknames. I've kept to the tradition.'

'There is a world of difference between a special name and a nickname. Didn't your husband have a special name for you? One he whispered when you and he shared a bed?'

'My relations with Leofwine have no part in this conversation. He is dead.'

'There we both agree.'

She bit her lip. Kal struggled not to pull her into his arms again, kiss her thoroughly and demonstrate why she needed to start living.

'My family call me Cynehild.'

'Cynehild is far too formidable for our current conversation. Cyn works much better. What is wrong with me having a special name for a lady who has become a friend?'

His special name for her as a friend? Cynehild fingered her mouth. Her lips still tingled from that brief touch. And she knew she wanted more. She had been within a heartbeat of snaking her arm about his neck when he'd ended the kiss. He'd ended it—not her. She had to hang on to that. Men had different ideas about such things from women. He had done it for a specific purpose, not because he found a widow like her attractive.

She had overheard her father speaking to their neighbour just before she'd left, both of them lamenting upon how she'd lost her looks and how it was a blessing in disguise that she wouldn't be searching for a powerful husband.

Kal kissing her had been a tease. Theirs was a fake betrothal and it would end as soon as they had both achieved what they wanted. There would be no marriage in which he later fell in love with her, as Leofwine had done. In her experience, solid and true love came at quiet times, with shared memories and working together, rather than suddenly, like the heat which had infused her after Kal's kiss.

What she felt for Kal was the burgeoning of desire, and desire always faded eventually. He didn't even know what sort of person she was. He was a *good* man, her heart argued. But she ignored it. One did not become a Deniscan *jaarl* without doing something significant.

She released all the air in her lungs, feeling steadier. 'You need to get more rest now that your belly is full.'

'Yes, Cyn, as do you.'

His soft, husky tones resonated in the room, curling about her insides.

'I would offer you my bed, but you have already declined it for reasons best known to yourself. I'm willing to share, help to keep you warm should you change your mind.'

'I never change my mind.'

'The offer remains open—and, Cyn, know that I have never forced a woman. Your choice, not my demand. Always.'

Cynehild stared intently at the fire, but the image of their bodies entwined on that bed refused to go out of her head. What truly frightened her was the fact that she didn't recoil in horror. Some part of her thought it an excellent idea, and wondered why she was being prudish.

If she was being totally honest with herself, that brief touch had made her feel far more alive than she had since well before Leofwine had died. Every piece of her thrummed with anticipation at the thought of encountering it again.

Cynehild continue to stare at the fire while she heard Kal move towards the bed and reminded herself of all the reasons why starting anything with him was bound to lead to heartbreak and sorrow. This betrothal was only for show. They would not be becoming man and wife. She had no intention of being his mistress either. She'd lose any authority she had in her father's house if it became apparent that she had done something so untoward.

And she knew she still loved Leofwine. If he came through that door right now she would throw herself at

him and cover his face with kisses. But that was an impossibility. Leofwine was in the ground and had taken
her heart with him. Lust was wrong. Everyone told her
so.

'Cyn? Have you fallen asleep? Do I need to carry
you to bed?'

'Allow me to worry about my needs. You look towards
getting well—and that means sleeping alone.'

'Such a cruel Cyn. Not even one little kiss to send me
off to my dreams?'

Cynehild wrapped her shawl more tightly about her
body. 'Certainly not that.'

Chapter Seven

Was she doing the right thing?

It was one thing to agree with Kal in the middle of the night to gain more intelligence and quite another to do it. How Ansithe would laugh—her ultra-cautious older sister, deciding to take a chance without a well-thought-out plan. Ansithe only knew the old Cynehild—not the woman who travelled on her own, saved a wounded warrior, actively plotted to discover a deadlier enemy and longed to learn how to play *tafl*. Cynehild wasn't entirely certain about the lady she was becoming, but she liked her. She liked being considered good for more than keeping house, nursing and making cloth—things which Leofwine had kept pronouncing to be her 'proper sphere'.

Leaving her men to watch over the slumbering Kal, she decided to act on her instincts. They did need to know more about what was happening at the hall. And this was the best compromise. Luba should be alone in her cottage at this time of day.

'Luba?' she called out, knocking loudly.

'My lady? I warned you to stay away.' The elderly

woman hurried out of the barn, wiping her hands on her apron. 'Does Icebeard still live?'

'Kal lives. I…that is Icebeard requires information.' She held out her second-best shawl. 'I remember how much you used to admire my dark green shawl. I think this one will go well with your colouring.'

'Oh. A gift for me?' The woman straightened her apron. 'I was just checking on the grain for the animals, seeing how much we have left until the new grass grows.'

'Kal… Jaarl Icebeard wants me to learn what is happening at the hall. You will know everything, Luba. You always had such an eye for detail, and an ear for an interesting story which far surpassed any of my husband's warriors.'

'Men only *think* they know things.' Luba tapped the side of her nose. 'My son-in-law continually spouts on and forgets my people have lived on these lands since time began. My husband was the same. The mess he left when he died… It is a wonder I can stand in front of you.'

'Has your son-in-law heard any more about Icebeard's disappearance?'

'My daughter says…' Luba lowered her voice to a conspiratorial whisper '…that at the hall Lady Toka speaks about witches and frost giants. She says that Icebeard has been enchanted and sups with the Fairy Queen, but others are muttering about the dark deeds of Mercians.'

'Who is this Lady Toka?'

'A Dane. Recently wed to Jaarl Icebeard's cousin, and a very cold fish that one. But she spotted my daughter tending our geese and demanded she serve in the hall, which is where she met Haddr, so I suppose she isn't all bad.'

'Is your daughter contented with her choice?'

'It was Haddr who pushed for the union and convinced Jaarl Icebeard. And, my love potion helped matters along.'

A loud whistle sounded on the wind. Cynehild froze.

'People still come for my remedies.' Luba glanced over her shoulder. 'Please go. Tell Jaarl Icebeard I keep your secrets close to my heart.'

'I'll return tomorrow.'

'Lady Cynehild, you are taking a terrible chance.' Luba gave a crooked smile. 'Have you used the herbs yet? He is a handsome devil, that one. I've no wish for you to take any risks.'

Cynehild feigned ignorance of which herbs Luba meant. 'I am far too busy. I'm trying to ensure Kal regains his proper place with the minimum of bloodshed. Then I will place Leofwine's sword and leave without glancing behind me.'

'Lady Cynehild, romance is wasted on you.'

The lengthening shadows marching across the cottage floor told Kal he'd slept through most of the day. He wriggled his toes underneath the furs. He struggled to remember when he had last slept for such a long time or so soundly.

Had Cynehild done as he'd requested and sent word to Luba? Or had she overruled him in the interests of safety? He regretted even mentioning it.

He stretched. The dark abyss remained, but now he could think properly around the pain.

His dreams had mainly been of Cynehild's mouth and how it had moved under his, before they had become more detailed and erotic, replacing his bleak memories of leaving his late wife's grave.

Cyn had been right. He'd lived through his wife's death years ago. He knew that guilt over what he'd failed to do would always haunt him, but bringing her or their son back to life was impossible. And as the memories of how he'd attempted to honour her memory returned the solid ache in his chest faded. In his heart, he was more than ready to live his life again.

Cyn had been most insistent that they would not be repeating their kiss, but he knew he'd felt her lips soften under his, and her cheeks had coloured when he'd teased her about sharing his bed.

Kal resolved that tonight Cyn would sleep in that bed. But he would not go in it again until she invited him to be there with her. He wanted to be the one who vanquished the demons which plagued her sleep.

'Cyn?'

No answer. Not even from her men.

The cottage was empty except for him. He slammed his fist down on the furs. He hadn't realised how much he'd counted on her being there when he woke. If she returned, he would have to be more cautious. He'd have to give her reasons why she should welcome his kisses and touches rather than assuming she would.

He was about to call her name louder when he heard raised voices—Cynehild's and a man's, a Dane's. Arguing.

The brave but foolhardy woman.

The man's voice sent a prickle down his spine. Friend or foe? He concentrated on the black abyss which was his mind. Nothing. No clues. Just the darkness.

The one thing he knew was that he could not show weakness to a warrior. Weakness would have his enemies circling like a pack of wolves, ready to bring him down.

He was under little illusion about what would happen if the true extent of his injuries was known. Far too many coveted his position and wealth. And what could happen to Cyn, if his enemy decided to strike at him through her?

Wincing, Kal removed the bandage from his head, stood and focused on the open doorway. Because the wound was at the back of his head, it would remain hidden as long as he faced the stranger.

When the world ceased spinning, he picked up Leofwine's sword. It was lighter than he recalled. He practised a swing. He stumbled to his right, but stayed on his feet.

'Your mother-in-law is correct.'

Cynehild's voice floated towards him.

'The Jaarl Icebeard hasn't been kidnapped or enchanted by anyone. Nor is he being held here against his will.'

'Wake him.'

'He sleeps until he decides to wake.'

'My Jaarl would never behave in that way—making a marriage contract with a Mercian lady. He detests them and their overly precious ways, their fluttering lashes and feather-brained thinking. Stand aside.'

Kal winced. If that was truly what he'd thought about Mercian women, then his former self had never encountered the force of nature that was Lady Cynehild. Overly precious? Inclined to flutter her lashes without a coherent thought in her head? How wrong he'd been. Lady Cynehild exuded competency, courage and common sense.

'Except he has.' Cyn moved so that she stood in front of the doorway with her feet braced against the stile. Her hair was impeccably styled and she'd changed her gown to a more flattering blue one, which emphasised her waist and the curve of her hips. 'I warn you that you risk his displeasure at your peril. If you lay one finger on me, you will answer to him.'

Inside, Kal nodded in agreement.

'Jaarl Icebeard! Jaarl Icebeard!'

Cyn gestured imperiously with her right arm. 'Sit on that stone. Keep quiet. And remember to thank me later when you emerge in one piece.'

'I want to see him, so I will remain,' the man declared, his voice rising. 'If you have harmed a single hair on his head you will answer to me, Saxon witch.'

'Luba, I would ask you to control your son-in-law. I have explained that the shawl you are wearing is a present from me and that is the end of it.'

'Why is there all this infernal noise?'

Forcing all dizziness from him, Kal strode to the door and put his hands on either side of Cyn's neat waist, which curved out to her luscious hips.

'Why are there raised voices, Cynehild? Why are you out here rather than where you belong…in my bed? Whoever has disturbed us must pay!'

'Icebeard! I mean… My Jaarl…'

Kal knew he should know the voice, but he struggled to place it.

'Kal, you are awake.' She glanced over her shoulder. Her voice was light, but the pinching of her mouth showed her agitation. 'Luba's son-in-law Haddr demands to see you. Immediately.'

'You defied this excuse for a warrior in order to guard my sleep? Another reason, if I needed one, for you to become my bride.'

Kal peered over her head to the warrior, who stood with a raised sword and an angry expression on his face. The heavily scarred face framed by a mop of unruly hair resonated in his mind. He had the impression of clashed swords, standing shield to shield, pushing the enemy back. But beyond that his memories slipped away.

He tightened all his muscles and willed them to appear. Nothing. 'Haddr has always been far too impatient. Nearly cost us the shield wall at Basceng.'

'My Jaarl, I explained about that and you forgave me. Several times.'

'No doubt you have an explanation for this intrusion as well? Let us hope it is a better one.'

Haddr shuffled his feet. 'Rumours about your whereabouts swirl in the hall. My mother-in-law has a new shawl. I wanted to know why she had it, and she came out with a story which led me to believe she was up to her neck in mischief.'

Kal inhaled and Cynehild's scent, faintly floral intermingled with sunshine, wafted up. The scent reminded him of summer days and hope. He had not realised how much that had been missing from his life until it had returned.

'Rumours about me always swirl.' He put an arm about Cynehild and shifted her to the right, so that they were standing with touching shoulders. 'I believe I asked for privacy in my message, so as to get to know my bride, not to have all and sundry invade and ask questions.'

'Message? What message?' For the first time Haddr appeared nonplussed. 'Your cousin failed to mention any message.'

'Does the Jaarl's cousin confide in you?' Cyn asked in a firm voice. 'I had understood you were not in the inner circle.'

The man gave a nervous smile, sheathed his sword and bowed low. 'My mother-in-law sometimes stretches the truth, pretending to know more than she actually does, my lord. My wife was certain that this was one of those times. There are disturbing rumours, my liege. North-men have been seen in our lands. There is talk of a band of Mercian mercenaries prowling the outer limits, and a powerful witch well-versed in enchantment.'

Luba gave an audible sniff from where she stood. 'Poppycock rumours. Jaarl Icebeard has made a betrothal which will benefit everyone. Even if some refuse to see it that way.' Here she gave Cyn a pointed look.

Cyn leant into his shoulder. 'It is a betrothal which could unite two peoples or tear them apart. I agreed with Icebeard that we both had to exercise caution.'

Haddr gaped. 'So Lady Cynehild's laying of her husband's sword was a diversionary tactic? But you mocked her for it, my lord. Said she likely had something else in mind and you weren't inclined to give the meddlesome grieving widow anything!'

'I wished to keep our betrothal a secret until the moment was right. Why should I spoil the wagering—particularly as everyone was going to lose?'

Kal frowned. He'd mocked Lady Cynehild? So he *had* been arrogant. But he couldn't rid himself of the notion that her desire to lay the sword hid another motive. Haddr had hit on the crux of the problem—his own actions seemed out of the ordinary.

'I'm learning all your secrets, Kal. Mocking me now?'

Cynehild's light voice brought him back. He captured her fingers and raised them to his lips. 'The mockery was before I encountered you, my lady, and I shall regret it until the day I die.'

She withdrew her fingers. 'I will hold you to your word.'

'Thank you.' Kal glared at Haddr. 'Next time, believe your mother-in-law.'

'I have served with you and Alff since Basceng. You've never had time for women beyond the bedroom. You prefer them with soft thighs and quiet tongues.'

Kal glared at him. 'I never wanted to marry any of the women who graced my bed in the past. Lady Cynehild will be my wife. I trust you understand the difference?'

Haddr gulped and muttered his apologies.

'What will you tell my daughter?' Luba jabbed a bony finger at Haddr. 'To stop getting strange notions in her head and that her mother's words should be trusted like they always were before?'

Haddr shuffled his feet. 'My bride made a mistake. I will be the one to inform her. But by Thor's hammer, I don't relish the prospect.'

'You must trust your mother-in-law in future. Your Jaarl commands it.'

At Haddr's distressed face, Kal felt the laugh which had been building inside him boom out, faintly rusty, as if he had rarely laughed before now. Cynehild joined in, as did Luba. And after a few breaths Haddr also laughed, but with far less enthusiasm.

'I don't know that I've ever heard you laugh in this country, Icebeard.'

'You see what being betrothed has done for me?' Kal pulled Cynehild tighter against his body. Her curves seemed to fit naturally against him. 'I used to laugh a lot, Haddr.'

'My bride said—'

'Your wife is wrong. Twice in one day. I suspect that it will do her good when you inform her of this fact.'

Cynehild put her head on his chest and appeared to be

the picture of a contented and devoted woman, but Kal caught the flash of fire in her eyes and the faint snort of another barely suppressed laugh.

'Very wrong indeed.'

Haddr's frown increased. 'I've never known you to run from a fight. You live the way you want and force others to accept it.'

Kal stiffened. 'Which fight am I running from? Who seeks to challenge me? You can't leave it there, Haddr.'

Haddr tugged at the neck of his tunic. 'I merely meant you taking a wife. Yes, your cousin will be less than impressed that it is a Saxon woman, but you don't care about his opinion...not really.'

'My cousin has no say over who I marry.' Kal took his arm from about Cynehild's shoulders.

'Kal kept it secret for my sake and mine alone.' Cynehild stepped forward. 'I, for one, am very grateful. Can you imagine how it would have looked if we'd failed to suit? The harm which would have been caused between Danes and Mercians? Kal has been more than gracious in granting my request. It is hardly his fault if people ignore his message.'

'Everyone who works the land will be very happy,' Luba said, coming to stand by her son-in-law. 'My lady was well liked when she last lived here.' She sniffed. 'Unlike some I could mention... Her lord could be overly proud, but then he wasn't a great warrior—not like Jaarl Icebeard.'

'Luba—one shouldn't speak ill of the dead,' Cynehild rebuked.

'My lady, I beg your pardon, but one must state the truth. You may have idealised Lord Leofwine, but I certainly did not. I wiped his bottom when he was a baby.'

Kal inclined his head, trying not to wince at the sudden rush of pain as he did so. A tiny piece of him rejoiced that Cyn's late husband appeared far from universally loved. 'There are reasons why I am the Jaarl, Haddr. An advantageous match will assist me in holding these lands.'

Something akin to annoyance flashed across Haddr's face but was quickly masked. He gave a cheeky smile and looped an arm about his mother-in-law. 'I agree, My Jaarl. I had the honour of serving with you on the battlefield. Your sword skills were more than a match for all your opponents.'

His sword had once matched any on the battlefield, but now Kal knew he'd struggle to take even the simplest of food to his mouth.

How long could he last as a leader of men if he made mistakes with his sword? He knew he wanted peace, but he had to be able to defend his lands or they would soon be overrun.

Kal made a sweeping gesture with his hand. 'This is my way of ensuring that everyone is satisfied.'

'Through disappearing for a few days? You have frightened everyone. Your cousin is particularly certain that you have come to harm.'

Tyrant. The word hammered in his brain while Kal sought in vain to recall what Alff looked like.

'My cousin sees shadows where there are none.'

'You have always confided in him before. Never were there two cousins closer than you and Alff.'

'My message must have been lost or not passed on.' Kal gave a careful shrug and hoped Haddr would accept the excuse.

His cousin… Alff. He frowned and tried to grasp

wisps of shadow. A large man, with a booming voice and even quicker temper, but one who had been steadfast in the line.

'It is possible. Alff has been unwell in recent days,' Haddr said.

'How unwell?' Cynehild asked.

'He has suffered from a fever and has taken to his bed. Jaarl Icebeard teased him about it before he disappeared…asked him why he was sulking like a woman.'

Kal exchanged glances with Cynehild. Not only had he been hit over the head, but his cousin, the man he was supposed to be so close to, had been seriously ill.

'Sulking like a woman?' Cynehild said drily. 'His fever could explain why he has forgotten to pass on the message, though.'

'It was just banter, my lady,' Haddr said before Kal could open his mouth. 'They always trade insults—particularly in the practice yard.'

'I see.'

Kal shifted uncomfortably. Alff had not deserved teasing if he'd truly been ill. 'My reasoning holds true whatever the state of my cousin's health. My estate can handle a few more days without me. I plan to be otherwise occupied.'

This time he managed to plant a kiss on the corner of Cyn's mouth. She started to turn her head away, but he gave a warning frown. Immediately she snaked an arm about his neck and allowed him to capture her lips properly.

He lingered, enjoying the way her mouth slotted against his. She moaned slightly. He let her go and stepped back. His body thrummed, seeming to waken from a long winter's sleep. Her eyes had darkened with passion and her fingers instinctively lifted to explore her swollen mouth. He struggled to bring his breathing back under control.

Luba wore a self-satisfied smile and tugged at her son-in-law's arm. 'Seen enough?'

'I believe your experiment is a great success,' Haddr called out. 'These lands will be a safer place once you are wed. You need an heir.'

'Taking things slowly remains the best course,' Cynehild said, drowning our Haddr's words. Her chest rapidly rose and fell. 'Caution before all else.'

Kal went over to Haddr and put an arm about the younger man's shoulders. 'You see what I must contend with?'

Haddr stepped away and bowed low. 'I understand now, my lord.'

Luba tugged harder at Haddr's sleeve. 'Those two wish to be alone. My lady, it is well that you took a notion to stop at my humble abode. Who knows what rumours could have been flying about as the message has gone missing? I'm sure that Haddr will keep your secret, Jaarl Icebeard.'

'Your men are loyal to you, My Jaarl. But Alff is terribly anxious about you. Surely you will permit me to—'

'No,' Cynehild said, laying her head against Kal's chest again. 'You gave me your word, Icebeard. We will see this through and make sure we are compatible before announcing our union to the world. We must have a few more days.'

'Anyone with eyes can see you are compatible,' Haddr said with a laugh. 'I look forward to wagering on this.'

'No, the Lady Cynehild is skittish about such things…' Kal winced as the black pain raised its ugly head again.

The scene swam in front of him. He leant on Cyn, and although she staggered a little under his sudden weight she managed to keep him upright.

'It might end my run of bad luck,' Haddr wheedled.

'Leave now. Keep silent and you will be rewarded in due course,' Cynehild said in a firm tone.

'My mother-in-law's new shawl *is* very fine...' His gaze flickered over Cynehild as if he were weighing up whether she would be a good match for His Jaarl or not. His lip curled slightly. 'If this is how you wish to proceed, my lord, then who am I to deny you?'

'Who are you, indeed?' Kal answered.

Haddr walked away arm in arm with Luba. Luba's voice, arguing that he should show more respect and that this match was in their interests, could be heard even after they had disappeared from view.

Kal released a long breath and stumbled to a stone bench. Haddr had appeared to believe the ruse, even if he was not entirely happy with it. But how much longer did they have until he was unable to resist telling the secret?

Cynehild put her hands on her hips as she returned from conferring with her men. The low moan from the bench in the sunlight demonstrated that Kal's confrontation had taken more out of him than he wanted to admit. He was worse than Wulfgar in many ways, insisting that he was fine when he was clearly not.

'Back to bed with you, Kal.'

'My lady's wish...' He attempted a bow but went off balance again.

She rapidly came to his side and caught his bulk before he crashed to ground. His lips turned upwards.

'Arm about my shoulders. Hang on to me,' she gasped.

'Who could ask for a better nurse?'

'Why, because I fail to get cross with you when you do something stupid, like taking off your bandage?'

'That and you have the most amazing eyes.' A dimple played in the corner of his cheek. 'Made you blush.'

'Allow me to do my job.'

She led him back into the cottage, sat him at the table and started to examine his head. Despite the removal of the bandage, the wound remained scabbed over. If he wore his hair differently it would be possible to cover the wound and no one would guess about his injury.

All the while she attempted to ignore the pulse in his throat and the way his eyelashes swept down over his eyes. 'I wish Father Oswald, the priest from Baelle Heale, was here. He'd find a way to make you behave. You need bed rest for *days*, not a few hours.'

Kal sat up straight. 'We don't have days, Cyn. Haddr possesses an uncanny inability to keep his mouth shut when asked a direct question.'

'Your memory is still flawed.'

'I have remembered that about him. There was also something important about his marriage to Luba's daughter. It will come to me…'

Cynehild busied herself with tidying the already tidy cottage. All the flaws in her plan were becoming self-evident. No doubt everyone in her family, particularly her father, would be delighted to tell her of the mistakes she'd made if she ever returned to Baelle Heale. She should have stuck to women's tasks. Except it was too late for regrets. She had to go forward with the plan and hope it would be successful.

'I suppose the time we have depends on the questions

he's asked? I thought we gave a pretty good impression of being betrothed.'

'That's one way of looking at it.'

She bustled about with the fire and put more grain on to soak. Little jobs, but they restored some small measure of calm.

'Should we move?' she asked finally, hating the quaver in her voice. 'Back to the cave?'

'How will your Brother Palni and these fabled men find us then?' His tone of voice echoed the sort she used with Wulfgar when he woke from a bad dream. 'A panicked reaction never solves anything. We can account for my injury if necessary. What is truly troubling you?'

'Our story is easy—you were on the way to meet me and were attacked. We decided this was the best course to follow. We keep to the story we gave Haddr if it comes to it.' Cynehild gave a decisive nod, altering the subject and not answering his question.

'Haddr did not appear that surprised.' Kal held out his hand. 'Can you get me a knife? A block of wood?'

'What for? We are having porridge. You should be resting.'

'I will need to be able to swing a sword with some degree of accuracy sooner rather than later.'

'But what does a block of wood and a knife have to do with anything?'

'I want to carve,' he said. 'Last night I struggled to get a spoon to my mouth. How can I command men in battle if I can't feed myself? My late wife said I was a genius at working with wood, and that was why she first noticed me. Keeping my hands busy will help me to think. Like you and your spinning. You do it because you are battling your demons.'

'I don't have demons.'

'Your hands are rarely still. I suspect your demons may be winning.'

Her throat clenched. He'd noticed. 'I can control them…when I spin. I miss my son, among other things.'

'And I can control mine if I carve.'

His quiet words filled the room, but Cynehild saw the stillness with which he held his body. 'Your lack of coordination will be to do with your head injury. Your skill will return.'

'If I have to fight, then I need to practise. You refuse to let me stand. Allow me to do this. Please.'

His words made her insides twist. What harm could carving do?

She left the cottage and returned with a block of wood and a small knife.

'Outside. Being in here reminds me of a tomb,' he said.

'We have a roof over our heads, and it might rain.'

'My eyesight will be better outside. And it isn't raining yet.' He went outside and sat down on the low stone bench in front of the cottage. 'Join me with your spinning? Unless you have something else to be doing?'

Cynehild opened her mouth to explain about her other chores, but the words died on her lips. 'It seems the best way to ensure you don't get into mischief.'

A soft huff of a laugh escaped his chest. He gently nudged her shoulder. 'I thought you liked spending time with me.'

'Are you planning on carving anything special?'

'I need to get my eye in. I thought to make something for your boy. A horse. Little boys like horses, and they like it when their mothers return to them with a gift.'

He made a swipe with his knife, missed the wood and cursed.

Cynehild's eyes opened wide at the unexpected answer. It would be easy to start liking Kal, but it would be a mistake. They were enemies and had to remain that way. Except she knew that wasn't quite true—not any longer. At some time over the last days he had become something more than an enemy—not yet a friend, but someone she could like.

'For Wulfgar? Why?'

'I want to thank you for not flinching away from me earlier, when Haddr was here. You played the part of besotted bride-to-be very well.' His eyes deepened to dark pools. 'Our rehearsal last night clearly worked.'

Cynehild bent her head and pretended an interest in her spinning wheel. He was making something for Wulfgar. She wished Wulfgar was here with her, so that he could meet the man who'd made it.

'I knew what was needed. You are right not to fully trust anyone.'

He made another swipe with his knife. This time it connected with wood. A long spiral curled off the block and fell to his feet. 'Does that include you?' he asked.

'I certainly mean you no harm,' she answered, turning her head away from his intense gaze.

The gold hidden in the church belonged to Wulfgar. She wasn't robbing someone she liked; she was liberating something which rightfully belonged to her son. And she would confess to Kal what she'd done—but not just yet. She couldn't risk spoiling something which had somehow become precious to her.

'No harm at all,' she said.

'I will take that for now.'

Chapter Eight

'We agreed to rest after you had managed to get the horse's outline done.'

Cynehild had returned to the cottage after ensuring her men were settled for the night to find Kal had made another makeshift pallet on the floor of the cottage out of straw, a cloak and some of the furs.

His smile caused her breath to hitch and her blood to warm. She put a hand to her temple and concentrated. She'd worked it out earlier, after she'd seen to her men. Her reaction to him was simply because they were around each other all the time and she was unused to men flirting with her.

Her men mainly stayed in the barn, guarding the covered cart and enjoying the break from travelling. None of them wanted to deal with an irritable Deniscan, but after some persuasion they had volunteered to be his sparring partners in the coming days.

Now, she rapidly explained the situation to Kal.

'And your conditions for this promised treat?' he asked.

'You stop pushing yourself.'

'I will if you do. It is far harder to sleep sitting up than lying down.' He gave the makeshift pallet another pat. 'Your very being proclaims exhaustion, Cynehild. Your son would say the same if he saw you.'

She pressed her lips together. 'You've no idea what my son would say.'

'Who is being stubborn now? Humour me. Try the bed and see what you think.'

Instead, Cynehild poked the cloak spread over one of the furs and moved the pillow with her toe. A crudely carved horse peeped out. 'Is it finished? Oh, Kal, you can really tell it is a horse!'

A smile split his face. 'I worked on it while you were gone. I intend on making a set.'

Cynehild curled her fingers about the horse. Wulfgar would adore this. She could almost hear his excited squeak. Once he saw it, she doubted he'd pay any attention to her. Although he might even give her a hug, like he'd used to, instead of proclaiming that he was too old. Her heart ached with longing to hear his voice and to inhale his little boy smell.

She understood the horse's significance. It was a gift beyond words. Kal didn't know her son but he'd made something which would light up his face.

'You're very kind. The perfect gift.'

'It is the sort of thing I wanted as boy. My father had a captive who carved a set of horses for me when I was young, before he was ransomed. When Ranka was pregnant I made a set for my boy...the one who died. She told me to stop because I was tempting the gods. Maybe I did.'

Cynehild forgot how to breathe, and then remembered she actually had to take in air.

'I'll be fine dozing on the bench where I spent last night,' she said. 'Luba has brought me more carded wool. I have plenty to be getting on with.'

She gave an awkward shrug. She struggled to remember when anyone had last seen to her welfare in this way. Brother Palni might fuss a bit, but no one really bothered to ensure she was comfortable. She was the one who was supposed to have all the answers where matters of the household were concerned. Her father certainly felt that was the case. And Leofwine had never been able to do anything special for Wulfgar—something he had regretted at the end.

'My mother always taught me that a man looks to the comfort of his women.'

'I'm not your woman.' Her cheeks burnt as if she had been sitting in front of the fire tending the ash cakes for too long. 'Get that idea out of your head.'

A dimple flashed in the corner of his cheek. He patted the freshly made-up pallet. 'So, if you don't want the comfortable bed, are you asking me to share the pallet I've just made instead? Normally I like to know a woman longer, but for you I am willing to make an exception. We can share the ground without a problem.'

'The bench.'

'You'll tumble off in your sleep. I'd have to stay awake all night, waiting to catch you.' His voice lowered to a soft rasp. 'Where would that leave us? Exhausted for no good purpose.'

'Is there such a thing as being exhausted for a *good* purpose?'

'Yes, without a doubt.' His voice slid over her skin like the finest fur. 'Are you asking me to show you?'

Cynehild sank down onto the wooden bench. His

words were painting enticing pictures in her head. Yet Brother Palni said that she looked like a rapidly aging crone. Kal must be playing some sort of game with her. He could have no idea about her attraction to him, or why she'd spent such a long time outside, trying to get her heart rate to go back to normal.

'It was not what I meant. You know that. Stop trying to twist my words.'

'Am I? I'm merely attempting to understand your reasoning for declining the bed.'

'My reasoning?' Cynehild reached for a stick and poked at the fire. The sparks fell bright and then winked out. Desire was like that—burning hot until it left only ash.

'The only reason I can think of why you'd prefer a pallet on the rush-covered floor to the comfort of a bed is that you require my arms about you.'

'In your dreams!'

'I'd prefer to be in yours.' At her gasp, he gave a shout of laughter. 'You're fun to tease, Cyn. You are wearing your totally shocked face, but your eyes are glowing with anticipation.'

'Glowing with anticipation? More like exasperation.'

He hung his head. 'Are you terribly angry with me, Cyn?'

'Find another pet name for me. I've never been a Cyn.' *Not now at any rate.*

Her husband had sometimes called her 'Cyn dear' when he was being exceptionally affectionate. It felt strange to hear it on another man's lips but not unpleasant, and what was worse, she longed to hear it again. It made her feel alive…as if her future contained more than simply being a daughter, a sister and a mother.

She hugged her arms about her waist. Even if Kal insisted on using that name, it didn't mean they were going to make love or do anything of that nature. She'd spent the better part of the day trying to forget what his mouth had felt like against hers and how it had sent her blood racing. Now, just when she'd considered she had her emotions under control, he went and did something like this.

'Someone must have called you Cyn once. It suits you. Cynehild is far too formal and stiff for a woman whose mouth constantly curves upwards into a smile.'

'It does?' Cynehild explored her lips with her tongue. 'I hadn't realised.'

'Your smile brings light to the cottage.' He lay down on the pallet he'd arranged. 'I'll be sleeping here. It's a shame to allow the bed to go empty, but that's your choice.'

He closed his eyes and pretended to snore.

'I won't sleep,' she told him. 'My so-called demons, remember? You might as well be comfortable in the bed. We'll need your sword arm before too long.'

She winced. She'd voiced her fears out loud—that Haddr would be unable to resist spreading gossip and then they'd have Kal's men here, including the person who had tried to murder him. Her men were primed and ready, but they were only two against who knew how many warriors.

'My arm will be strong enough when the time comes. My head has already improved immeasurably after the tisanes you've brewed. And I am hereby willing to swear on the healing power of porridge and carving wooden animals.'

'I hope and pray that it will be.'

'Lie awake, then. Gaze at the rafters. You will be no

good for anything if you fail to rest properly. Sitting up and spinning wool is about as far from resting as you can get, to my mind.'

'You are more of a mother hen than Brother Palni.'

'Something that I'm better at than the monk? Good.' He closed his eyes. 'I've been quite jealous of him and I keep thinking up ways to surpass his goodness.'

Cynehild struggled not to laugh. Kal in this mood was hard to resist.

'I can see you smiling,' he said.

'How can you? Your eyes are shut,' she protested.

'I can sense it. Go on. Let me hear you laugh. You want to.'

Cynehild gave a cross between a snort and a laugh. 'You win. Brother Palni and I rarely get on.'

Kal opened his eyes and stared directly at her. 'I like it when I win…particularly with a lady I admire. Some might say I am very good at winning—which is why I was appointed Jaarl.'

'You think?'

'Becoming one takes a good deal of skill, patience and luck. I remember my father saying that once. Far better to be born one.'

She stifled a yawn. 'Have you remembered how you became one?'

'That story will need to wait until after you sleep. Now, lie down properly on the bed. Do as you are told for once.'

The bed did look very inviting. A wave of tiredness washed over her. 'You can be quite irritating.'

His eyes danced. 'All the more reason why I should take the floor, Cyn.'

Cynehild tried to ignore the warm pulse of heat which coursed down her spine at his tone. He was right—rest would solve her problem of being attracted to him. 'You're not going to let me win on this, are you?'

'Not when it is something that matters. Sometimes, my stubborn lady, you must give way and accept the inevitable.'

The dying fire made strange shadows on the rafters, shifting in the slight breeze. The wind had picked up outside, howling and driving rain against the roof, but sleep refused to come despite the softness of the bed. Cynehild toyed with the idea of rising and doing more spinning, but she suspected that if she moved, Kal would wake. Currently his breathing was a steady counterpoint to the rain.

Lately she'd feared sleep because of her dreams about Leofwine, and not doing as he had instructed. Now, though, every time she closed her eyes she remembered Kal's touch on her waist and the way his mouth had briefly moved over hers. She barely knew the man but he made her feel alive.

And she was about to rob him. It didn't matter that he probably didn't even know the gold existed. It was buried on his land.

Cynehild tried to turn her thoughts to more mundane matters—like who would Brother Palni bring back with him? If she was lucky, it would be a few of Moir's men. If she was unlucky, it would be her brother-in-law himself—or, worse still, her sister too, riding like an avenging angel.

She and Ansithe had always fought as children. They'd grown closer after Ansithe's marriage to Moir, but Cynehild knew Ansithe wouldn't understand why she'd taken this risk. She suspected, though, that Brother Palni had guessed about the coins…where they'd come from and her reasons for insisting that they continue.

It had all been much easier when she hadn't actually known who Jaarl Icebeard was and hadn't had to consider that he might be a caring person and she would want his regard. All she knew was that she wished Leofwine had never given her this burden in the first place. But because she had taken it on she would continue to the end.

She brought her knees up to her chest and hugged them. A wave of loneliness swept over her. She wasn't entirely sure she wanted this to end. With Kal, she felt part of a team, wanted for herself. Was sharing a few kisses with him so wrong?

A sudden low moan made her sit up straight. She listened in the darkness. 'Kal, are you all right?'

Kal began to thrash about on the makeshift pallet, shouting out, 'Help me. Please someone help. Dying!'

She rushed towards where he lay. His hands were flailing about but she caught them and held them still. He instantly stopped. His eyes blinked open and he stared at her as if he'd never seen her before. She let his hands go and one touched the side of her face, smoothing back a tendril of her hair.

'You are safe?' he asked.

'We both are.'

His eyes fluttered shut. 'I need to know you are safe.'

He mumbled a word, a name that she couldn't quite catch. It was probably his wife's. Cynehild's heart constricted. Regardless of what he might say, or what she might hope for, he was clearly not yet over her.

She had started to tiptoe away when he moaned again.

'You are fine, Kal. You are safe. We should have bandaged your head again earlier. If you are not careful, you will start bleeding again. Kal…please. You need to be quiet.'

His eyes snapped open. 'Cyn? You are here? You haven't left me? You haven't died on the road? I dreamt my enemy had found you and I was too late to save you.'

The tension leaked out of her. 'I'm here. I'll stay until it's time for me to go.'

'I was dreaming, wasn't I?'

'Your dreams vanish when you wake,' she said, in the sort of voice she used when Wulfgar had his night terrors. 'You are among friends—people who care what happens to you. Close your eyes and sleep again. All is well and safely gathered in.'

'Am I safe?' He raised himself up on one elbow and looked about him as if he didn't recognise where he was. 'Truly?'

'No one will harm you here.'

'Good.' His mouth curved up. 'I'm glad you are here with me, Cynehild. I want… I want to be good for you.'

'I'm sure you will be.'

'But am I good enough?'

'Be quiet now and rest.'

She started to move away, conscious suddenly that she was dressed in her under-gown and her hair was unbound. The cold from the floor seeped into her feet.

'Stay with me.' He caught her fingers. With a deft tug he pulled, and she tumbled down into his embrace.

She lay against the hard planes of his body. There was not any fat on him. She put a hand on his warm chest. The temptation to lay her head against it nearly overwhelmed her.

'Kal, really… Be sensible. This is the worst thing for you.'

'Hush.' He put a finger to her lips. 'You will spoil everything. Remain with me.'

Her mouth tingled where he'd touched her. 'How?'

'You talk too much.'

His other arm tightened about her, pressing her curves against his body. His lips were only a breath away.

'Kiss me. Let me feel your mouth against mine. Properly.'

'Kiss you?' She moistened her aching lips.

His eyes fluttered shut. 'Please.'

Giving in to impulse, she bent her head and tasted. His mouth was like sunshine and warmth after a cold winter. She knew in the sensible part of her brain that she should not be doing this. She should get up and move away. He'd allow her to go. But she stayed with her lips pressed against his. If she tried hard enough, maybe she could pretend she was dreaming too.

His arms tightened about her, drawing her closer so that she could feel every inch of his hard body through her thin gown. Her legs moulded to his. His lips parted and she delved inside, tasting and tangling her tongue with his. Her whole being became infused with heat. And she knew she wanted more.

He twisted so that she was below him and he loomed over her. His mouth traced a line of kisses down her neck. Her body arched upwards, seeking his hardness.

A sudden snap from the fire sent a cloud of sparks

flying into the air, highlighting his cheekbones and the size of his shoulders. She trailed a gentle finger down his cheek and his mouth curved upwards in a masculine smile. His mouth roamed her face, raining small kisses on her cheekbones, the line of her jaw and the corner of her mouth.

'Sweetling…' he murmured against her earlobe.

At the generic term of endearment, Cynehild stiffened. Leofwine had been like that when they were first together, during those months when he'd kept his old mistress—always the endearment and never her name. That had come later. She hated remembering the awful loneliness of being a bride of convenience.

She pushed against Kal's chest. 'No.'

Instantly he rolled off her and she scrambled to standing.

'What's wrong?' he asked.

Cynehild smoothed down her under-gown, which had become scrunched up to the top of her thighs in the madness of their kisses. 'I am many things, Kal Randrson, but I am not just a warm body in the night.'

He ran his hand through his hair. 'A warm body in the night? You could never be that.'

'You called me sweetling. I could have been anyone. I'm me. When we join, I don't want to be called by someone else's name.'

'*When* we join? That's an improvement on *if.*'

She snorted and hugged her arms about her body. 'You are muddying the subject.'

His gaze slowly travelled the length of her, seeming to take in all her curves and her unbound hair. 'I have no idea why you are so angry, my lady. I thought you wanted this. I meant no harm with the endearment.'

'It's not my name.'

He hesitated for another breath. Then, 'Cynehild. My lady. Are you satisfied?'

'I am now.' She forced her fingers to relax. 'You were having a bad dream. I came to you because you started calling out. I did not come because I wanted to climb into bed with you. I wish that to be made clear.'

'You were part of the dream.' He gave a slow smile. 'A very pleasant part of it. And the reality was much better than the dream.'

Cynehild ignored the curl of warmth which was even now circling her insides. She knew precisely what had nearly happened. She was hardly some innocent maiden. She'd forgotten how good it felt to be held in a man's arms. If he hadn't called her sweetling she would have stayed in his arms and they would have joined.

She glanced upwards, towards the blackened beams. She knew that if Leofwine had been the one to survive she would have expected him to have other liaisons, even marry again. But she wasn't him. And what she felt for Kal wasn't the same as her feelings for Leofwine. What did that make her with all her protestations about how she'd always be true to Leofwine?

She tried to think about something other than the way Kal's mouth had moved against hers. Or how alive her body had felt. It had taken all her willpower to step away from him.

'My lady, know that whatever happens between us, it is your choice.'

'We should both get some sleep. As you pointed out earlier—the morning will bring new challenges.'

'I am sorry if I disturbed you, my lady. It wasn't my intention.'

'I am pleased everything is well with you.' She nodded towards her bed and gave an exaggerated yawn, knowing her dreams would revolve about a hard-muscled body and soft lips moving against hers. 'I find I am beyond exhausted.'

'Sleep, my lady. I will attempt to keep quiet for the remainder of the night.'

'I will appreciate that.'

She settled down and pulled the furs tight about her. Her body thrummed with frustrated disappointment. She tried to ignore it. When she joined with a man she wanted it to be for the right reasons—not simply to keep warm in the night.

Kal savoured the first rays of sunshine reaching inside the cottage. He had made a mistake earlier with Cynehild—calling her by an endearment. Her reaction had made him wonder anew about her relationship with her late husband. He might not have been the paragon of all virtue that she proclaimed him to be. He drew hope from that.

Kissing her properly and exploring her soft contours had gone beyond all his previous imaginings. His body ached for her and her alone, but he was aware that Saxon ladies had a different view of such things from the Danes.

'You're awake.'

Cynehild appeared in the doorway. She was dressed in her gown which effectively hid most of her alluring curves. Her hair was carefully done and hidden away under a *couvre-chef* instead of falling about her face like a glorious golden cloud as it had done last night. Kal's body responded instantly to her presence and he concentrated on the wall in front of him rather than looking at the object of his dreams.

There was little he could tell her which would make the awkward situation better. He knew she considered their alliance to be a platonic pretend relationship—one which would of necessity end in a few days' time, when her man returned with reinforcements. He had to find a way to change her mind and make her see that they could make their relationship work for real.

It had come to him when he'd glimpsed the first streaks of rose in the sky that the answer to his problems was marriage to Cynehild—a proper marriage and not one merely for convenience.

Despite everything she'd been through, she held the people of this land in her heart. He could see that. It was one of the reasons he admired her spirit. However, he suspected that while she might be attracted to him, she would be resistant to the idea of making their temporary liaison permanent. But he knew he had somehow been given this chance to turn his life around and he was not going to ruin it.

The early dawn gave her skin a radiant gleam and his heart asked him who he thought he was kidding. He wanted to sink into Cynehild and enjoy her many charms with an intensity that frightened him. He wanted it even knowing that her heart belonged to another. But how did one compete with a ghost—particularly a ghost whose lands he now held?

'Do you normally get up this early?' she asked, coming to stand beside him.

'It's my normal habit. From what I can recall.' He risked a smile up at her and saw her eyes grow warm. 'I like to spend a little time thinking in peace.'

She walked back to the open door and looked out. 'I will start looking for Brother Palni's return today. I'm assuming that he hasn't got lost.'

'Does he often get lost?'

'It has been known to happen.' She smiled. 'Once he is here, we can plan the next phase of our strategy. I think Ansithe and Moir might travel with him.'

He blinked rapidly. He needed more time alone with her before her sister arrived. 'So quickly? Surely it will take a little while for him to assemble a sizeable force of men. We need a show of strength rather than a quick raid.'

She gave him one of her sideways glances over her shoulder. Her lips parted, as if she was about to say something, but then she closed her mouth tight.

'I'm just offering my expertise…saying what I'd do if I were your brother-in-law.' He wanted to believe it as well. He sent a silent prayer up to any god who might be listening—he needed more time to show her how good they could be together.

'I suppose you're right—assembling a large force could take some time—but my sister will insist on moving quickly.' She rose up on her tiptoes and peered out, as if she was searching for the smallest speck of dust which might signal their arrival. 'I hope Brother Palni remembers that I only want enough men to be able to give you authority. Not an invasion force. We should quickly discover who wanted you dead.'

Kal tapped his fingers together. He had to know how long he had. 'Once they are here, you plan to go to the church, lay your husband's sword and go, having decided that we don't suit. Do I have that right?'

'Why wait? You say your enemy will immediately

challenge you. We will stay for the fight, to ensure its fairness.'

She put her hands on her hips, drawing attention to her curves. Kal was forcibly reminded of how well her body had fitted against his last night. If they stayed here he'd be tempted to take her in his arms again, and there were many reasons why that was a poor idea right now.

'Shall we go for a walk?' he asked. 'Your men can remain here in case Brother Palni arrives in our absence.'

Her lashes hid her eyes. 'Where to?'

'Just in the general area. I thought it might assist my memory. I can ask one of your men to accompany me if you are too busy.'

She shook her head. 'I'm not too busy. A walk might be a good thing. We can go slowly and return if it proves too much for you.'

'Excellent.' He held out the rough carving he'd done of a warrior. 'Your son's next piece.'

'How many do you mean to carve?'

'As many as it takes.'

'What do you mean?'

'I've deprived him of his mother for a considerable time. These are a bribe to make him think well of me.'

'He is unlikely to meet you, but if he ever did I'm sure he would see what I see—a man who wishes to do what is right.'

He put his hand to his chest. 'With one hand you take away hope and with the other you make me proud.'

She took the carving and weighed it in her hand. Her smile was like the sun coming out from behind the clouds and it gave him the courage to go on.

'I would enjoy that walk very much.'

Chapter Nine

The state of the woods impressed Cynehild. In her mind, she was expecting to see the neglect of Leofwine's final years—the years when he had concentrated on the growing threat of the Deniscan instead of caring for his people. But these woods showed signs of being used, with fresh coppicing and logs stacked neatly.

Throughout their ramble she kept finding reasons to glance over at Kal, telling herself that it was because she feared him collapsing rather than because she simply enjoyed looking at him. But each time she caught herself doing it she knew the lie grew bigger and the attraction became harder to deny.

'We should return. My men will wonder where we are,' she said, when she had run out of excuses in her own mind. Today Kal showed no sign of falling or needing assistance to walk.

'They were very reluctant to allow you to go off on your own with me. Brother Palni's orders, apparently.' Kal inclined his head. 'The good brother appears to have left a number of instructions about the way you and I are to be managed.'

Cynehild smiled inwardly. It almost sounded as if Kal was jealous. Something inside her twisted. She had no right to hope that Kal had any feelings for her. Even hoping was a betrayal of Leofwine. Except he was cold and dead in the ground...

She *couldn't* have these feelings of desire for this Deniscan. Brother Palni was right—by looking after him she had become too close to him. She was the sensible forthright sister who had now become a widow with a child. She was not in the least like her youngest sister, Elene, who had yet to marry and was given to extravagant displays of emotion. Or her middle sister, Ansithe, who possessed a quicksilver temper. She took pride in being the steady one, who considered her beloved son's future before her own.

'Your strength begins to return, but it will quickly fail if you do too much,' she commented.

'I'm grateful you have allowed me to carry Leofwine's sword on my belt. I feel naked without a weapon.' He stopped suddenly. 'I've sworn to protect you, Cyn, even if you disbelieve me.'

'Do I look as if I disbelieve you?'

He captured her chin with his fingers and turned her face to the left and the right, studying her. The now familiar curl of warmth entangled about her insides. Just when her lips had parted to welcome his kiss, he let go.

'You look like a woman who needs convincing.'

His soft laugh played on her skin like sunlight chasing shadows.

Cynehild firmed her mouth. 'Let's hope you are not put to the test any time soon.'

Liking him had crept up on her. She wanted to spend

time with him in a way she hadn't wanted with Leof-wine—not even when she had known she loved him.

Back then she had accepted that men and women had different spheres which rarely touched. Leofwine had had his routine and she'd had hers. He'd no sooner weave than she'd wave a sword. Except now that he was dead she'd learned to do all manner of things usually left to men—like inspecting outbuildings, ensuring there was enough grain and making plans for having her son prop-erly trained.

Leofwine wouldn't recognise the woman she'd be-come. She wasn't even sure she recognised herself. But she liked her feeling of accomplishment. And, having seen Moir and Ansithe together, she wondered if there was another way to organise a marriage.

She pushed the thought away. She wasn't planning on marrying again. Her life was going in another direc-tion altogether.

'It is a well-balanced sword,' Kal said. 'A pity that it cannot go to your son.'

'You will need a sword when we return to the hall. It will give you a reason as to why you are not carrying your own. Why you left it at the hall. Because you knew I would be giving you this one.'

His brow lowered. 'But I didn't leave my sword at the hall.'

'I know that. But whoever has it is either the culprit or knows who it is. It is the best lead I can think of.' She waited and steeled herself for his mockery.

He nodded, accepting her idea. 'When the time comes, you will still be able to go into the church and lay your husband's sword in front of the altar—although it remains a mystery to me why he wanted you to do it in the first place.'

'I suspect he considered that somehow it would show Wulfgar his heritage.'

'But you didn't bring your son with you. Did I make that a condition of my agreement?' He hesitated and a shy smile hovered on his lips. 'I have a vague recollection of thinking it might put you off your journey if I didn't allow him to come with you.'

'No, he is still too young to travel.' Cynehild pretended an interest in the skeletons of old leaves which dotted the path. 'Also, in not bringing him I wanted to show you that I have no designs on your lands. His heritage may come from here, but his future lies elsewhere.'

'Very sensible.'

'My brother-in-law suggested it would be a wise move to emphasise this when I arrived. Apparently, your temper is notoriously uncertain.'

'Moir sounds like a man who thinks about consequences.'

'He is far wiser than I first considered.' She briefly told him of the events which had led to their meeting and her sister's eventual marriage to him. 'I owe him a great deal for trying to reunite me with Leofwine when he was captured by the Danes. Despite Moir's efforts, my husband ended up dying from the treatment he received at the hands of his captors, but before he passed we were together for a brief time. It is a memory I will always treasure.'

A muscle tightened in Kal's jaw and his pace quickened.

She hurried to catch up with him and caught his arm.

'This is supposed to be a walk, not a race, or we'll have to return to the hut for you to rest.'

'Your husband was lucky to have a wife like you.' Each word was carefully enunciated. 'I hope he appreciated you and kept you safe.'

'He kept me safe until he couldn't any longer...' A confession about the hidden treasure threatened to spill from her lips. 'What was your wife like?' she asked, before she did confess.

She didn't even know if the treasure was still there. It might have vanished long before Kal had arrived. Someone might have guessed that Leofwine would hide something he could come back for—particularly after his wagons were attacked. She'd always wondered if it had been outlaws and not of the Great Heathen Horde. Nothing else had been overrun. But Leofwine had told her not to be silly and to stop worrying. And if it wasn't there she would have to find another way to ensure Wulfgar's future.

Kal stopped. 'We were both young. We married for the wrong reasons. She wanted to escape from her family, and I wanted a family because mine had all died. Then the crops failed. She thought I should go and join the Army, but I wanted to stay at home until our child was born. I was away taking our last cow to market when she gave birth. When I returned she was dying of fever with the crying baby next to her. She passed that day, and the baby boy lived only two more before dying too. I swore I'd make something of my life as she had wanted me to do.'

'What do you want now?'

He turned his face from hers. 'To live my life in peace. I've seen enough of war. This land needs to heal. I think that is why I gave permission for the sword to be laid. I'm certain of it.'

Cynehild flinched. Kal's simple assurance made it far harder to keep the truth from him. 'You don't know how much your words mean to me,' she said finally, tumbling into the shifting pools of his eyes as he turned back to her.

'I know I fell in love with this land the first time I set foot on it.'

His gaze drifted down over her travelling dress—the one she'd chosen that morning for its practicality.

'It was like a beautiful woman wearing an ugly dress—neglected and overlooked, but with potential that took my breath.'

'An ugly dress? Are you making a comment about this gown? Brother Palni hates it with a passion, as does my sister Elene. It may be brown and loose-fitting, but it is useful for travelling.'

'Will you allow me to call you beautiful?'

She toyed with the tweezers which hung from her belt. 'The land responds well to your touch.'

He threw his head back and laughed. 'You are attempting to change the subject. Why?'

'I will admit that a part of me wanted the land to be less than it was. Leofwine disliked farming. It bored him and his steward—Luba's late husband—who was worse than useless.'

Kal's eyes turned serious and he raised her hand to his lips. 'I'm pleased you see that the land needs me. It needs a beautiful lady who will love it as well.'

She froze. Her heart resounded in her ears. Was he saying what she thought he was? How to respond? She didn't know what she wanted to say to that. She wasn't in love with him. She liked the man she knew very much. But was the Kal she'd encountered the real Kal, or was he still suffering the after-effects of the blow to his head?

Her responsibility lay far to the west of here, with Wulfgar. Would Kal be willing to take on the son of the man who'd once owned these lands? Or would he see him as a threat? Not now, when he was a little boy, but when he was a grown warrior? How could she even ask him when she hadn't confessed her true purpose here?

'Cyn…? You don't have to answer me now.'

A noise like men shouting floated on the breeze. The tension in her shoulders released. Her confession would have to wait.

'Can you hear voices?' she asked. 'Do you think we'd better investigate?'

'Voices? Is that what the sound is?' He cocked his head to one side. 'You're right. Angry voices. Which direction are they coming from?'

She listened harder. 'They don't sound like Northern voices, but I could be wrong. I'm not very good on Northern accents. And they seem to be speaking your language rather than mine. It could be that my brother-in-law has arrived and wants to know where I am.'

A muscle jumped in his jaw and his hand went to the sword. 'Or it could mean something else. Someone else.'

Cynehild clenched her fists and tried to control the panic rising in her. Not all Northmen were bad—she knew that. And Kal was in no fit state to be defending anyone. 'Someone else? What are they saying?'

'Trust me to protect you. Trust my sword arm.'

Cynehild planted her feet firmly on the ground. Men had always seemed to consider her brainless where battle was concerned. She'd accepted it from Leofwine, but she refused to accept it from Kal.

'My husband used to keep me in the dark about the dangers we faced when we fled the Great Army, but I won't have it from you. I'm a grown woman—not some maiden given to fainting. If my men are in danger, they need to be rescued.'

He lifted his brow. 'Apologies. I thought to protect you and keep you from panicking.'

'Panicking is a luxury not afforded to widows with small sons.'

'I'll bear that in mind.'

The shouting began again. Curses and shouted questions about Icebeard. Cynehild's heart sank. Moir and Brother Palni would not be demanding those sorts of answers. Haddr had talked. Kal's time of healing had ended.

'Danish. Not Northern.' Kal cursed Haddr with a particularly colourful oath.

'Haddr has betrayed us so quickly?'

'It will be accidental. His mouth always runs like a river in the evening, after he has drunk his ale. Our secret time is over—and without your additional men arriving.' He put a heavy hand on her shoulder. 'I must return to the hall.'

'Brother Palni left strict instructions—'

'Do you want to save your men?'

'Of course.' Cynehild frowned. Despite her earlier show of bravado, a solid lump of panic occupied her middle. Her stomach heaved.

'My going to the hall is the best way to do that. You must trust me on this.'

'I do…but I still worry.' She wrapped her arms about her aching middle. 'Brother Palni made me promise.'

'But I gave him no such promise.'

He put his hand on her arm. A pulse of warmth radiated out from it.

'Stay behind in these woods, near the hut. Keep out of the way. Wait until I deal with these men and return or until your own men arrive.'

'Allow *you* to deal with it?' She made a suitably disgusted noise with her throat. 'Grant me strength. I stopped running away after I left these lands the first time. I stand and fight. If they kill you and torture my men they will learn I am here anyway and then hunt me down.'

'Your bravery puts me to shame. The Nourns truly smiled on me when our paths crossed.' He inclined his head. 'I will take any help offered. But I haven't decided yet what my next move will be. I want to see if I can get a good look at the men. Taking time to pause and assess the situation can win battles.'

Time to pause. He made it sound as if her men were already lost. She remembered suddenly how Leofwine had been—who he'd left behind. 'I promised to keep those men safe. They volunteered to stay behind to guard us. I can't abandon them. I won't do that—not again. Not ever again when I'm in charge.'

'Ensuring their safety is my priority.'

Cynehild gnawed her bottom lip. The tension in her neck eased. Kal understood. 'What do you need?' she asked.

'Ideally a place to spy out the land…somewhere we can't be seen.'

'There is a slight rise over there which might afford a decent view of the cottage. I discovered it when I came back from Luba's. Would that suit?'

A smile spread across his face. 'You are as clever as you are beautiful, Cyn. If you'd been a warrior, the Great Army would not have stood a chance.'

Her heart did a little flip. She tried to tell herself that she didn't really know him—not as he had been before the accident—and that he might often make flirtatious comments to women when he wanted them to do something. Certainly Luba seemed ready to melt over him. Except he did listen to her and he respected her opinion.

'I will take that as a heartfelt compliment.'

'Very much so.'

Kal followed Cynehild through the undergrowth to a small overhang which afforded him a decent view. Below them was a guard of men, several of whom Kal vaguely recognised as belonging to him. One of the Danes slapped one of Cynehild's men in the face.

Cyn stifled a cry and looked away. Kal kept a hand on her shoulder, pinning her in place.

'Should you show yourself?' she whispered. 'They are your men. Aren't they?'

Kal shook his head, trying to rid it of the buzzing. If those men were not loyal to him he could be leading Cyn into a trap. 'Not here. We need to go to the hall. Whatever happens they will bring them back alive. They won't dare execute them without further orders.'

Cyn's face drained of colour. 'Surely these must be your men? They answer to you. They will obey your word.'

'Circumstances altered when I was struck on the head. I've no idea if they have come because they want to make sure I'm alive or if they want to make sure I'm dead. Or if they have come for another purpose entirely.'

Her flesh quivered under his fingers. He longed to pull her into his arms and whisper easy platitudes, but she had requested the truth.

'Haddr appears to be missing.'

She shaded her eyes with her hand. 'You're right. He isn't here. We need to carefully consider what to do next. Perhaps we should try to make for Moir Mimrson's hall and beg his assistance—unless you think that will take too long and my men will die.'

He firmed his mouth. His Cyn had not panicked or demanded. His admiration for her courage grew. 'Do you know the way?'

'I know the general direction.' She made an imprudent gesture with her hand, accidentally dislodging a rock, sending it flying down the slope.

One of the Danes glanced upwards and gestured with his bow.

'Keep down,' Kal muttered. 'Crawl backwards. Slowly. Without making a noise.'

She began to crawl, but her left foot became entangled in her skirt. A great tearing sound reverberated. She swore a loud oath—the sort ladies were not supposed to know.

Kal put his finger to his lips. 'Impressive,' he muttered. 'I've not heard that one for a long time.'

'My foot became stuck in my gown.' She rucked up the gown so her lower limbs were exposed.

He attempted to ignore the enticing curve of her calves. 'That is the trouble with wearing women's clothes.'

'Something like that.'

When she had gone far enough, Kal put up his hand

and she stopped. He rapidly joined her and helped her to her feet.

'We will go this way.' He started off down a faint track which instinct told him looped back to the hall.

'Where are you going? The cottage is that way.' Cynehild pointed in the opposite direction. 'My men remain in danger. Abandoning them is unthinkable. They'll start searching for us.'

'We're going to my hall.' He ran his hand through his hair, wincing as he caught the lump on his head. 'If I have it wrong, direct me. We need to go quickly, by a back route, and we must get there before those men return. If they search, they must not find us. Searching will delay them until I can plan a welcome they won't soon forget.'

Her mouth dropped open. 'You want to go to your hall, where you know your would-be assassin lurks?'

'It's the best way to save your men. I must take my rightful place there again and I'm going to require your help, Cyn. I'm sorry.'

'Sorry for what?'

He pushed a lock of her hair back from her face. 'For putting you in danger. But I'm left with no other choice. If it is any consolation, you are just the sort of person I want by my side in this venture.'

Cynehild's stomach knotted. She didn't know who was crazier—the man proposing the scheme or her for going along with it. 'Flattery is unnecessary. You are right. The only sensible way is to go to your hall as soon as possible.'

'Excellent. A woman with common sense. You trusted me back there—trust me again to get your men back alive.'

Cynehild examined the clouds skittering across the

sky. Trust him? Her heart whispered that she should…
with everything. She hardened her mind. Not with her
son's future. She was the only person who could secure
that.

'Should we wait for Brother Palni, perhaps? He can't
be too far away now. We need men with strong sword
arms—nothing has changed that. The prudent choice
might be to wait.'

'If we continue to wait and do nothing those men die.'

Cynehild pinched the sides of her nose and tried to
quell a sudden feeling of being sick. She'd proudly proclaimed that she wanted to be a part of this, and now she
wanted to run and hide.

She stiffened her spine. Going back to being a protected woman would mean giving up what she liked
about herself now. The woman she'd been when Leofwine had first gone off to war no longer existed and she
didn't miss her.

'What are you going to do once we get to the hall?'
she asked around the lump in her throat.

'Reveal myself. It is impossible to try people for the
murder of someone who is alive.' He dropped a kiss on
her forehead. 'Your bravery does you credit.'

'I'm not brave. I'm petrified,' she admitted in a rush,
and waited for the kind of snort of laughter that her late
husband would have given.

Silence.

'Me too—but we're both going to do it anyway,' he
said.

The hall, with its great gables of newly hewn tim-
ber, rose in front of Kal as they rounded a bend. A lake

shimmered in the sunlight off to its right. Images flashed through his brain, making the pain in his head unbearable.

He put his hands on his thighs and attempted to control it. In that brief breath he seemed to be back in Ribe, walking towards Ranka, where she waited for him to rescue her from her father's so-called tyranny. Then that image became overlaid with the building of this hall. It was as if all his memories were coming at once, speeded up. His stomach roiled as a wave of dizziness passed over him.

Then Cynehild gave a small cry of shock, and he was jolted back into the present and his responsibilities towards this woman's safety.

He wished those memories of building this hall were stronger, but already they were slipping away from him. Had he enjoyed creating it? Or had it been a burden? Why had he chosen those particular carvings?

Questions for another time and place.

'Is everything all right?' Cynehild asked, putting her hand on his shoulder. 'Can we keep going? Or do you need to regain your strength? We've travelled here without pausing for a breath. Your body has been through too much.'

Kal concentrated on breathing steadily and the pain receded. 'Surprise is our best weapon. The men at the hut will soon return here with their captives. Alive— not dead.'

'I will take your word for it. You're the warrior...'

Cynehild nibbled her lip as if she feared saying more. Kal silently cursed her late husband. She might have loved him, but he knew in his heart that Leofwine hadn't treated her the way he should have. He had this one chance to show her that he could treat her as she deserved to be treated. He simply needed that unattainable luxury—time. He needed her brother-in-law not to arrive with his men too soon, but he also knew he needed that support if it came to a fight.

Rather than taking her in his arms and holding her close, he squeezed her hand. Her fingers tightened around his. He released her and put his head on one side, listening to the everyday noises.

The compound was far too quiet for his liking—almost as if it was hushed, waiting for something. He wasn't sure if it was always this way or had become like this in his absence, but it had a distinctly subdued air, and there was no one practising in the yard or repairing things—the little aspects of life which he would have expected to see at this time of day.

He set his jaw and summoned all his remaining energy. 'We keep going forward. There is no time to lose. I'll rest when my task is done.'

She put her hand under his elbow. 'Your task won't be started if you rush about like this.'

'Wasting time won't save your men.'

He took a step and the world tilted. He stumbled over a stone and nearly went sprawling face-first on the path.

'Sit.' Cyn pointed towards a flat rock. 'Sit until your colour is restored. The men who have captured mine are some distance away.'

'How can you tell?'

'If they'd returned there would be shouting and intense activity. People would already be hunting us. We're close enough to hear when those men arrive back and to take action if necessary.'

'Can I argue with common sense?'

'No.' She gave him a gentle push towards the rock. 'Sit.'

As he sank down his legs nearly gave out, but her hand was there to break his fall. He patted the stone next to him. Their shoulders touched as they looked towards the hall.

'What do you think of it?' he asked when the extreme dizziness had passed. 'I want to say that I built it on the ruins of the old hall which stood here, but my memory is faulty.'

Her cheeks paled in the sunshine. 'Ruins? You mean the old hall was not still standing?'

'Someone burnt it to the ground before I even arrived.'

Her teeth nibbled at her lower lip. 'And the church? Does that still stand?'

'Some of the roof has gone, but the altar remains with its stone cross.' He held his breath, waiting to see if she believed him. He wasn't entirely certain he believed himself, but he knew he didn't want to be responsible for destroying what had once been her home. 'I hope my memory has not played me false. But I'm sure I kept it to allow the villagers freedom to worship their god.'

She tapped a finger against her mouth. 'The church must have remained standing or you wouldn't have given me permission to come and visit it.'

'True enough. You will be able to keep your vow and lay the sword.'

He willed her to tell him why it was so important to her. It surely went beyond simply honouring her husband. But her gaze slid away from him.

'My vow is why I'm here.'

He shifted uneasily. How did he fight a ghost? How could he make her see that he wasn't her enemy? That he wanted the best for her in the future and that future included him?

He stood and held out his hand. 'Enough rest. We have a battle to face.'

'Hopefully it will be more of a homecoming,' she said.

'Do you really think so?'

'The very air exudes a prosperity which was lacking when Leofwine was in charge. He meant well, but there was always another war or battle to fight.'

She deftly twisted her hair so that it was once again hidden beneath her *couvre-chef.* When she'd finished, she'd become far more the Mercian lady than his Cyn.

'I know what it was like when we left. Beloved, but a little faded about the edges. You saw Luba's reaction— she likes having you as her overlord.'

'She disliked your husband?'

'She was his old nurse…' Cynehild sighed. 'She and her husband argued for us to stay and fight, but Leofwine thought we'd be better served by fleeing to my father. It would bring safety for his family, anyway.'

'Is there more? What else did your husband fail to do? Did he not manage to rescue any of your belongings?'

She pretended to take an interest in the ground, kicking a pebble so it skipped along the road.

'What is it, Cyn?'

'Are you going to go straight into the hall? Or stand and call from the yard that you have returned?'

Kal let her avoid his question and instead tested the weight of her husband's sword in his right hand. His mouth was parched, as it always was before battle. Right now, he wanted to believe he possessed enough strength to wield the sword effectively.

He made a practice swing and winced internally. His aim was worse than an unblooded warrior's.

Cynehild simply watched him try again, without saying anything or offering to help.

'Do you have a better plan?' he asked, lowering the sword. 'I suspect my enemy will be amongst the men at the cottage, determined to see the end of me. At the hall there will be some left who are loyal. I must believe that, Cyn. Someone must be loyal to me. Not everyone can want me dead.'

She kissed him on his cheek. 'I know people will be loyal to you.'

He glanced up at the clouds, unable to speak for a moment. He wished he could explain that he wanted her to stay with him, that he had never met anyone as honest as she was. But the words stuck in his throat.

'You can come in with me or stay behind in the safety of the shadows. Your choice,' he said.

'As long as you allow me to walk shoulder to shoulder with you, I will go in with you. We face this together. If you need my help, you must squeeze my hand.'

Shoulder to shoulder? Her courage threatened to unman him. Most women would have been desperate to hide. But this was far from Cynehild's fight and her safety was paramount.

He opened his mouth to refuse, but swallowed the words when he caught sight of her determined face. 'I would be honoured to walk like that with you.'

Her being glowed, as if he had given her some great present. He hated himself. A better man would have found some way to keep her from any chance of harm.

She looped her arm through his. 'We are taking a risk, but you have to trust the people who live on these lands.

If your attacker thought everyone loathed you, he would not have hesitated to strike you down in public. Yet he kept to the shadows when you were alone, hitting you from behind like a coward.'

Her wise words did much to bolster his confidence. He hadn't considered it in that way before. Maybe he wasn't the tyrant he feared he must be. Maybe his attacker was in the wrong.

'I trust you will be able to rally your men without me, but I am here if you need me. And thank you.'

'For what?'

'Believing I can contribute. People used to say I would only hinder on such occasions. Not so much since my sisters and I managed to defeat some Northmen, including my new brother-in-law…'

He struggled to keep a straight face, but his heart soared. Her husband had discounted her usefulness. It made him glad that he hadn't given in to his instinct and tried to protect her by keeping her away from the situation. He resolved that he wouldn't ever shut her out. He would show her that he was different from her husband.

He caught her hand and raised her palm to his lips. It trembled at his touch. *Slowly. Slowly.* If he was granted the time, he'd show her that things could be so very good between them. He released her hand. She instantly curled her fingers around her palm, as if she was trying to cling on to his touch.

'I've no idea why the Fates have allowed our paths to cross, but I'm grateful.'

She pointed towards the hall and her face became a study in determination. 'We go and reclaim your lands.'

'I promise your safety will not be compromised.'

'I'm counting on it.'

Chapter Ten

Kal dimly recognised the people in the yard, but their actual names and relationships to him slid away from his mind.

One elderly man dropped the bucket he carried and milk spilt out. A younger man missed his stroke with a pitchfork. But no one said anything. They simply watched in shocked silence.

Kal's gut ached. Maybe he'd been overly optimistic about the sort of welcome he'd receive. What had he done to these people? Had he truly been bent on serving his own needs and not thinking about others?

'Stay close,' he whispered, coming to an abrupt halt. He surveyed the ground in front of him. If he made his stand here, Cyn would still have the possibility of escaping to the shelter of the trees and then eventually finding a horse and making her way to her brother-in-law's. 'Whatever happens, trust me. Do what I say, when I say it. Without question.'

'Whatever happens, I will trust my own abilities. I don't have to lean on a man.'

'But it would be pleasant to lean on me. I would make it my business to ensure it.'

Her cheeks flamed bright red. 'I'm a widow with a child, not a maiden to have her head turned with such talk. Concentrate.'

'What does being a widow have to do with anything?' He put his hand about her waist. 'You do yourself a disservice, my lady, if you believe you are unattractive because you are a widow and a mother.'

'Hush. Someone approaches.'

A brawny Dane had started towards them, his hand on his sword's hilt and a distinct wariness in his step.

Kal frowned, trying to place him. Friend or foe? He recalled a shield wall buckling, a sword arching through the air and this man's hand in his as Kal pulled him to safety.

Kal clapped his hands together. 'A fine welcome this is. No one speaking. Everyone staring.'

The Dane stubbed his foot against a cobblestone and sent his sword flying through the air. It fell within a few feet of where Kal stood with Cynehild.

'Jaarl Icebeard, is it truly you? And you are alive?'

'Who else would it be?' Kal reached down and retrieved the sword, holding it out to the man. 'You should have a care. Keep a tight hold, lest you lose it again in a shield wall.'

'You are not a ghost? A figment of my imagination come to haunt me?' The man eyed the proffered sword warily.

Kal dropped it at his feet. 'Come here and see. I'm flesh and blood. And my shade would have better things to do than haunt you, Gautr.' Kal held out his arms, thankful that the man's name had just come to him. 'What is all this about?'

Gautr enfolded him in a hug while tears streamed down his face. 'You are a sight for a troubled mind, but beware—rumours of your death are everywhere. Your cousin went today to deal with the murderers, even though no body had been found. He knew where a nest of outlaws lurked.'

A nest of outlaws? Cyn's men... Kal silently thanked the Fates for their foresight in having most of the men leave.

'Understood, Gautr, son of Agathi. I know I can count on you in any fight.' Kal pounded the man on the back and then stepped away.

Gautr clapped his hands together like a young boy, instead of like the hardened warrior he undoubtedly was. 'It is you! Everyone—our Jaarl has returned. He is not dead on some hillside as Alff claimed! We need to greet him properly.'

A loud roar filled the yard, replacing the silence.

The news of who had proclaimed his death thudded into Kal. His cousin had claimed he was dead. His very being rejected the notion that Alff had had anything to do with it. He and Alff had always looked after each other.

'We will go into the hall. Me and my lady.' Kal put his hand firmly on Cyn's back and urged her forward. He leant down so his mouth touched her ear. 'Things are far worse than I feared. We need to stay together, no matter what happens.'

Her face became shuttered. 'Obviously.'

'My lady?' An elderly woman darted across the yard. She dropped into a deep curtsy in front of Cyn. 'Is it truly you? You are a fair sight for sore eyes. How does

the little one fare? We had heard you and the late lord
had a bonny son. Is the young man with you?'

Cynehild's smile lit up her face. 'Ursula, it is good to
see you. My son grows very well indeed, but he remains
with my father back in Mercia. He is far too young to
undertake such an arduous journey as this one.'

'You are here with the master, my lady?' the woman
asked, grabbing Cynehild's arm. 'Without any men?'

'He hasn't kidnapped me, if that is what you are asking.'

'We had understood you were travelling in a large
group, and well-armed. We feared it would go badly for
you if you arrived here while Jaarl Icebeard remained
missing.'

A cold shiver went through Kal. The person behind
the attack had placed these rumours well. Cynehild had
very nearly walked right into a trap.

'But Jaarl Icebeard is not missing. He has been with
me. We've been deciding if it would be wise to weave a
separate peace.'

'You were with Jaarl Icebeard all this time?' The
woman belatedly gave a curtsy in his direction. 'Truly?'

'We would hardly be here like this if it wasn't the
truth.'

Kal took Cyn's arm from Ursula's and strode towards
the door without a backward glance. When he reached
the top step, he turned to look back at the yard. In the
time it had taken them to walk to the door the nearly
empty yard had overflowed. Kal scanned the faces of
the people nudging each other, seeking the familiar. His
head started pounding. The last thing he wanted to be
doing was to be standing here.

Cynehild gestured towards the increasing throng with a tight smile.

'The Lady Cynehild and I are betrothed.' Kal ensured his voice rang out over the cobblestones. 'Having plighted my troth to this woman, I have returned to ensure the continued peace and prosperity of these lands.'

A ragged cheer went up in the yard. Kal smiled down at Cynehild's twinkling eyes. His people's simple pleasure at the news of his survival and betrothal showed him that he commanded their respect, and possibly their love. His attacker had struck from the shadows because he feared striking in the open.

The muscles in Kal's neck eased. He stood a little straighter. With Cyn's help he would survive the coming days and discover the truth. Because of Cyn he had hope. His only fear was that Brother Palni would return before he had convinced her to stay.

At his knock, the great door swung inwards, revealing a blonde woman dressed in a gold-embroidered gown with a crown of intricate braids topping her head. But a network of fine lines had started to appear around her mouth and eyes, and her small mouth was turned down in a petulant pout.

'What is this noise about? You were given work. You are being disrespectful to your Jaarl's—'

Her mouth dropped open and she went very white.

'Kal, is it you? I'd understood… That is, we had heard…'

She shielded her eyes with her hand and recognition rocked through Kal. Toka—Ranka's much older sister, the woman who had tried to sabotage their marriage, stood in front of him, seemingly in command of his hall.

How had he allowed that to happen? How could he have forgotten her base betrayal of him?

'Where have you been?' Her talons dug into his arm. 'Alff and I have been frantic. Alff was certain the Mercians had done away with you. There have been rumours about war bands of Mercians prowling about these lands, and you know what a lot of thieving cowards they are.'

Kal firmed his mouth and disengaged his arm from the vice-like grip. More rumours of Mercian outlaws? How many gangs of supposed outlaws were there? His stomach roiled. Had he believed this about the Mercians as well? If he had, he'd been wrong.

'Where is Alff? Fetch him.'

'Alff rose from his sickbed for you. He leads today's search for the culprits who abducted you. Why would he be hiding in the hall when his lord is missing?'

His cousin must have been the one to spread the rumour about the reason for his disappearance. Kal's guts churned even more. Alff and he had been so close as boys, and now Alff was his right-hand man…

'I've been with my intended bride, Lady Cynehild. We have come to an understanding. But it appears some misunderstanding has grown in my absence.'

He rapidly made the introductions, taking his time in naming Cyn's antecedents.

Toka's reaction was immediate. She put her hand over her mouth and her eyes bulged. 'The widow of the last Mercian lord and you? Betrothed? Haddr mentioned a woman, but I thought he'd been drinking too much!'

The final word rose to a crescendo of a shriek. He almost smiled. Luba, unlike her son-in-law, had kept her word.

'Do I need to consult you about my plans, Toka?'

'No, but it would have been appreciated.' Toka's knuckles shone white against her gown. 'We've been worried, Icebeard. I'd hoped you might show some small consideration for your family—but when have you ever done that?'

He noticed how she said his name, with a curl in her lip. 'Where did you think I had been?'

'You went off without a word. I considered you had gone for a walk after… Never mind. You had been keeping secrets, and you were always good at that. You have never paid the slightest heed to those who might be concerned about you.'

Kal narrowed his eyes. Toka made it sound as if he was arrogant, running roughshod over everyone—the worst sort of leader. But Toka and he had rarely seen eye to eye. He wished he could remember why Alff had decided to marry the woman. Perhaps he'd done it and then informed Kal. The thought of her had always obsessed Alff.

'You of all people should know better than to worry about me—particularly after I'd had words with my cousin.'

She made a little cat's paw with her hand. 'I told Alff that you would turn up, and that he was being unduly worried after your intemperate words. But then you didn't.'

What had they had words about? Kal concentrated, but hit the black abyss again. 'Alff knows I always turn up.'

'He would rise from his deathbed for you.' Toka's mouth pursed as though she'd tasted a sour plum. 'Not that you'd care or notice…such things as human frailty are beyond you.'

Kal winced. Had he really been like that? He knew he pushed himself, and made demands to get the results he desired, but surely he thought of others too. Surely his road to this hall had not been littered with the bodies of men who trusted him.

'This Alff—is he your husband?' Cynehild asked, fluttering her lashes and tucking her arm more tightly about his, as if she was ready to prop him up should the need arise. 'I want to get everything straight in my head. Kal and I have been discussing other matters. But it is important for the new lady of the hall to understand the tangle of relationships.'

Kal had to admit that Cyn did a good impersonation of being utterly brainless when she wanted to. The intensity of her gaze gave the game away to Kal, but he suspected Toka would only hear the breathlessness of her voice and dismiss her as feather-brained.

'Yes, Alff's my husband and Icebeard's closest advisor. His cousin. His last remaining blood kin.' Toka widened her eyes and put a hand to her head, as if it pained her to think about Kal's folly. 'Icebeard, I'm astonished you never confided in him your intention to meet with this…this person. Let alone contract a ruinous marriage which will sow discord throughout these lands. Perhaps the rumours about her being a witch are correct and she has enchanted you.'

'Show respect to my betrothed,' Kal growled.

Toka tossed her head, making her braids slither like glittering snakes. 'Sometimes, Icebeard, I wonder if you really have not learned lessons from your previous encounters with Mercian women.'

'I believe I'm not like other women—from my country or yours.'

Cyn laid her head against his chest and somehow it felt right to have it there. Kal put his arm about her waist.

Toka's mouth opened and shut several times in rapid succession with no sound emerging. 'We shall have to make sure you are well looked after, *my lady*. I run the household, as I'm married to my lord's cousin and therefore the senior ranking woman. Also, Icebeard's adored wife was my sister.'

Cynehild did not miss a beat. 'It is something we both share—the loss of beloved spouses.'

'He spoke to you about Ranka?'

'And the child he lost.'

Toka's smile became almost fanged. 'We must also speak about Ranka soon, Icebeard.'

She turned her back on Cynehild and began to discuss the hall and all the mundane things which had occurred in his absence.

Cynehild lifted her head from his chest and stood on her own two feet. 'Of course, once I become mistress here, in truth, I will require things to be done my way. That goes without saying.'

Kal kept his face impassive. Cyn's quick thinking had given him the clues he needed to work out what had happened. It was Alff's doing that Toka was here. Toka had always been clear about her intention to progress in life through marriage, and Alff had always sworn he'd have no woman but her.

'I wouldn't trust either of them,' Cynehild murmured out of the side of her mouth, while maintaining a pleasant smile on her face. 'She is less than pleased to see you.'

'Toka dislikes surprises unless they are of her own making.' Kal gave her hand a squeeze, to show he understood. Thankfully Cynehild allowed her hand to rest in his while Toka continued with her endless speech.

'I wish to get my lady settled. She shall be sharing my chambers,' Kal said, when Toka finally paused to take a breath.

There was a rapid blinking of her eyes. 'Does she have any belongings with her?'

'Alff will be bringing them all directly.'

Toka gave him a surprised look. 'Alff has seen the pair of you?'

'Not directly,' Cynehild said, putting her arm through his. 'We have been staying a little way from here. But if he has gone to investigate the so-called Mercian outlaws, he will have discovered my covered cart. I hope he will save me the trouble of having to send someone to fetch it. But one can never tell.'

Her voice sounded very light and innocent, but Kal caught the deadly expression in Cynehild's eyes.

Toka drew in a sharp breath. 'I see.'

'I hope you do.'

Cynehild placed a kiss against Kal's cheek. He knew it was only for show, but the touch gave him courage. He would use this time to convince her to stay with him. He simply had to stay alive long enough to ensure he discovered who had attempted to kill him and then show Cynehild that he was the sort of husband she needed— for herself and for her son.

'Being with Kal has been a revelation.'

Toka drew her brows together. 'If I had not seen you together and heard the words from your lips I would not have credited the tale. You always were one for games, Icebeard.'

'I must marry sometime, and Cyn fits my needs far better than I had hoped.'

He hoped that Cynehild would hear the truth in his words.

Kal's private chamber surprised Cynehild, with its well-appointed tapestries, its set of semi-precious stone *tafl* counters, carefully placed on a board made from in-laid wood, and—dominating everything—its massive bed piled high with furs. Intellectually, she knew he was supposed to be a successful warlord, and she had seen the amount of gold he'd been wearing when he was at-tacked, but she wasn't prepared for the unabashed luxury of his accommodation.

The opulence was in stark contrast to the self-effac-ing man she'd thought she knew, and a reminder that he had played his part in the invasion of her homeland. Whatever was between them was a pretence and a sham. Pretending it was otherwise was a delusion. There was no future for them as a couple. There could not be. She had to keep in mind who he truly was, and not who she wanted him to be.

Even so, her heart kept whispering that she was being too hard on him.

'Did you carve these animals?' she asked, running her hand along the intricate carvings on the headboard to take her mind off the gloomy prognosis of where their relationship was headed. She wanted it to have another ending, but she couldn't see how that was possible. 'It is a true labour of love to create something like this for such an intimate room. Few people will see it, I mean. I thought such things needed to be displayed for every-one to admire?'

He gave a little boy's pleased smile at her words. 'Do you like them?'

'You have a real talent…for something other than war.'

'*Had* a real talent.' Kal drew his brows together, which gave him a stern look. He seemed lost in his thoughts now that they had returned to the hall. 'My skill appears to have deserted me for the time being.'

Cynehild felt for the little carved horse and rider she'd placed in the pouch she wore. 'For a first effort it wasn't bad. You made a horse. And Wulfgar will love the warrior.'

'And if I wanted that warrior to be a bear?'

'A bear?' She turned it over in her hand. 'You adapted it to the requirements of the wood. It is a good thing in a warrior, Kal, to be able to adapt to the battle which is being fought.'

His smile warmed her down to her toes. 'You always know the right thing to say to make my heart easier.'

'You're hardly a failure,' she said. 'We need to concentrate on the things which must be done—such as working out who wants you dead.'

'I heard a voice, Cyn. Someone telling me that I was a tyrant and I must fall. That person wanted them to be the last words I ever heard.'

'Did the voice belong to your cousin?'

Slowly Kal shook his head. 'More guttural than that—and why strike me then? If my cousin wanted a serious quarrel with me then he possesses the right to challenge me for the leadership of this band of warriors. Any of my men can do it. I only lead because my men see that I'm capable of doing so. I suspect someone will challenge me today, when Alff returns. Be ready to grab a horse with your men if I should fall.'

Cynehild firmed her mouth. While she might instinctively distrust his sister-in-law, she had no proof that Toka was behind the attack. 'Hadn't we best discover if you left your sword here? It might give you a clue as to why you were up on Hangra Hill to begin with, if you did.'

He opened an iron bound trunk and drew out a sword which had gold inlaid on the handle. The sword gleamed silver in the torchlight.

He swore loud and long before tossing it back into the trunk. 'My second favourite sword, but my first is not here.'

'Then, as I've said before, whoever hit you will have the missing sword or know where it is.'

'I suspect you're right. I keep trying to place the voice…the one that called me a tyrant just before I was hit from behind.'

Cynehild frowned. 'Can you remember yet if it was male or female?'

'That still continues to elude me.' He paused. 'Could a woman have hit me hard enough to break my skull? Would a woman even be tall enough?'

'Toka is tall for a woman, and she has taken an instant dislike to me, that is clear.'

'My sister-in-law was always prickly. She was several years older than Ranka and liked to boss her about. Toka's poisonous words about my lack of ability to provide for my family dripped into our marriage and eventually Ranka became exactly like her.'

'It seems odd that she should be here if she feels so strongly against you.'

'I'd never refuse my cousin's wife a home.'

Cynehild stilled. She had to be so careful here. If she accused the wrong person everything could go wrong.

But she had no real idea why Alff was at the cottage, interrogating her men.

'Do you think Alff had something to do with the attack?'

Kal tapped his sword against his leg. His brow furrowed as if he was trying to think. Cynehild waited, despite the temptation to fill the silence with noise.

'We will know soon enough.' He looked away. 'Alff will bring your men here. He won't risk leaving them—particularly as they will demand to see me.'

'You're sure he won't kill them?'

'The Alff I remember from Ribe is overly cautious. He dislikes making a move unless he's certain that everything will go well for him. Your men will remain alive.'

She noticed he didn't say they would remain free from injury. Brother Palni's warning about becoming entangled in Deniscan affairs thundered in her mind. But it was far too late for regrets. She had to go forward and do her best to keep her men, herself and Kal alive, until Brother Palni returned with Moir's men.

'You remain in grave danger,' she said, instead of confessing her growing fears.

'Tell me something else.'

He picked up one of the *tafl* counters from the board and tossed it in the air. He caught it once, tried a second time and this time dropped it. He swore softly.

'You will get better every day, Kal.'

'I need to be better now. I need to be ready. Whoever did this to me remains out there, poised to strike again.' He shook his head. 'Alff will return very soon. What if he does challenge me? What if I fail to defeat him?'

Cynehild plucked the counter from the rushes and put it in his palm. 'Toss it again. Keep your eye on the counter. Practise. We will make use of the time before Alff arrives.'

He tried again, missed and cursed.

Without making a sound, Cynehild retrieved the piece and gently threw it to him. This time he caught it. They played the game of catch several more times. His reactions were slow, but improving.

'Thank you for agreeing to stay with me. You will be safest in this chamber rather than in private quarters of your own...until the bulk of your men arrive.'

'How else could I play a game of catch the counter with you? By far the best use for *tafl* pieces, if you want my opinion.'

He caught the counter and tossed it into the air, sending it spinning. 'You would be a natural if someone taught you the intricacies of the game rather than chiding you for making mistakes like your husband did.'

'How did you guess?' Cynehild wrinkled her nose.

All those irritations and slights from Leofwine kept coming back to her—the little things she'd sworn she would forget. She had loved him, but he had wanted a very specific sort of wife. Once she had found it easy to be that sort, but now she'd tasted independence and the freedom of making her own decisions. She had to wonder what Leofwine would have made of her...

'Playing with a woman can be stimulating. My late wife and I used to play.' He gave a crooked smile. 'She had honed her skills against her sister and was very hard to beat. But I found a way which was pleasurable for both of us, no matter who won.'

Cynehild carefully rearranged the counters. *A way which was pleasurable for both of us, no matter who won.* Making love, she had no doubt. She ran her tongue over her lips. Leofwine would never have suggested that sort of thing. It might have been fun with Kal… It might still be fun with Kal, whispered a small piece of her.

Was there any harm in indulging in a little fun? No one would ever know or guess. When Brother Palni returned she would go back to being the sensible widow instead of a woman who played *tafl* with…with her lover.

But she still had a task to complete. How could she have him as a lover if she intended on taking the hoard of gold?

'What sort of plan do you have for when Alff returns?' she asked, to direct the conversation away from potentially fraught topics.

'It will evolve in good time.' He held out Leofwine's sword. 'You keep this.'

Cynehild grabbed it. The solid weight reminded her of her duty to get that gold for her son's future. She rapidly put it down at the foot of the bed. 'You think I need to be armed?'

He let out a long breath. 'Is there something bothering you? Out with it, Cyn. Let me know the worst. Confide in me.'

Confide in him? About the true nature of her task? Ask him for advice on what to do about Wulfgar's training? She knew she should. She opened her mouth, but the words stuck in her throat.

'What is it that you want? Truly?' he whispered, before she could confess.

The words twined themselves about her insides. What she wanted was not to have to do her duty. What she wanted was to feel cherished and not to have this promise to Leofwine hanging over her head. Was that wrong of her?

The bed appeared to be growing larger with each breath she took. She stepped backwards. As if sensing her thoughts, he walked over to it and started rearranging the furs.

A lock of hair fell over his forehead. Her palm itched to smooth it. But she knew the action would be just an excuse so that she could 'accidentally' tumble into his arms.

'Your cousin will be returning soon. Hopefully my men haven't suffered too badly. I need to be thinking about that, rather than where I am to sleep.'

He straightened the pillows. 'This bed is yours, not mine, while you are here. It's up to you if you invite me in or not. But I will be here in this chamber with you. Then my cousin, or whoever is behind this villainy, will not be able to use you to get to me.'

'What?'

'I can't risk someone trying to strike at me through you. You are under my personal protection. I want to assure you that nothing will happen between us unless you desire it.'

She hugged her arms about her waist to stop herself from launching at him and hugging him tight. 'Once Brother Palni returns—'

'You will go. So you refuse to start anything with me which cannot be permanent. I know. My memory is hazy about the time just before my injury, but it remains perfect about afterwards.' He tilted his head. 'Have you considered that nothing is permanent? We never know what might happen. Sometimes we all need a warm body in the night.'

Cynehild gulped hard. *A warm body in the night.* Instantly forgettable. That was all she'd be to him if she gave in to the increasing curl of heat in her belly.

She began to pace the room. 'This is the first time I have been back here since we fled. So many memories of little things I'd forgotten... When Leofwine died I swore I wouldn't— But look at me, going on about my memories when yours remain missing.'

'I'd hope those memories bring you happiness, but you are far too restless for that.'

After her second circuit of the room, he put his hand on her shoulder and she immediately leaned against his reassuring bulk. A violent shivering overtook her and she knew her legs were about to give way. She turned into his chest. He stroked her head until the shivering stopped.

'If being here failed to affect you there would be something wrong. I understand. Remember, I lost my wife.'

She forced her gaze to remain at the point where his tunic gaped open. 'You are kind—not at all what I expected from a Danish warlord...particularly one with a reputation like yours.'

His brow instantly lowered. 'Let's hope nobody else has noticed the change in me. I like being kind, but until my enemy is vanquished I must appear to be the same man as I ever was.'

A reminder, if she needed it, that Kal's actions now might not be the way he'd used to behave. Brother Palni's warnings rang in her mind again. She was attracted to this Kal, but would she have been attracted to Icebeard?

'I'm sure no one will mention it. But I for one like how you are now.'

His mouth grazed her forehead. It would be easy to sink into the kiss, but also it would be wrong.

She leant back against his arms. 'Let's return to the hall now that you have your own sword,' she said in an overly bright voice—the one she always used when she

wanted Wulfgar to do something. 'You can pretend to
be giving me a tour, but you can use the time to familia-
rise yourself with the ground in case it comes to a fight.'

His arms released her abruptly. 'Your wisdom is something to be cherished. It shows why you will make a
formidable opponent when we do play *tafl*. You think
several moves ahead.'

'I didn't promise to play,' she said to the rushes. 'You
twist my words.'

He put a finger under her chin and raised it. 'You
didn't have to. And we will play like a man and a woman
play—for pleasure.'

Despite all her promises to the contrary, she could feel
herself drowning in his eyes. Her mouth ached.

She tentatively wet it. 'I…'

'Know that I want you, Cyn.' He brushed his lips
against hers, stepped away and watched her with hooded
eyes.

Cynehild kept her body still. She bowed her head and
fussed with rearranging the pleats of her gown, hating
it that a large piece of her heart wanted his easy words
to be true. 'I will bear that in mind, but concentrate.'

'My first encounter with Alff will be on my terms,'
he said.

On his terms. She knew what leadership challenges
could be like amongst the men of the North, and it was
not beyond reasoning that whoever had done this to Kal
had anticipated that there would be a fight if he reap-
peared, and wanted to keep him off balance.

'He won't wish to fight you straight away, will he?'

'If he wanted that he would have challenged me directly, instead of hitting me on the head and leaving me

to die.' His brows knitted. 'I want Alff to be innocent, Cyn. He was my best friend once.'

'We will find the culprit. I have faith.' Cynehild forced a smile.

'I am pleased somebody does.'

His easy words made her whole body seem lighter. The moment of desire between them had passed. She knew what to expect, and that was why she wouldn't be taking him up on his offer of a lesson in anything— most of all pleasure.

Chapter Eleven

The sound of horses' hooves rang out in the yard as they were halfway through their tour of the hall and its surrounding buildings. The conversation had been deliberately light in case anyone overheard them.

Throughout the tour Toka had been conspicuous by her absence, but Cynehild suspected that she was lurking somewhere—a bit like a spider. She knew she should not judge people on first impressions, but there had been something about the woman and the way she had done her hair which had made Cynehild instinctively distrust her. She wished she'd asked Luba about Toka when she'd had the chance, instead of getting the gossip on various people she'd known long ago.

'Are you ready?' she murmured to Kal, while pretending to be pointing out the barns.

Kal's lips were a thin white line and he didn't answer her. Silently she prayed that he would be able to withstand this ordeal until Brother Palni arrived. The monk had to be no more than a day or two away—three at most. She would keep Kal alive until then.

'Shoulder to shoulder,' she whispered.

He put a steadying hand on the small of her back. It took all her self-control not to lean into it. Her body drank in reassurance from his touch.

'I would not have it any other way.'

The horses came into view. Behind lurched her covered cart. Cynehild stifled a gasp. Her men were trussed up and slung across the backs of the lead horses. A burly man with a faint yellowish tinge to his skin walked beside them. When they entered the yard, he pushed at her men's bodies so that they lay in the dirt, kicking one to ensure he didn't rise.

Her men lived—but barely.

Cynehild clenched her fists, aware of her own powerlessness and how alone she actually was.

'Toka! Toka! Where have you hidden yourself, woman!'

'What are you doing, cousin?' Kal boomed out. 'Why call for your wife before you greet your liege lord?'

He took a step forward, putting his bulk between her and the man, and Cynehild knew she wasn't alone.

The man who must be his cousin stared at him, slack-jawed. All the colour drained from his face.

'Kal? You are here?'

'Are you going to answer me properly, cousin?' Kal boomed out again. 'What are you doing, abusing those men? What crime have they committed? Release them.'

'Cousin? Is it really you?'

'When last I looked this was my hall and you were my cousin and sworn liegeman—Alff, son of Alfuir.' Kal opened his arms and started forward. He appeared every inch the warrior lord. 'Have I altered that much in the short time I've been away?'

'Husband! Your cousin is here!'

Toka ran into the yard. Her crown of braids was now slightly lopsided, with one braid hanging down, and her gown bore smears of dirt, as if she'd been trying to take a shortcut through woods. Her chest heaved as if she'd been running.

Her smile shone with false brilliance. 'Isn't it wonderful?'

'You have returned, my liege...'

Alff's hard gaze flickered over Cynehild, making her feel like something which had been scraped from the bottom of a shoe.

'With a woman, no less.'

'With his wife-to-be, husband,' Toka said.

Kal drew on all his training and focused on breathing steadily rather than answering either Alff or Toka straight away. He had to wait for mistakes and errors rather than jump to conclusions. Who precisely was his enemy?

'Did you think I'd been left for dead somewhere?' he asked, when he was certain of his temper. 'Surely you knew it would take a lot to kill a man who stood his ground.'

Alff blinked rapidly. 'You know me, Icebeard...ever faithful to you.'

'That's good to hear. And it is good to see you up and looking so healthy after your recent illness.'

Again, that rapid wetting of Alff's lips which Kal distrusted. And both his skin and the whites of his eyes had a distinct yellowness to them which surprised him.

'I've been seriously ill. Ask my wife. I only rose from my sickbed because you went missing. Someone had to take charge. We have been frantic.' He inclined his head.

'But you have been merely dallying with a pretty woman. How like you, cousin, to forget others.'

Kal ignored the jibe and gestured towards the prisoners. 'I asked you to release those men. I'm unaccustomed to having to ask twice.'

'They are outlaws—they were up to no good and have refused to answer our questions. That cart is full of women's clothes.'

'They serve my betrothed. Release them now.' Kal snapped his fingers.

The men accompanying Alff did not move.

'I expect my orders to be obeyed or there will be consequences, Alff. Are you and your men prepared for those?'

A low murmuring arose from the crowd. Several of the men, including Gautr the Dane from earlier, started forward, but Kal held up his hand, stopping them. If Alff wanted a fight then it would be on his terms—not Alff's.

'Husband, please.' Toka held out her hands. 'Our cousin's safe return should be a matter for rejoicing, rather than arguing.' She gave Kal a significant look. 'But who can blame you for acting with good intent when things have been kept hidden from you, supposedly his closest advisor?'

Kal counted to five, tightened his muscles and readied himself for Alff's challenge. But Alff hunched his shoulders and turned his face away, conceding the point. His cousin had always been a bit of a coward.

One of Alff's minions undid the ropes. Kal made careful note of the man and his scarred hands, as well as the others who had ridden out with his cousin. He would find reasons why they would be leaving his service in short order. Not immediately, because that might cause further rebellion, but before the next Jul and the swearing of oaths.

Cyn rushed over to her men and tried to raise them up, but failed. Her pinched face revealed that her men had been treated far worse than they'd feared.

Kal gestured towards his men. 'Take them to the infirmary. We will demonstrate to you what true Danish hospitality is like, my lady. Your men will be made whole again.'

Cynehild dusted the dirt from her hands and curtsied, dropping suitably low. 'Thank you, Jaarl Icebeard.'

Kal winced, despising the way the name fell from her lips.

'What game are you playing, Icebeard?' Alff had stalked over. His cold gaze flickered over Cynehild, taking in her generous curves. 'When did you *ever* want to marry a Saxon—particularly an overly plump one? Have you bumped your head and lost all reason? Forgive me, my lady, but my cousin…'

'This is Lady Cynehild of Baelle Heale. Her late husband used to be lord of these lands.' Kal inclined his head. 'I trust you understand my reasoning? You must remember my stated intention is to hold these lands until my final breath.'

Alff gulped—hard. 'I knew you had allowed the lady to travel here. I counselled against it, but you overruled me. I see now that you have made further plans without consulting me. Weaving peace is a good strategy…if you can stomach the woman.'

A wave of dizziness passed over Kal. Instantly Cyn noticed and started forward, but Kal shook his head and gestured that she should remain with her men.

'You didn't think I would allow such an opportunity

to pass me by, did you? Are you sore because you have lost your wager about who I would marry? I did warn you not to bet on my bride as you'd never guess who she was.'

Alff's pale cheeks became infused with rose. 'That much is true. You did warn me.'

'We suit far more than I'd considered possible.'

He hoped that Cyn understood his words. He knew he couldn't give her his entire heart—not yet. That had turned to stone a long time ago and was only just beginning to thaw. But he could give her his warm regard and his friendship, and his fidelity in the bedroom. Their marriage did make sense—not just as a feint, but in truth. He simply had to convince her why it was right for both of them.

'But why make us think something dreadful had happened to you?' Toka asked, linking her arm with Alff's and whispering something Kal didn't catch in his ear.

'My message must have been lost.' Kal shrugged. 'Now I've returned, prepared to wed a suitable lady, as my people asked me only a few weeks ago.'

The crowd roared its approval and he relaxed a little. The men for the most part were with him and not Alff.

'I heard a tale that the Mercians had enchanted you. I presumed it meant they had somehow overcome you.' Alff rubbed the back of his neck. 'Trust Haddr to have made a mistake.'

'Where is Haddr? He is not with you?'

'He decided to stay at home today, but he blurted out the tale yesterday evening, when he was somewhat the worse for wear after losing heavily at dice,' Toka said. 'I don't think he is happy in his marriage. I can't think why you championed it, Icebeard, after I warned you that it would not be good for anyone.'

Kal noticed the slight pursing of Cyn's lips. The description of Haddr's drunken tale had been almost too pat, and Luba had already proclaimed how contented her daughter was.

Haddr had difficulty remembering where to stand in a shield wall, or which way to wheel when the enemy pressed them on the flank. His failure had been part of the reason Kal had planted his own feet at Basceng and stopped the shield wall from crumbling. About all Haddr was good for was the sheer, mind-numbing hard work of rowing. And yet there had been a reason why he'd agreed to this marriage. He knew in his heart that he'd wanted peace, and Luba's family commanded the respect of the village.

'I was worried about you, Icebeard… Toka was worried. This behaviour is unlike you—keeping yourself absent from your men, sending no proper message. Have our recent quarrels destroyed your trust in me?'

The faint pounding of Kal's head became a steady throb. Quarrels over what?

'Tales grow in the telling, Alff, that is all. Thankfully I decided to show Cynehild my hall today. No great harm has been done other than a few cuts and bruises which will heal.'

Alff blinked. 'Harm?'

'I would hate to think that anyone would do something untoward towards those men. My lady's men are my men now. You moved to strike against them without fully investigating their presence here. Compensation must be paid to them, Alff. Your Jaarl has spoken.'

Alff's mouth opened and shut several times. 'I thought you were in danger. Why must you try to pick fault with me? Why must you always prove Toka right?'

'Indeed...' Kal drew his sword. 'What is it that you sought, Alff—leadership of my *felag*? I'm not minded to give it up just yet.'

Alff watched the sword uncertainly and stumbled backwards. 'Now, see here, Icebeard—'

'Spare my husband! He rose from his sickbed to save you.' Toka fell to her knees and raised her arms in supplication. 'How were we to know you wanted a betrothal with a woman like that? Look at her.' She gestured towards Cyn. 'Even now I'm not sure I truly believe you. You are playing some sort of game, and I won't have my husband sacrificed for your paranoid thoughts.'

Cynehild's generous mouth became pinched. It was true that her travelling gown did nothing for her colouring, but her curves remained magnificent and the fire in her eyes shone.

'I am looking at her and I am very happy with what I see.'

'But she is not your type. She looks nothing like my sister.'

'You've no idea about my type, Toka.'

Toka took several steps backwards. 'You declared that your heart was buried with my sister when I suggested you start looking for a bride less than a month ago—and now this. You kept us in the dark, and now you seek to blame Alff for assuming the worst! Where is your fabled justice in that?'

Kal flexed his hands. Toka had caused problems in his marriage to Ranka. Would he have accepted her now that she was married to his cousin? Kal firmed his mouth. No, he'd have barely tolerated her at best, he decided.

'Do I confide my secrets to you, Toka? Have I ever done so?'

She raised her hands. 'Then don't blame Alff. Blame me. I felt that there was something odd in Haddr's tale and sent him out there. Rumours about outlaws have been swirling since we arrived in this place.'

'Look into your heart, Kal,' Alff added, moving behind his wife. 'You know I could never go against you. I've no idea what this woman has been saying about me or the Danes. But I have always been your most loyal supporter. Toka has as well, since our marriage. Why would you doubt this?'

'I'm concerned that your men did not follow my orders when I asked them to release their captives.'

'A momentary hesitation, that is all. The shock of seeing you so well when we feared you dead. After all we have been through…'

Kal growled in the back of his throat.

Alff lost more colour in his face. 'I do apologise, cousin. It won't happen again.'

'We must feast instead of quarrelling.' Toka clapped her hands and various servants brought out horns of ale. 'All here wish to welcome your return, Icebeard, particularly with such an…intriguing companion.'

Alff staggered to one side. 'I'm not sure if a feast is a good idea, wife.'

'Nonsense. You always enjoy feasts.'

Kal put an arm about Cynehild's waist and she immediately moved closer, so that his body could be supported. This skirmish might be over, but he had no proof that Alff had been behind the attack. Until he had proof, he refused to act against his blood kin.

'Let us feast and raise a glass to friendships and my betrothed. But first I need to ensure my lady greets her new people properly.'

* * *

Having old retainers come up to her with tears in their eyes, thanking her for returning and taming Icebeard, was especially hard for Cynehild. Several of them asked after Wulfgar, remembering him from when he was a tiny baby and telling her how much they'd missed him. But no one asked how Leofwine had died.

She hated to think about disappointing them again when she left. In her heart she knew that Kal would stay on these lands and fight to the last drop of his blood. *He* would not have fled.

She stayed until the last person had kissed her hands, and then went with Kal back to the bedchamber.

'You were patient with the villagers,' he said.

'They seemed pleased to see me, but they want you as their *jaarl*.'

Kal practised a swing with the sword. 'Your popularity outshone your husband's.'

'If you'd known that, would you have truly sought my hand?'

He put the sword down. 'It's something I should have considered.'

'No matter; I would have rejected the offer. Peace-weaving is hard, and I've my son's future to consider.'

His eyes deepened to dark pools, making her want to drown in them.

'So there's no room left in your life for yourself?' he asked.

She hugged her arms about her waist and spoke to the floor. 'I was certain of that before I left Baelle Heale.'

He went over to where the *tafl* board was set up and began to move the pieces as if he were searching for a pattern. 'Has something happened since to change your mind?'

Cynehild stiffened her spine. This wasn't real. The sooner she returned to her old life the better. Except she liked looking into his eyes and feeling as if someone saw her as a woman again.

'Nothing. Our current agreement suits me.'

He crossed the room in two strides and stood a breath away from her, lifting a hand to her face. 'We could discuss altering it to suit both our advantage and our pleasure.'

He had said nothing about love or respect.

Cynehild swallowed hard, tried to ignore the warm fluttering in her belly and fought against the urge to turn her face into his palm. 'We need to expose your enemy. Brother Palni has not returned with reinforcements. You could still lose everything. *I* could lose everything.'

His hand returned to his side. 'Always so serious, Cyn.'

'My men need me. They've been injured.'

He nodded. 'I've requested that they have the best care.'

'I will feel better once I've seen them. Alone.'

Despite the elderly servant's protestations that Toka ran the infirmary and none could enter without her permission, Cynehild stared the woman down and was allowed to go in.

'I came as soon as I was able.'

Cynehild went and knelt by the pallets. Her men appeared shaken, and somewhat cut and bruised, but otherwise fine.

'I've brought some herbs from the cart which should assist.'

Using the mortar and pestle in the infirmary, she rapidly made up a poultice for each of them, under the watchful gaze of the elderly servant, and placed the mixture on the worst of their injuries.

'You should be up in time for Brother Palni's arrival.'

'Brother Palni will have our hides when he arrives,' one of the men said.

'Why?'

'We were supposed to prevent you from going to this here hall on pain of death,' the other one called out. 'We gave our sacred oaths. Brother Palni doesn't want you here without him. He said... Well, he said that seeing how you were a widow, your head could be easily turned. You might be tempted to do something foolish. He said he saw how you looked at the Jaarl.'

'My head could be turned?'

Cynehild did not bother to hide her incredulity. Brother Palni considered her to be lacking in basic common sense. If she had not come to this hall with Kal, these men would likely be dead now. Brother Palni was wrong about her. Being a widow did not mean that she was dead inside. She lived and, what was more, she was fully capable of making her own decisions.

Her next task was to enter the church and check that all remained intact. From the outside, the church appeared neglected. She expected all the gold and silver which had adorned the altar to be long gone, but no one knew that Leofwine had buried the rest of his hoard there. It should have remained undisturbed. Wulfgar's inheritance...

A wave of guilt swept over her. She missed her son

with every fibre of her being, but once she recovered the treasure she'd lose Kal. She knew that deep in her heart. How could he care for her when she'd only come to rob him? Would he understand her motives for doing so?

Yet telling him of her quest would cause more uncertainty. She needed him to keep her safe until Palni arrived and, more importantly, she wanted Kal to remain looking at her as if she was an angel for as long as possible.

But she was an angel with a dark secret.

She pressed her hands against her eyes.

'You should leave immediately,' one of the men urged. 'Take a horse and return to Baelle Heale and your son. Brother Palni will understand.'

If the monk had had his way, she'd still be doubting her ability to do anything beyond spinning, she thought bitterly.

'We will wait for Brother Palni to return before we leave. I've made a promise to Kal—we will help him regain his hall and discover who has tried to blacken my name,' Cynehild said firmly.

Both men looked suitably ashamed, mumbling their apologies.

'Good. Get better. I may have need of you yet.'

'Where are you going, my lady?'

'I have a betrothal feast to prepare for. Thankfully, Alff thoughtfully brought my cart. My crimson gown will be the most suitable, I wager.'

Cynehild smiled. Toka was about to see that Mercian ladies could be elegant and well turned out. Dismiss her with pointed looks as somehow inadequate and unworthy? That was not going to happen. She would be dressed in her finest gown. And she wasn't going to think about how Kal's eyes might gleam in appreciation. That dress always made her hair appear more golden and her lips ruby-red...

'My lady, are you sure that is wise? What would your father say?'

'That Mercia must triumph.'

'Cousin.'

Kal finished drying his hair after his dip in the lake. If he was going to his betrothal feast, there was no way he would go as he currently was.

'Cousin.'

'I've come to apologise,' Alff said.

'Apologise?'

Kal raised an eyebrow. He'd half expected Alff to seek him out. It was why he'd openly bathed in the lake, rather than using the sweat hut.

'I should have known you had something up your sleeve when you decided to permit that woman onto your lands.'

Alff's words practically tripped over themselves in their rush to be said. Kal wondered if Alff had decided to approach him or if Toka had encouraged him. Over Alff's shoulder Kal scanned the yard. Toka was nowhere to be seen, but Alff glanced back twice, as if he expected to see her.

'I never considered you might want to marry a Mercian,' he said, dropping his voice to a hoarse whisper. 'Never. Not after what you said about her and her kind.'

Kal schooled his features. 'Do I always need to confide in you?' He strongly suspected that he'd been less than kind about Cynehild in the days leading up to his accident. He regretted that now. His only consolation was that he hadn't known her or experienced her generosity of spirit.

Alff shuffled his feet. 'Not in the slightest. I wish you'd given me some warning, though. Everyone thought you'd met your end, Kal. Toka kept muttering about witches and enchantments and making my head ache. When I dared to complain, she told me the witch must have enchanted me as well, because her remedies refused to work. How was I to know you wanted to bed the Mercian widow? I hope she is worth the trouble you've caused.'

Kal clung on to his temper by the slenderest of threads. Bed Cyn? He wanted to grow old with her.

The thought rocked him. That sounded like more than friendship and regard to him.

'It surprises me that you call me Kal instead of Icebeard.'

'Icebeard is for the others, to instil respect, but we are blood.'

Alff gave one of his charming smiles, which reminded Kal of how it had been when they were young. Back then, most people had considered Alff to be the one to become a *jaarl*. Now he looked tired, with his sunken eyes and sallow skin.

'You know that, don't you?' he asked.

Kal looped the linen cloth about his neck. 'You seem at pains to ensure I do.'

'I've been unwell.' Alff patted his stomach. 'Every time I eat my stomach pains me more than I've let Toka know. Today is the first day I've been up since you departed that morning, in high dudgeon over my refusal to go hunting with you and try out that new crossbow of yours. Perhaps you would have confided in me then.'

Alff had refused to go hunting with him and had remained in bed ill. And he'd gone to the hill with a crossbow, not a sword. Kal picked up a stone and skimmed it across the lake. The crossbow had obviously been taken. But who had it now? And where was his best sword?

'Do you intend on being at the feast?'

'I wouldn't miss it.' Alff scrunched up his nose. 'I don't suppose she's had many other offers.'

'Why do you say that?'

'She is hardly a slender maiden, and her tongue is supposed to be overly sharp. You remarked on that when you gave her your permission to travel here. You wanted to know why she was coming, and if there was any truth in the rumours about her husband's buried treasure.'

Kal concentrated on the still waters of the lake. Treasure? Cynehild had made no mention of it. Was that what she'd been hiding from him? It was entirely possible that her husband had given her instructions on how to recover it before he'd died.

After what they'd shared, Kal would have liked to think that she would confide in him, but it was looking increasingly unlikely that she had.

Why had he given her permission to come? Had he hungered for more treasure? What did Cynehild intend to do with it if she found it?

His head ached from the dilemma. He needed to know her secrets.

'There are reasons why we needed time alone before we made an announcement, Alff. My reputation is far from the most congenial, and it has gone before me. She had every reason to consider me a tyrant.'

At the word, Alff's hand trembled as he tugged at the neck of his tunic. Sweat appeared on his forehead. 'Just know that I am here for you. That is all I ask. I would never challenge you for the leadership. You know that.'

'I will. I do. Blood, cousin…blood is thicker than water.' Kal spied Cynehild's skirt. She was going back into the hall. 'I appreciate your concern.'

'Are you ready to go? Or do you need more time.'

Kal appeared in the doorway to the chamber just as Cynehild finished adjusting the belt of her dark red gown. His hair glistened as if he had sprinkled it with diamonds, and he'd changed into a linen shirt adorned with gold embroidery. A short fur-trimmed cape was thrown about his shoulders. In the short time they'd been apart, he had become Icebeard.

'I'm as ready as I'll ever be.'

She tried to smooth the wrinkles out of her gown. She'd lost some weight on her journey, and the gown flowed better on her hips, but it seemed her breasts were larger than ever. She strongly suspected that she would look like a giant dun cow compared to the slender Toka.

'I like a lady who decides not to waste others' time.'

'My men are recovering. Luckily there were some healing herbs in the cart, so I could make up the appropriate poultices.'

'They'll come to no further harm. My word still holds sway here.'

'You proved that earlier.' She gave an uneasy laugh. 'You are truly Jaarl of these lands.'

'That colour suits you,' Kal said, taking her arm.

He smelt of spring sunshine.

'It makes your hair look even more golden.'

'Do you think your enemy will attack tonight? Do we need a plan?' she asked, trying to keep her gaze away from the sculpted shape of his mouth. 'I like to have an inkling of what I'm supposed to do.'

'My enemy will be biding his time…'

Kal explained in a low voice about his cousin's attempted apology.

An uneasy prickle went down Cynehild's spine. Kal seemed to be waiting for something from her. His cousin couldn't know about the treasure, could he? No one did.

'You think it is him?'

'I don't yet know, but I'm pleased you will be at my side. You make a fine addition to this hall, even if for just a short while.'

'I'll endeavour to play my part well.'

He tightened his grip on her arm, pulling her closer to him. His mouth grazed the top of her head, making her more aware of him than ever.

'I'm counting on that.'

Chapter Twelve

The hall filled rapidly with men and women—his retainers. Kal struggled to recognise any of them beyond Toka and Alff and a few of the others. Haddr and the heavily pregnant woman Kal presumed was his wife were there, but Luba was nowhere to be seen.

Despite his earlier claim of feeling unwell, Alff had appeared, leaning on Toka's arm and keeping up banter with various men. He sat down a little way from Kal. Close enough, but too far away to engage in ready conversation.

Several of Kal's retainers came up and wrung his hand, declaring that he was a lucky man to have Lady Cynehild as his betrothed.

He agreed, particularly as her form-fitting deep red gown and the golden cross about her neck showed that she could play the imperious lady. However, he preferred her as he'd first seen her, with her hair unbound and her dress only hinting at her curves.

His fingers itched to unwrap her and explore her lush figure for himself. If she gave her body to him, he knew he could convince her that staying and giving this betrothal a real chance would be the right thing for both the Mercians and the Danes.

'There are rather more here than I thought there would be,' he said, lifting her hand to his lips. 'I appear to command far more men than I considered possible.'

'How many desire their lord's marriage to a woman like me?'

'It is something to consider. Everyone appears pleased with the notion.' He jerked his head towards where Alff sat, downing draught after draught of ale, leading the toasts with increasing gusto. 'Now my cousin has pondered the notion, he also appears taken with the idea. One would almost think he'd thought of it in the first place.'

'Not everyone is pleased.' She nodded towards where Toka hovered, directing various maids to fill up the tankards. 'Toka still seems put out.'

'She dislikes my happiness.'

Kal pinched the bridge of his nose, trying to get rid of the buzzing in his ears. He couldn't help feeling that he'd missed something obvious—something which connected his late wife's death with his present situation. The memory slipped away again, and he couldn't even be certain that it was a true one. Toka was efficient, but he knew there was a coldness to her...something missing deep within her.

He brought his fist down too heavily on the table, willing his missing memories to return. All conversation stopped and a sea of faces turned towards where he and Cyn sat. He gestured for the people to go on talking and the hum of conversation slowly resumed.

Cyn immediately put her hand on his arm. 'Are you too tired for this?'

Kal shook his head. 'The feast must be endured. My

enemy is here, even though he decided not to challenge me earlier. I can feel it. All we require is one little error from him.'

'There hasn't been one so far.'

'My enemy allowed you to find me. I take that as a point in my favour.'

When Kal's men started wrestling, and then wagering on the outcome, Cynehild declared they would return to their chamber. Ribald shouts rang in her ears, making her cheeks flame. She'd never cared for those aspects of a war band feast when she'd presided over them as a young bride. Leofwine had always excused them, saying it was his men's way of showing their appreciation.

'My lady is to be respected. Always.' Kal glared at the men and the comments ceased.

Her heart turned over. It would be easy to begin to believe that this betrothal could become real, that they could make a success of the marriage and that love could blossom. She missed a step. *Love?* Was that what she felt for Kal? She didn't even truly know him.

Once in the chamber, she stared up at the beams to avoid looking at the suggestive tapestries. Whoever Kal married would be a lucky woman, but it wouldn't be her. What they had was desire, and that was all too fleeting; true love took time to blossom and build. It was a lesson she'd learned a long time ago.

Her heart whispered that her sister Ansithe had known quite quickly about her feelings for Moir, but Ansithe had always been impetuous. Cynehild took great pleasure in making lists and having a settled routine. 'Cautious Cynehild', Ansithe had used to call her.

'I've heard worse language,' she remarked, after Kal

had closed the door to their chamber. Someone had lit
several reed lamps and dotted them about the room.
'When I was a bride it used to shock me, but I learned
to ignore it. My husband used to tell me that men must
be allowed their jokes.'

'Those remarks undermine my authority,' he said,
lighting several more lamps, so that the room was bathed
in a gentle glow, making the tapestries shimmer. 'It surprises me that your husband allowed them.'

She plastered a smile on her face. 'Leofwine wanted
to keep his men happy. And in time I learned to stop
being so overly sensitive.'

'We'll have to disagree on this point. Your husband
should have protected you. You were a living symbol of
his power and prestige, if nothing else.'

'He protected me in other ways.' Cynehild forced a
laugh. 'What does it matter now? I'm sure your men
won't try it again.'

'They'd better not.'

'Despite our earlier agreement, you should have the
bed,' she said, before he could start making up a pallet
and she lost her nerve.

He remained standing just inside the door. 'To take
the bed while you are on the floor is not the way I was
raised. There is room enough for both of us.'

'I know...' Her voice was far too breathless. 'And your
cousin or his wife might decide to accidentally check
on us.'

His eyes danced in the lamplight and a dimple flashed
in the corner of his mouth. Belatedly she realised she'd
given him the excuse he needed.

'I'll admit they might do something like that,' he said.

Impulsively she caught his hand and gave it a squeeze. His fingers tightened about hers. Somehow it felt right.

What happened tonight would have nothing to do with her real life. Soon enough Brother Palni would return, she'd place the sword in the church and return to her everyday life. Back to existing rather than being truly alive. Back to being Wulfgar's mother—and a grieving widow, she corrected her errant mind. But tonight she required something different—something just for her.

He brushed her hand with his lips and let go. 'Cyn...'

'I can easily sit up until you fall asleep, if it will make things easier,' she said before he rejected her. 'You will need your wits about you. We may have wrong-footed your opponent today, but tomorrow will give him a chance to regroup.'

'You need to rest.'

He smoothed a strand of her hair from her forehead. The simple touch sent a flurry of flames coursing through her.

'I require your clear-headed thinking until your brother-in-law arrives with his men. My own head has a constant dull throb. It is better than it was, but I remain injured.'

'You need me to think for both of us?' she asked, forcing her aching lips to form the words.

Life would be easier if he just swooped her into his arms and kissed her senseless. The choice would be taken from her then. She curled her fingers into a fist. A large part of her longed to be honest and admit that she needed to be in that bed with him. She wanted to feel alive again.

'My mind is working more slowly than I'm accustomed to,' he said, tucking his chin into his neck and stepping backwards. 'You covered my lapses brilliantly tonight, with your quips and little jokes. I owe you another debt. More than I can ever repay.'

He watched her with hooded eyes, waiting for something.

She sighed inwardly. The moment had passed. He hadn't given in to temptation. She should feel overjoyed that nothing was going to happen between them, but all she felt was a profound sense of loneliness. She'd wanted to be held.

'Some day you will repay them.'

'Do you want gold?'

He removed one of his arm rings and held it out to her. She dreaded to think how much it must be worth. It alone was probably worth more than all of Leofwine's hidden gold.

'Take it and it is yours.'

'Why would I want that? I'm not greedy.' She forced a smile and tried to change the subject to a more suitable topic. 'I'm simply grateful that my men have suffered no lasting harm.'

An uncertain expression flickered across his face. Cynehild winced. Had she inadvertently hurt him through refusing his gold?

'They appear well-settled,' he said, placing the arm ring on top of his trunk. 'No worse for what has happened to them. And I've ensured Alff will compensate them before they leave.'

'They'll appreciate it.'

She shifted her weight, knowing that this might be their last true chance to speak intimately. She should confess about Leofwine's gold and explain, but for just one night she wanted to feel like a woman.

'In the morning…'

He put a finger over her lips. 'The morning has to wait. We have tonight, and the night was made for... sleeping.'

'Sleeping?'

'What else is night-time for?' he teased.

'The lamps are nearly out...'

'Do you require darkness?' He put his hands on either side of her face and lowered his mouth to a breath away from hers. 'Tell me what you want me to do, Cyn, and I will do it. I want to make today's terror go away. I want you to feel safe with me.'

Cynehild's arms curled about his neck. His mouth was temptation personified. She knew she had to act now or regret it for ever. Later, when she'd discovered the gold and her men had returned, she'd confess, and explain why Wulfgar needed to know that his father had cared for him. If she chose the right words Kal would understand. But not now. Now she wanted to be in Kal's arms.

'Hold me. Make me forget what is out there, waiting for us.'

His arms came about her. He managed to engineer a tumble onto the bed, where the furs came up to meet them. 'That is a request I can fulfil.'

She smoothed the hair from his forehead and bent to capture his lips. His mouth instantly opened and their tongues tangled before retreating. His hands roamed down her body, tracing the outline of her curves before encircling her waist and pulling her body firmly against him.

His hard arousal pushed against the apex of her thighs, dispelling her last lingering doubt about his attraction to her. A wild exhilaration filled her—their feelings were mutual. She groaned in the back of her throat.

He rolled them over so that he was on top of her. He cupped her face between his hands. 'Why are you doing this?'

She traced the line of his jaw. His skin quivered under the pads of her fingers. 'All my life I have done what is right and proper. I've walked a very straight and narrow path. Tonight, I want to forget that exists. I don't know what will happen tomorrow. What I do know is that you make me feel alive. We're adults, and I like to think we both want this. We know it must end, yet neither of us will look back on this time with anything but joy.'

She was proud of her answer. Her declaration wasn't about spending the rest of her life with him, or even loving him. It was about what would happen for this time out of mind when they were together. And then it would be over. They would both get on with the rest of their lives. Their desire would become ash.

She didn't have to worry about any consequences as she still had the pouch of herbs Luba had provided her with to make a tea. Their affair had an end in sight; it was not a prelude to marriage.

Deep within her, she knew those thoughts were a lie. She wanted more, and a way for them to be together, but she needed him to say it first.

He watched her without saying anything for a long heartbeat. Then he raised her hand to his lips, turned her palm over and kissed it. 'I agree to your conditions. Joy it is.'

A tiny stab of disappointment swept through her. No protestation that their affair should be a prelude to a real marriage? But she was the one who had made the rules.

She curled her fingers around the kiss. 'Excellent.'

'Talking is overrated.'

His mouth went to hers and drank from it. The fire banked inside her exploded. She forgot everything except the sensation of his mouth moving against hers. She tugged at his tunic, slipping her hands under the cloth. He reared up to help her remove the garment. Her hands travelled slowly over his back, feeling each indentation. The power in his muscles contrasted with the gentleness in his touch.

His teeth nibbled at her earlobe. 'One of us is overdressed. Shall I help you remedy that? Your gown is far too pretty to ruin.'

She nodded.

His fingers worked at her belt and then tossed it to the ground. Then he removed her gown before his mouth traced a line down her neck. His hands cupped her full breasts and teased the nipples, rolling them between his thumb and forefinger until they became hardened points.

Her breath came in little gasps and she clawed at his shoulders. He eased her down and lazily lowered his mouth to the first nipple. His tongue drew circles on her under-gown, caused it to dampen, before he turned his attention to the other nipple.

As her body wriggled the wet material rasped against her nipples, submerging her in a primitive fire. Her body arched upwards, seeking relief from the heat, but encountered their remaining clothes.

She tugged at his trousers. 'Please...'

His eyes darkened and he returned to her mouth and feasted, tangling her tongue with his.

Slowly he inched her under-gown upwards, until his fingers were able to play in her nest of curls. Round and round his fingers roamed over her most sensitive skin, until she was slick with wanting him inside her.

She moaned in the back of her throat before the world exploded about her in a haze of stars.

As she became slowly aware of her surroundings again he reared up and removed his trousers, freeing his arousal.

He moved her palm to it. 'Feel it. See how I want you. Put me where you want me.'

She ran her fingers down the silky hardness of him and tightened her hand, moving it back and forth. He groaned and put one hand over hers, keeping it there while his other hand returned to the apex of her thighs.

The wanting grew inside her again, becoming more urgent with every breath, and she knew what she had to do.

She twisted so that he was positioned between her thighs, and then she wrapped her legs about him. He thrust forward and filled her completely and utterly.

They lay there entwined until she slowly began to move her hips, then faster and faster, until the world exploded around her again.

Kal slowly drifted back down to earth in the aftermath. He struggled to think when he had enjoyed himself as much. Already he could feel his body hardening again within her. Once could never be enough. He wanted to spend the rest of his life exploring the hidden peaks and valleys of her body.

'Now that you have seen how good it can be between us, Cyn, stay with me. Trust me with the secrets you are keeping. Trust me to look after you,' he urged.

She murmured slightly and he realised she had drifted off to sleep. He slowly eased himself out and gathered her close to him. Her hand splayed on his chest and he kissed the side of her temple and made all sorts of silent promises.

If only this was not the last time they joined. He knew he'd lied when he'd told her that he accepted her conditions. He wanted so much more than one night. He wanted her regard and her trust. He wanted her to explain why she'd left her beloved son and come on this journey, why her promise to her late husband still drove her. And until she did, he knew he could never hope to convince her to give them a chance.

Chapter Thirteen

Cynehild sat bolt upright. Her under-gown was tangled about her legs and places she'd considered long dead ached. It took her several heartbeats to orientate herself. Kal's breathing was even and his arm was flung about her, holding her against his nakedness.

She whispered a small prayer of thanks that it had been dark and he'd been spared the full horror of her body with its network of silver scars from her pregnancy and her overly generous curves. She was under no illusions. She knew that she had passed her best.

She lay still for a few heartbeats, drinking in his scent and revelling in the way she felt—as if she could accomplish anything. Except she had no real idea of how to proceed. Since she'd been young, she'd always had a plan, a mental list of what she wanted to accomplish. Today, she had nothing.

The room had become marginally lighter and she knew dawn must be near. She listened, but the sounds in the hall were muffled. She suspected there would be a late start to the day after last night's feast. Few people would be about. It would be her best chance to investigate the church and discover where Leofwine had hidden the gold.

She meant what she'd said last night—she didn't require Kal's gold. She wanted the gold her late husband had left for their son because of what it represented.

She rapidly removed Kal's hand. He mumbled something indistinct but remained asleep. In the faint light he appeared impossibly handsome, and she knew she'd lied to herself last night—one night with him was not going to be enough. Her desire for his touch remained as strong as ever.

It would be easy to believe that somehow they could make something of this—except she had other responsibilities. How could she ask him to look after her son, a boy whose presence might cause difficulties for him? People might whisper that she'd married him just so that her son could reclaim these lands. And would Kal even be willing to train Wulfgar, knowing whose son he was? She could not leave her son behind in Baelle Heale. Her child was the most important part of her.

She quickly dressed. Back in her travelling clothes, she felt like the woman she knew she was, rather than this mysterious being who had made love with Kal far into the night.

'I'm sorry,' she whispered, shutting the door with a click. 'Sometimes things can only be right temporarily, and this is one of them. I need to start thinking with my brain, instead of other parts of me. I need to remember what and who is important.' She closed her eyes, holding her breath. When her stomach had settled, she released it. 'I can do what is required of me. And I will do it. Now.'

Grey-rose streaks painted the sky when Cynehild entered the ruined church which stood a little way from the new hall. It was the only building in the entire complex which was made from stone rather than from wood. Several of the stones were carved with Latin phrases. The door had been pulled off its hinges.

Inside, a small altar had been set up at one end, but it was clear from the muddy puddles and bird droppings that the church was seldom used these days. A faint musty scent clung to it. However, someone had recently left a small bouquet of spring flowers beside the altar— a sign that not everyone had forgotten what this place had been used for.

Cynehild cleared the dead leaves from its top and placed the bouquet in the centre.

Once this building had been at the centre of life on the estate, where incense had burned and the murmurs of priests had been heard, particularly in the early morning. Now all was deathly silent.

She went and knelt in front of the altar, asking forgiveness. For what, she wasn't entirely sure—last night's pleasure or the fact that she was here under false pretences and about to rob a man who had been nothing but kind to her. She suspected it hardly mattered. All she knew was that she'd made her promise and she needed to hold true to it. But the thought didn't make her task any easier.

When her knees began to ache, she stood, dusted her hands off and began her search.

Leofwine had sworn that when she was in front of the altar, laying his sword, she would be able to tell from the way the statue of the Virgin Mary was placed where he'd secreted the hoard of gold. She'd presumed he meant under the flagstones, in front of the altar, but now, being in this place, she was no longer certain. And the statue had vanished, taking with it its vital clue.

Her heart sank. Did that mean the gold had gone as well and she'd endured all this for nothing? Had Leofwine's request truly been all about ensuring Wulfgar reclaimed these lands?

She went down on her hands and knees, feeling about on the flagstone floor, trying to discover a tiny carving to which the statue must have been pointing. If she could find that, she'd discover Leofwine's hiding place.

All the while she kept thinking that she'd come too far just to lose everything.

One of the flagstones slipped slightly. She feverishly dug with her fingers, trying to get a better grip on the stone. This had to be the one.

And then her hands stilled on the cold rock.

It was one thing to think about an unknown *jaarl* she was taking the gold from, and quite another thing to consider it was Kal—the man who had restored prosperity to this place.

She placed her hands flat on the stone. She was going about this the wrong way. She needed to confess her mission to Kal and ask him for his help. He owed her a life debt. More than that, she liked him and respected what he'd done here. She couldn't stand the thought of him looking at her with hatred or disgust—not after he'd encouraged her to believe in her own abilities.

In that breath, she hated Leofwine for giving her this task, Kal for being decent and not the power-hungry Deniscan *jaarl* she had considered him to be, and most of all herself, for thinking she could do this.

She couldn't. She had to tell Kal the truth and decide

the way forward with him. She had to hope he'd see why she'd done it and why she'd kept her quest a secret.

A calm serenity swept over her.

'I wondered when you would come here today. I had a bet with my husband about it. Before breakfast, I said. I do like being correct.'

Toka's precise nasal whine echoed in the deserted building.

Cynehild froze. Her hands carefully eased the stone back into place. 'Is there anything wrong with me coming here?'

'Not in the slightest. I just knew you would—and I reckon Icebeard knows it as well, even if he doesn't want to admit it.'

Cynehild took her hands away from the stone. Toka could have no idea why she was there...what she was looking for. No one knew. Leofwine had sworn that no one else knew.

When she trusted her breathing, Cynehild forced her legs to stand and turned to face the woman. She felt amazingly calm and serene.

'I was at prayer. Is it surprising that I should wish to pray in my old church? A pity it has seen so much trouble since I last worshipped here.'

A tiny smile played on Toka's thin lips. 'If you ask him, I'm sure Icebeard will remake this place for you. He seemed quite besotted with you last night. But I have seen such obsessions come and go.' She fluffed her hair. 'I've often asked myself—why doesn't he remarry? It would make life much simpler for everyone. But he never has. My sister was going to leave him after the baby came and make something of herself. We even had the right warrior lined up for her—someone who knew how the world worked and who had prospects. Except she died.'

'Kal has proved your prediction wrong. He has made something of his life.'

Toka's face contorted. 'Ranka despised him. After a short while she knew there was no good in him.'

Cynehild pressed her lips together. Her heart broke for Kal. She'd witnessed his grief and guilt over his wife and child. His late wife, if her spiteful sister was to be believed, hadn't deserved any of it.

'That was her sorrow, then. I've seen his decency and honour.' She made the smallest of curtsies.

'You simply mistake his intentions. He is playing a game with you because he requires something. I know him better than you do, and I've never seen his so-called honour.' Toka's mouth twisted. 'You're a naive fool if you believe otherwise. But I hear he is good in bed, so maybe that is all a lonely widow needs.'

Cynehild took several deep breaths and allowed the woman's words to flow over her. If she started shouting Toka would have won a small victory, and she wasn't minded to allow her to win even that.

'I'm not in the habit of discussing my sleeping arrangements with strangers.' She forced a smile. 'I'm sure you'll understand my reasoning. Do you go explaining to everyone who asks where *your* husband slept last night?'

Two bright spots appeared on Toka's pale cheeks and she suddenly developed a great interest in the various objects which hung from her belt. 'Very wise.'

Cynehild forced her back to stay straight. She gestured towards the faded bouquet. 'Part of the reason Icebeard seeks to marry me is to unite our two communities. Refurbishing this church will demonstrate that he respects mine.'

'That doesn't sound like him—discussing anything with a woman.'

Cynehild edged away from the stone. 'You'd be surprised. He is very easy to talk to. It is why I shall always treasure the time we spent alone before we arrived here.'

'He can be single-minded when he desires something. My sister discovered that to her cost.'

'If you think so little of him, why do you remain in this place? Surely your husband has lands of his own.' She waited with bated breath to see if the woman took the bait.

The woman gave a half shrug and toyed with her belt. 'They say that the former lord—your late husband—hid a veritable fortune before he left. In this very church. Did you know that? Or did he keep that piece of information to himself? What do you truly want here, Lady Cynehild?'

Cynehild concentrated on the fading flowers. A rumour. She should have considered that. And any number of people could have spied Leofwine when he'd buried the gold in this church, despite him swearing otherwise.

'You mustn't believe everything you hear. I know I don't.' Cynehild gave a decided nod. 'Particularly rumours whose source is so vague. *"They"* are always saying things which are false.'

'Icebeard and my husband have spent time searching for it but never found anything. I swear Icebeard must have lifted every stone in this building looking for it— but then he lusts after gold. It is why he wears so much of it. He has it now, but he didn't have any when my poor sister required it.'

Sweat started to pool at the base of Cynehild's neck. She knew Toka wanted to frighten her and she had to resist the urge to flee. Toka considered her to be a frivolous woman with barely any thoughts in her head. Why was it that some women thought so little of other women?

'Kal hasn't asked me about any gold which my late husband might have hidden.' Cynehild forced a quick smile. 'We've been busy with other things. You can understand how it is...particularly when you meet your soul friend.'

Soul friend—that was a good way to describe Kal and the way she felt about him. She didn't love Leofwine any less. It was more as if her heart had grown and could accommodate Kal as well.

'What will you tell him when he asks? He is bound to,' said Toka.

'That I came here to lay my husband's sword at the feet of his ancestors and fulfil my promise to him in that way.' Cynehild gestured with her hand. 'I suspect my husband had a romantic notion that somehow the people would see the affection he held them in and would then offer some affection to my son. I am afraid I'm far more hard-headed than that—I am here to carry out my husband's request, but my son remains elsewhere, safe.'

'And your marriage? Will your son come here after the marriage, seeking to reclaim his inheritance, displacing more deserving warriors?'

Cynehild gulped hard. The woman was truly like a spider, spinning various webs to trap her. 'My son is my concern, not yours. Why are you so intent on causing trouble? Are you frightened of me?'

'Trouble? Frightened of a woman like you?' The woman blinked several times. 'I came to let you know that my former brother-in-law may seem charming, but there is a dark side to him. How do you think he gained his *jaarldom*?'

A distinct chill went down Cynehild's spine. Toka might speak of Kal being ruthless, but the woman had ice in her veins, and she clearly disliked even using Kal's name. She would be willing to wager that Toka had something to do with Kal's injuries, even though she suspected the woman preferred to keep her own hands clean.

'Through being an excellent war leader—the same way my brother-in-law gained his.'

The woman's gaze turned scornful. 'You are such an innocent.'

'Cynehild—here I discover you. I've been searching for you.' Kal strode into the ruined building.

How much had he overheard? Cynehild's stomach twisted into tight knots. She knew she needed to confess, but not with Toka listening. What she had to say was for Kal's ears only.

'Kal, I came to the church for my morning prayers. I'd hoped to be back before you woke, but I was detained.' She nodded towards Toka. 'Toka seeks to instruct me in how best to please you.'

Kal's eyes flickered between the two women. His expression hardened. 'I shall be taking Cyn back to my chambers now, Toka. Your storytelling must wait for another day. I believe I am perfectly capable of instructing my future wife in what gives me pleasure.'

'I look forward to continuing our discussions, Cynehild. Particularly as I can see that you are someone who values the truth.' Toka curtsied and left.

Cynehild swallowed hard. Kal's eyes were frosted

with ice. She struggled to see the gentle man who had held her. 'My husband—'

'Your husband hid his gold in this place, rather than take it with him,' he said.

'You knew that?'

'Any number of helpful villagers seeking to curry favour told me when I first arrived. I have searched it but found nothing.' His face was set in hard and unforgiving planes. 'If there ever was a hoard, it vanished before I ever arrived.'

'Your memory returns?'

'Yes, although patches remain missing. I am many things, Cyn, but I'm not stupid. Know that I always intended on giving you safe passage to lay the sword. Maybe I was cruel enough to wonder how you'd react when you discovered the missing hoard. Maybe I wondered about your son and if you intended the laying of the sword to be the first move in an uprising which would deprive me of my lands. Maybe I planned some sort of retribution.'

Cynehild's throat worked up and down. She'd been wrong to dismiss Brother Palni's fears. 'What are you going to do to me? I only wanted to show my son that his father truly cared for him. I wanted to show him that following a promise, even when it is hard, is the right thing to do.'

He watched her without making a move towards her. 'I assumed you were like the other Mercian ladies I'd encountered. I was very wrong indeed. You are nothing like them.' He held out his arm. 'Are your prayers finished?'

'I was nearly done when Toka interrupted me.'

'Take your time. I will wait.'

Cynehild knelt for a little while longer, aware that

she was being watched and that her mind refused to give her any words which would make right what she'd done to him.

She rose unsteadily, aware that sweat had pooled at her back. Leofwine had made it seem so easy, but it was far more difficult than she'd considered. She would have walked straight into a trap. Kal would never have allowed her to take the gold, even if she had somehow managed to discover it.

Her stomach twisted. Did she truly know him? They had only spent a relatively short time together. Maybe some of the things Toka said about him had a ring of truth…

Cynehild instinctively rejected the idea. Toka was trying to stir up trouble, plain and simple. Once they'd discovered the identity of Kal's attacker then she was going home without a backward glance. She had to hope that she would escape with her life and without losing too much of her heart.

She had more to confess, but not here in what remained of this church.

She wiped her hands against her gown. 'I'm ready to return to your chambers now.'

Chapter Fourteen

Kal breathed more easily when they reached the confines of his chambers. When he'd woken to find Cyn gone he'd panicked, certain his enemy had captured her, and he'd not relaxed until he'd discovered her confronting Toka in the church.

Toka's prattling about the supposed treasure Cynehild's husband had hidden had made matters worse. Kal had a vivid memory of searching for it, but after digging the stones up he'd discovered an empty cavity under one of the flagstones near the altar. If any treasure had been buried there, it was long gone, stolen away—possibly by whomever had burnt the hall down.

He knew that without Cynehild he would be dead now. He owed her a great deal more than any non-existent hoard of gold. It failed to matter why she'd travelled here, but it did matter why she was here now. She'd saved his life. She'd demonstrated her value was worth far more than any amount of gold. He simply had to convince her of that.

The pain in his head eased.

'Why did you go to the church on your own?' he

asked carefully, silently willing her to tell him the truth about her intentions. He wanted her to show him that she trusted him to do the right thing.

She bowed her head. 'When I woke, I was unsettled. I wanted to go somewhere I used to find solace.'

Something deep within him where his heart had once resided cracked. Despite everything they'd shared, she still distrusted him.

He put his hands on her arms. 'The person who tried to kill me remains at large. They may yet try to attack you. Can you blame me for being worried?'

She gave a bleak-eyed smile. 'If Toka is to be believed, your enemy wouldn't bother with me because you never keep your women for long. One night is usually more than enough for you.'

He flinched. Toka's remarks held more than a ring of truth. He knew that after the disappointment of his marriage and the horror of his wife and child's deaths he'd shied away from commitment. But he'd always made sure that the women involved knew the limitations of any liaison with him.

Then Cyn had tumbled into his life and he knew he needed her to stay with him. This wasn't the all-consuming passion he'd borne for Ranka and her body before they'd married, but something very different and no less powerful. The power of it frightened him. He cared greatly about her and her future. He wanted to be a part of it. He wanted to be a father to her son—the sort he hoped he'd have been to his own son.

But he couldn't find the words to tell her this—not yet. It was far too new and unsettling.

Kal knew his unseen enemy had to remain in ignorance about the nature of his feelings for her or he'd use them to destroy him. His throat tightened and he forced his lungs to fill with air. One problem at a time.

'Maybe I have never met the right woman,' he said in a quiet voice.

She looked up at him with big eyes. 'I'm not the right one either, Kal.'

His heart squeezed tighter. He couldn't lose her now.

'Why did you take the risk after I warned you about staying close to me?' he asked. It was either kiss her or discover answers. Knowing what he fought against gave him a better chance of winning. 'Were you searching for the fabled treasure?'

'The treasure which Toka spoke of?' Her gaze slid away from his. 'Is that the treasure you mean?'

'Did your husband ask you to find it? Right now I'm very glad he's dead, because it is a monstrous thing to ask of anyone—let alone a lady like you.' He tightened his grip on her arms. 'How could you have hoped for success?'

She twisted away and he let her go. 'I gave my word to at least try. If there was any treasure, I'm sure it is long gone. You saw how the church has been ransacked.' Her voice quivered on the last word. 'My husband never expected that. I think he thought churches were sacred... incapable of being destroyed. I don't know what he thought, but it was naive. Maybe he didn't think at all, but he wanted me to know he'd provided for our son.'

'Did he really hide something in the church, then? Or was it just a rumour?'

'He said he did,' she whispered. 'I gave him a promise that I would search for it, Kal. For our son.'

'What were you going to use it for? To raise an army? Defeat me? Do you hate me that much?'

Her eyes became unbearably bleak. 'Hate you? Maybe I did before I encountered you. But now you are my friend.'

Friend. The tight spot in his chest eased. She considered him a friend. 'Why, then, Cyn?'

'To pay for my son to be properly trained, instead of haphazardly like my father would do it. To ensure Wulfgar knows his father cared about him and his future, that he hasn't been left without anything at all.' She hunched her shoulders. 'Maybe I should have told you earlier, when we became allies. At first I didn't because I thought the gold belonged to Wulfgar, not you, and that you never needed to know. But after what we shared in the charcoal burner's hut, and last night, I don't know any longer...and it is tearing me up inside.' She drew an unsteady breath. 'I was going to return to you and confess all, but then Toka arrived and—'

'Cynehild...' he said, wanting to draw her into his arms but knowing deep within him that she had to come into them because she wanted to.

'There—now you know the worst of me. As soon as my brother-in-law arrives I will leave with him. I will not seek to rob you. And I understand if you never want to see my lying face again.' Her eyes flashed fire. 'I'm not the good woman you thought I was, Kal.'

His admiration for her grew. She wasn't asking for forgiveness but for understanding. He knew if the tables had been turned he'd have struggled to exhibit half the courage she had. He wanted to shout at her—*Love me, just love me and I will make everything better. Stop loving that man who made you risk your life for a selfish dream.* But he knew he couldn't. Cynehild's love for her husband was one of the reasons why Kal cared for her.

'When something consumes you, sometimes you can't think straight. I can understand you wanting to provide for your son far more than your wanting to lay a sword in honour of your husband.'

'Can you?' She put a hand to her head. 'Leofwine's excuse was threadbare—I see that now. In his delirium he must have thought Wulfgar would manage, when full-grown, to hold these lands in a way he couldn't. And I was arrogant in thinking you wouldn't understand my quest.'

'If you hadn't travelled, would I still be breathing? Many have searched for that treasure before you, Cyne-hild,' he said quietly. 'Haddr, in drink, kept coming up with more and more outlandish theories about where it might be. He even claimed that if he was allowed to marry Luba's daughter he would discover it and give me half.'

'I know Luba's husband was my husband's steward, but Leofwine swore he'd told no one the location but me.'

'On Haddr's wedding day I told him to be quick about discovering the treasure as you were travelling here. But it was only a joke, Cyn.'

Her mouth opened and shut several times. 'That is not the point. I lied. You are supposed to hate me.'

'Your being on that hill is precisely the point. You came to save your son, and in doing so you saved my life, giving me something far more precious than all my gold.' He took off his torc and the remainder of his arm rings and laid them at her feet. 'Will that be enough for his training? Is that all you require from this place?'

'That wasn't what I meant and you know it.' She balled her fists. 'I'm trying to find a way to apologise for my behaviour. Stop twisting things. I don't want your gold. I never did. I only wanted Leofwine's because… because…'

'Because you wanted to show your son that sometimes you have to do hard things. Because you wanted to believe Leofwine cared for you and your son like you wanted him to.'

'Yes.'

He lifted her chin. So brave and fearless. In her heart, she had to have known that her mission was doomed to failure, but she'd come anyway, holding true to a rashly given promise.

It frightened him how much he had come to need her and her belief in his goodness. He had a choice, she'd told him, and he had to make it now. He could try to destroy her memories of her husband and make war on the dead or he could tend to the living.

'Leofwine cared for you. He loved you beyond reason.'

Her mouth trembled. 'How do you know? You never met him.'

'He came back to die in your arms.'

She stuffed her hand into her mouth. 'And I loved him for that. I will always love him for it. Thank you.'

Kal pushed away the hurt in his chest. She hadn't asked him to love her. She'd been open about loving her late husband. He regarded the *tafl* board thoughtfully. He had until her brother-in-law and that monk returned. Time still remained to make her care for him, and making her care meant getting her back into his bed.

Her mouth quirked upwards. 'Your memory is getting better.'

'It is. I can now remember how I came here, what I did

here—I even remember teasing Haddr. But I still have no idea who hit me or why.'

'We will discover your enemy before I leave. I give you my word.'

'I've no reason to doubt that you will keep your word.' He opened his arms and willed her to believe in him. 'But allow me to say good morning to you properly. Please.'

This time, she walked into them. He bent and claimed her lips. Her mouth opened and he instantly deepened the kiss, trying to explain with his touch about his fears when he'd discovered her gone. Their tongues met and warred. The desperation in her kiss surprised him. He picked her up and carried her to the bed.

'This is the proper place to say good morning after such a kiss.'

Her response was to reach up and curl her arm about his neck, hold his face close to hers. 'We have this for such a short time,' she whispered against his mouth. 'How can I resist?'

His heart clenched. How many times had he said that sort of thing to women? The irony of the situation made his mouth taste bitter. But she was in his arms, and right now he would settle for that.

He placed kisses across her jawline and down her neck. 'Let me see you in the morning light. Let me enjoy your body.'

Her teeth worried at her bottom lip. 'I'm not sure you will like what you see. It might be better if we wait for darkness and keep the mystery.'

He stared at her, taking in her hair, the shape of her face and her curves...particularly her curves. How could anyone have made this woman think she was less than she was? He wanted to punish Toka for making Cyn feel that way, but he knew the problem ran far deeper than his poisonous ex-sister-in-law. People in Cyn's family had made her like this, and he despised them for it.

He leant forward and grazed her temple with his lips. 'Why don't you allow me to be the judge? Everything I have seen so far I have liked.'

Shadows remained in her eyes. 'Have you…?'

He took her hand and placed it against the bulge in his trousers. 'See. You excite me. You—not some mystery woman in my mind whose face I never see and whose body I can never touch.'

'I… I… That is, my husband and I… It was always dark when we were together.'

'What you did with your husband has no bearing on what you do with me.' He dropped a kiss on her mouth. 'That is in the past. This is now.'

Her tongue moistened her lips. 'I was always taught that darkness is necessary. Leofwine insisted on it.'

'I'm not your husband. I'm your lover.' His breath caught in his throat. If she denied it, his heart would shatter into a thousand pieces.

'Lovers…' she murmured. 'I suppose we are.'

'You need to feel and see how true lovers can behave. In this moment with me, Cyn. Nowhere else.'

She glanced at him from under a forest of lashes. 'I've no other plans for the morning.'

Kal's body instantly hardened beyond the point of aching. He doubted he'd ever want a woman as much as he did her. 'Then allow me.'

He quickly divested her of her garments, taking care to fold each one up before he turned back to where she lay on the bed. She attempted to hide her breasts and the nest of curls with her hands, but he firmly grasped her wrists in his left hand and held them above her head. He allowed his gaze to roam over her body, appreciating the way her full breasts spilled out and the gentle curve of her stomach. The network of scars which criss-crossed her abdomen begged to be tasted.

'There is nothing to be ashamed of. You are the most beautiful woman I've seen—even more so in the morning light.' He ran a finger down her flank.

A rose tint infused her skin. 'Truly? When I was a bride, I thought I was much prettier. My figure was better. My skin bears the scars from my pregnancy.'

'Fishing for compliments? Stop telling me what should excite me. I know my own mind. Like my battle scars, your scars show your courage.'

'Do you think that…really?'

'Let me demonstrate.'

He nipped her shoulder blade before making a trail of kisses down to the creaminess of her breasts. He cupped them and allowed their fullness to spill out of his hands. Then he teased each dawn-kissed nipple in turn until her eyes became dilated with pleasure. Slowly moving his mouth down her torso, pausing to kiss each silver scar which adorned her skin, he settled himself between her thighs.

'I plan to feast on you—if you have no objection.'

He waited, blowing a steady stream of air against her curls. Her mound bucked upwards and her nipples became hard points.

'I will take the risk…with you,' she said, between small pants.

'Excellent choice, my lady.'

* * *

He lowered his mouth and proceeded to part her curls with his tongue as he sought the sweetness of her inner core. His fingers caressed her full breasts.

Cynehild stiffened when his tongue lapped at her folds before going deep within her and then back to her hidden nub. No one had touched her that intimately before, but she felt no shame with Kal. The inexorable motion of his tongue combined with the pressure of his hands on her breasts caused her body to arch upwards again, seeking relief.

'Please!' she cried.

Her urgent plea made him withdraw. A smile crossed his face. 'I take it you approve of the way I am breaking my fast and will understand why remaining in bed with me in the mornings is something to be sought rather than avoided?'

She struggled to make coherent sense of his words while her whole being thrummed. 'You're hungry?'

'For something other than food.' His tongue traced a circle around her belly button. 'Something much more pleasurable…unless you require sustenance?'

She tugged at his shoulders. 'I'm hungry as well.'

He levered himself upwards so that his mouth was level with hers. 'Thankfully I know of a way we can both be satisfied.'

She opened her legs wide and welcomed the entire length of him. Then they began to move as one, and what she had thought she'd known about making love proved to be totally inadequate as wave after wave of intense pleasure coursed through her.

She cried out in joy and his shouts intermingled with hers. And as she slowly came back down to earth she knew that when she left she'd be leaving a large part of her heart behind. She'd fallen in love with Kal. He was her soul friend—not her mate but her friend. She could confide in him in a way she had never done with Leofwine.

The thought scared her. She barely knew him. With her late husband, the realisation had come quietly, after they'd shared many things. She'd known his faults and his virtues, but she'd never felt the compulsion to be with him. With Kal, she only thought she knew him, but she felt far more comfortable with him than she had done with anyone in a long time.

Kal kissed her shoulder, dismissing all coherent thought from her mind.

'You wear your serious face again. Does something concern you? For today, my men can get along without me.'

'My thoughts are unimportant. It seems strange for me to stay this long in bed.' She reached for her discarded clothes. 'I like to keep my hands busy.'

'Allow me to teach you to play *tafl* properly, then.' His eyes twinkled. 'You would be an excellent player, I know.'

He'd told her before that he thought she'd be good at it.

Her heart warmed. 'It will give us something to do as I am determined that you shall rest.'

He laughed. 'It will also give us a chance to think about what needs to be done about my attacker and develop a scheme to unveil him.'

'We can't do anything until my brother-in-law arrives.'

'That remains to be seen.' He inclined his head. 'But, whatever happens, I'm determined to keep you safe. I will not allow my enemy to harm you.'

Chapter Fifteen

'We need to find a way to force your enemy out into the open.'

Kal paused in setting out the blue and white glass counters for the next game in their *tafl* match. Thus far today, he'd won three and she had won two.

Given that she'd claimed not to be very good when they'd first started playing two days ago, he was more than impressed. Her grasp of strategy was excellent and her capacity for lateral thinking superb. In every way she was a worthy opponent.

And yet he knew with each passing day the likelihood of her leaving increased exponentially. Her brother-in-law would appear with his men and she would go. And he'd let her go because then she would be safe from his elusive enemy.

He was fairly positive Alff had something to do with it, but he lacked proof. Banishing him for no reason could result in a rebellion in his war band—something he refused to risk, and he suspected his enemy knew it as well.

'There is no "we" about it, Cyn. I will find a way, but you must be kept safe.' He softened his words with a smile. 'For your son's sake. He has already lost one parent. Someone must watch over him and keep your father in check where your youngest sister is concerned. She must be allowed to choose her own life partner.'

He waited to see if Cyn was ready to yield—for her son's sake if not her own.

She bent her head and spent a long time examining the *tafl* board. 'I thank you for your concern for Wulfgar, but whatever happens to me he will be well looked after. I would not have come here if I had not planned ahead for all eventualities. Without a plan, we are doomed to fail.'

Kal moved his first piece. His chance of winning her seemed more remote than ever. On the one hand he wanted the new contingent of men to arrive, as they would help to ensure her safety, but on the other hand he knew once they did he would lose all chance of winning her heart.

'This is not your fight.'

'It has become my fight,' she said, expertly countering his attack.

He tried to control the sudden lurching of his heart. 'Why?' he asked, watching her intently.

She rolled a counter between her fingers. He scarcely dared to hope that she might confess she had feelings for him. But with the slightest indication that she wanted more, he'd tell her about his own growing feelings for her and ask her to marry him.

It amazed him that on the battlefield he led men, never doubting victory would be his, but here, on a very different sort of battlefield, he was fearful of defeat.

'When we came here you promised me we would stand shoulder to shoulder. That means more to me than you might realise. You treated me like an equal.' She placed her counter down. 'Once Moir arrives, we will lose our opportunity. I will be taken off the board and your enemy—your opponent—will once again have the chance to strike you down.'

'Except I know about the danger now.' He ran his hands through his hair. Cyn had to see that he wanted to protect her. Without her, his life wouldn't be worth living. He needed her here with him, but he also had to know that she was safe. 'Stop worrying. I'm pretty good at looking after myself.'

He made a move on the board.

Cynehild immediately countered it.

'You always knew about the danger. Every *jaarl* must. But your enemy knows you and used your habits against you once before. I want to help, Kal. Before it is too late. Before I have no excuse to stay. Moir and Brother Palni will insist I lay the sword and go.'

'And our betrothal?'

'We both know why we contracted it. Look, I've a son waiting for me. I promise if you allow me to help I won't take silly risks.'

'I won't use you as bait for a trap. I could not look your son in the eye if I did.'

'I realise that. Alff has refused to fight you openly, so we need to retrace your steps on that day and see if there are any clues. What would be the most direct route to Hangra Hill from here?'

He stared at her in astonishment. 'You've hit on a point that I've failed to consider. Why was I up on Hangra Hill in the first place? Alff said I stormed off to go hunting with a crossbow, but I never go that way.'

'Do you think you staggered there after being hit, or had you gone there for some other purpose?'

'It is an area where several estates come together. Hangra Hill is owned by no one. There is a move to start holding a *thynge* there—a local assembly—so all our differences can be settled amicably.'

'Your attacker could be another *jaarl* or one of his supporters, then.'

Kal concentrated. The muffled voice rose up in his mind again—*tyrant*. It was personal. He should know the voice.

'It's someone from here. I'm certain of it.'

'If we retrace your footsteps and discover nothing new, we could consider setting a trap.'

'Perhaps more rumours of the golden hoard? Or would we then just catch Haddr looking for it again?'

'You don't think Haddr could be behind it?'

Kal concentrated on the board. 'Why would he be? He commands no respect in the *felag*. He owes me a life debt for Basceng. Besides, if he is the culprit, why did he not attack me when we were at the charcoal burner's cottage? Someone else must be involved, but I need proof. I don't want to make another mistake.'

'I want the culprit found before I leave,' said Cynehild.

She put her hand over his and he tightened his fingers about it. He wanted to swoop and carry her off somewhere to keep her safe, but if he did that he would be denying the bravery which made him love Cyn.

His breath caught in his throat. He loved her. But how could he ask her to stay? Particularly when she'd made it so clear that she would leave once her brother-in-law and his men arrived and return to her old life—a life which included not only her son but an entire community…

* * *

Cynehild carefully measured out the ground, keeping her head down, eyes focused, walking in tandem with Kal. In a few weeks' time the new ferns would have unfurled and the grass would have grown long, but for now she could follow the trail of broken dead ferns and the occasional set of footprints in the thick mud at the side of the barely visible path.

Kal had pointed out several which he knew were his from the way his left heel was worn. But there was a set of footprints which led back towards the hall which were not his.

It made the most sense that Kal had initially gone this way if he had headed directly towards Hangra Hill on that fateful day.

'It shows that we are on the right track,' she said, when he knelt beside another set of footprints.

'But there is no way of telling how old these are, and the rain will have washed most of the other prints away. What are you hoping to find?'

She glanced up at the clear blue sky. 'I've little idea,' she admitted. 'I keep going back to the fabled hoard. Perhaps your enemy thought the rumours were true and you were going on your own to get it?'

She couldn't explain her unsettled feelings for him, and how she'd started hoping that Brother Palni would take even longer to come. Once he and Moir arrived, they would force her to leave and she didn't have an excuse to stay. Begging Kal to make their betrothal real, so she and Wulfgar could live here with him as a family, was not part of their deal.

Her men trailed along behind them, keeping a respectful distance. Both had refused to stay in the compound when they'd discovered what she intended. They had argued with her that she ought to stay behind, but she'd refused. In the end, with Kal on her side, they'd agreed— on the condition that they would actually be able to do their appointed task of guarding her.

'It seems odd that you went so far away from the hall unarmed…particularly if you were meeting someone else,' she mused.

'I have a vague memory of hunting. I wanted to spend time on my own after quarrelling with Alff. I needed to think because it was the anniversary of my wife's death.'

'You must have been thinking about her when you were hit.'

He gave a half-smile. 'I must have been. I'd decided that nothing I could do would bring her or our son back. That I needed to start living again and find a new wife.'

He needed a wife.

Cynehild carefully turned her face away.

That need had not vanished. After she'd left he would have to marry. Maybe he would fall in love with some other woman and make her his bride, but she knew she didn't want that. She wanted him to love her and only her. Yet she couldn't find the words to tell him that.

She pushed the thought to the back of her mind.

Something glistened in the sunlight a little way down the cliff. 'There is some metal down there.'

She started to go after it, but Kal held her back. 'Let one of your men get it. No need for you to take the risk.'

'But—'

He put a finger on her lips. 'You were the one to tell me I needed to be able to accept help. Now I'm asking you to do the same thing. You don't need to keep proving your courage to me, Cynehild. You've proved it time and time again.'

'Have I?'

'Allow your men to help. Neither of them is wearing a skirt, to start with.'

She nodded and directed her men to retrieve the object. They quickly went down the bank, which was far steeper than she'd considered, and she was pleased she'd delegated the responsibility.

'I hope it's worth it,' she said.

'Whatever it is, it shouldn't be there.'

Her men brought up a small eating knife and handed it to Cynehild.

'Is it your missing knife?' she asked.

Kal frowned, turning the knife over in his hands several times. 'It is one I haven't seen for a long time—not since Ribe,' he said finally, securing the knife into his belt. 'And I'm certain it was not here when I walked up to Hangra Hill.'

'And you know it?'

'I know who it used to belong to, and that person is dead.'

'Your wife?'

'No, her ex-brother-in-law. Toka's first husband. I can remember hearing that he had collapsed and died about the time I left with the Great Army. He had a son from his first marriage.'

'How old would he be now?'

'More than twenty, I believe.' Kal put his hands on his thighs and gulped several quick breaths of air.

Cynehild pressed her fingers together. Once again Kal had pushed himself too far, and he would continue to do so if she wasn't here to stop him. She wanted to be there at his side, ensuring that he could cope. Once Brother Palni returned she would find a way to delay leaving until she was certain Kal had improved.

'Proof, if you needed it, that you were attacked by someone from your household rather than by a villager. Whoever it was hurried back towards the hall. We will go back there now.'

'Give me a little time,' Kal said.

His hand closed about the knife. The simple act of holding it had the memories of that day flooding back. He'd been hunting. Alone. He had not taken his favourite sword, but he had taken a crossbow. There had been a stag whose life he'd spared because he'd shed his antlers. And then blackness.

'Did you see any antlers when you found me?'

'Antlers?' Cynehild shook her head. 'Blood on the ground, but no antlers. We can go back and check if you like.'

'I didn't kill a stag because he dropped his antlers. I was going towards them to pick them up when someone hit me from behind. They accused me of being a tyrant and the voice echoes in my mind.'

'Having seen your hall, and the people there, I don't think you're a tyrant. I do think someone wants you dead, and now you've survived they want you to be off balance and seek to punish the people of this land, not look towards the obvious culprit amongst your own men. They want you to become a tyrant in truth, and provoke a rebellion against you. They wanted to strip everything from you.'

'Everything points towards Alff, except he was ill. He has pointedly told me that he did not accompany me and blames himself because I stormed off without my usual escort. You have seen his yellowish colour; it's clear he's been genuinely unwell.'

'Did he say what you had quarrelled about?'

'He didn't—but he became a changed man when he married Toka.'

Cynehild tapped a finger against her mouth. 'He has not risen today. Toka complained about it when I went into the main hall to see if I could help with the weaving. She refused my offer, saying I wouldn't understand the pattern.'

'Toka likes to stir up trouble.'

'Could she inherit the hall? If you died and then Alff?'

'She doesn't have a child.'

Kal concentrated. That stepson of hers would be a warrior now…

'It's unlike my cousin to be abed this long,' he said.

'Whoever your enemy is, they may wait until I leave to try again.'

He raised her hand to his lips. 'Then stay, Cyn. Stay for ever. Become a peace-weaver in truth.'

She withdrew her hand. 'We agreed—until my brother-in-law arrives. My son—'

'I would like to meet Wulfgar. Get to know him.'

'Lord Icebeard! Icebeard!'

Haddr's shouts echoed on the wind. Kal stiffened, but then dismissed the notion. Haddr was loyal to him. He'd been part of the *felag* since its inception—one of the first to swear fealty. He might have lusted after treasure, but he lacked the ambition to lead.

'Up here. Is there something wrong?'

Haddr climbed up the slope. 'Your cousin, my lord. He is dying—coughing up blood. He calls for you.'

Kal froze. 'Alff's dying?'

'Lady Toka sent me to fetch you.' Haddr struggled to catch his breath. 'I've been running around like a mad person ever since. I was about to go back to the cottage when I spotted Lady Cynehild's cloak.'

All colour had drained from Cynehild's face. 'Is there no hope?'

'He complained of feeling most unwell yesterday evening. Lady Toka discovered him this morning and she suspects poison. People are saying how Lady Cynehild kept going to the infirmary and mixing up potions.'

Cyn took a step backwards. 'I went to see my men.'

Haddr gave a shrug. 'You know how rumours get started. And there are more rumours of an army advancing from the East.'

It had to be Brother Palni with Moir's men.

Kal pressed his lips together. Haddr appeared edgy, as he always did before a battle. Someone wanted Cyn to take the blame for Alff's illness. He had to put her somewhere he could keep her safe.

'Why leave it so late to raise the alarm?' Cynehild asked. 'If he was so unwell last night, it strikes me as odd that Toka should not have spoken to us before now, rather than waiting until after we'd left the hall.'

Haddr fingered his sword while his eyes darted everywhere. 'All I know is that my lord needs to know what is happening.'

'I see.' Cynehild's jaw jutted forward. 'It seems very convenient, that's all. I'll return with you, Kal, and examine the patient. I know a thing or three about herbs. And Alff was ill before I ever arrived at the hall.'

'I hadn't considered that!' Haddr said, his mouth dropping open.

'These riders who have been sighted—they will go to the hall,' Cynehild continued.

Kal disliked his sense of foreboding. His enemy had made a move, but he needed to get Cyn to safety before she was put in mortal danger. If her family thought he'd done that to her he would never stand a chance of properly wooing her.

'That won't be necessary.'

'Not necessary? Why?'

'You need to go and wait for your brother-in-law and the monk,' Kal said in a low voice, and willed her to understand what he was saying—what he was asking her to do and why. 'Someone is trying to implicate you, Cyn, in whatever illness Alff has. Anger can quickly build. Keep away for now and allow me to deal with this alone.'

Annoyance flashed through Cynehild. Kal was behaving precisely as every other man in her life had, treating her as though she had no mind of her own. He wanted her to leave because he did not think she could contribute any more.

'It has become my fight,' she said. 'I care about what happens to you, Kal.'

His face became carved from stone and his brow lowered. In that instant she realised why he had such a fearsome reputation.

'Cynehild. Obey me.'

'Shoulder to shoulder,' she whispered. 'You promised.'

'That was then. This is now. Promises can be altered. You need to keep your mind on your responsibilities and on who waits for you back in Baelle Heale.'

Her duty to Wulfgar. Cynehild clenched her fists. Why was Kal being so obtuse? Other than the rumours that were flying around about Alff being poisoned, nothing had altered.

'I never, *ever* forget my duty to my son.'

'Icebeard, we need to go…before your cousin dies.'

Kal lowered his voice to the merest whisper. 'I once told you I'd never allow you to become a counter in this game I'm playing with my enemy. Stay safe.'

Cynehild shook her head, trying to lose the buzzing noise. Kal had decided his enemy had made a move against Alff. He was trying to keep her safe, but he was going about it in precisely the wrong way. He needed her ears and eyes.

'Let me help you.'

'Brother Palni gave orders that you were to remain at the cottage in the woods, so he and your brother-in-law will go there first. Meet them there and then bring them and the men to me. We may have need of them.'

He started off down the slope with Haddr following in his wake. Cynehild watched him go. Arguing with him would be futile. He'd made up his mind—he was going after his enemy alone. The king piece in *tafl* was finally making his move. Except this wasn't a game between two, and she still had a part she intended to play. If herbs were involved, there was one person who would know the likely poisoner.

'My lady, do you know the way to the hut?' her men asked.

'We're not going back there. We are going to see Luba. She has questions to answer.'

Chapter Sixteen

Kal quickened his footsteps, leading Haddr away from Cyn. He willed her for once to do as he'd requested and to wait at the hut, either for him or for her brother-in-law. She'd be safe there. When he had finished, he would go and confess his feelings for her.

However, his chest ached at Cyn's unspoken accusation that he'd betrayed her by excluding her from his plan. He couldn't explain and risk her not going to the relative safety of the hut, or Haddr understanding what he intended to do.

He glanced at the young warrior. Despite remaining injured, Kal reckoned he could defeat him in a fight. But he needed to ensure Haddr did not realise that he'd worked out the younger man's part in the attack.

'Are you coming? There is no time to lose.'

Haddr balanced on the balls of his feet, as he'd done when they'd been waiting for the Saxons to attack, and as he'd done as a young boy, when he'd waited for Toka to finish speaking with her sister.

Kal put a hand against a tree trunk and feigned weakness. 'I don't want to go too fast. My head still pains me.'

'That blow to the back of your head was really strong.'

'Not strong enough to kill me. You always did lack a certain strength in your arms, Haddr.'

Haddr skittered to a stop. 'Have you lost your mind, Icebeard? Everyone knows you are different now because of that woman. I have ever been a faithful member of this *felag*.'

'On your father's shade?' Kal held out the knife Cyn had discovered. 'I believe this once belonged to him?'

Haddr eyed it as if he was eyeing a writhing snake and Kal knew his hunch was correct. Haddr was Toka's stepson—the one who had disappeared.

'Where did you find that?'

'Did Luba tell you where the treasure was hidden after you married her daughter? Is that why you pushed for the marriage?' Kal asked, rather than answering Haddr's question.

Haddr might have hit him on the head, but he did not have the wit to plan something like this. That left two people who could have done so—either Toka or Luba.

Haddr straightened. 'What sort of stories has that Mercian woman been telling you?'

'Toka never seems to have much time for you. Not now and certainly not when you were a boy.' Kal concentrated, remembering what Ranka had once said. 'You were another woman's child and she resented caring for you. She hadn't realised that your father had had a child or she'd never have married him.'

'You lie. She did care about me. She reminded me of that when she arrived here. She promised me riches and power after you and Alff—' Haddr stopped, belatedly realising he'd said too much.

'And your persistent quest for Leofwine's treasure? Was that Toka's doing?'

'It is why I had to marry my ugly sow of a wife. Toka confided that there were riches for the right man, if I could get my wife to show me where they were. Only she and her mother claimed not to know.'

Kal set his jaw. Cyn had gone to the charcoal burner's hut, not to Luba's cottage. She was safe. But he had to eliminate Haddr from the game before Toka tried to use him yet again.

'Shall we battle here and now, or are you looking to hit me over the head from behind again?'

Haddr's face went dark red. 'You were supposed to die. Toka—'

'It wasn't my time—and thank you for confirming what I already thought. But Toka lied to you. She was never going to share anything with you.'

Haddr drew his sword. 'I will fight you. Here. Now. If you are not a coward.'

'Good.' Kal watched the younger man intently.

'You are not as good as they say.' Haddr rushed towards him, his sword raised.

Kal pivoted and allowed him to go past without engaging him. 'We haven't sorted terms yet.'

'No terms. You and I to the death.'

Haddr charged again. This time Kal was ready and shoulder-charged Haddr's outstretched arm. The momentum sent his sword spinning in the air.

Haddr stood completely still.

'You never did like to pay attention in training, did you? You should have agreed to terms when you had the chance.' Kal leant down and picked up the sword. 'Shall we fight properly now?'

'Icebeard… That is to say…'

'I never sought your death. I hoped you'd be content with the honours I bestowed on you. You had a wife, lands and a place in my *felag*, but that clearly wasn't enough.'

Haddr rushed at him again, going low and seeking to knock him off balance, but he mistimed his run and managed to connect with his own sword, which went into his stomach. He fell, bleeding from his mouth.

'Look after my child,' he murmured with his last breath.

Kal bent down and closed the man's eyes. 'Aye. I will ensure that happens.'

He shouldered the body and headed back towards the hall.

One down. The most dangerous ones still to go.

Cynehild concentrated on the smoke rising from Luba's cottage and tried to ignore the immense ache in her chest. Before meeting Kal, she'd worried that her heart had been buried with Leofwine, but now she knew it remained a living and beating thing. While a part of her would always love Leofwine for giving her Wulfgar, her whole heart loved Kal.

She wished she'd been brave enough to tell him that before she'd left him in the woods. What if she never had a chance to tell him? What if she was wrong about who was behind this and he was walking into a trap?

'My lady.'

Luba hurried out before Cynehild reached the door. Her shawl flapped in the breeze and covered half her face.

'I didn't expect you here. Not at all, since you are at

the hall. All is well because Lord Icebeard has returned. I heard tell about the fine feast to celebrate your betrothal. I would have come, but—'

'Alff has died.' Cynehild knew she was stretching the truth slightly, but she wanted to see Luba's reaction.

Luba's face paled to the colour of fine linen which had been left out in the sun far too long. 'Alff has died? Who told you? When did that happen?'

'Haddr. He came searching for us. He was quite upset about the development.'

Luba's face became stern. 'If anyone knows, it would be Haddr. He'd hear about it from that witch first.'

'What do you mean?'

'Alff wasn't supposed to die.' Luba straightened up and tucked the shawl tighter about her body. 'But I vow I didn't have anything to do with it.'

The sweat started to pool in the back of Cynehild's neck.

Alff had been poisoned.

Haddr was at the centre of everything.

Excuses kept being found for him. Kal must have had another reason for marrying him off besides wanting to keep the villagers sweet. If he was married, what couldn't he do?

Cynehild peered around Luba. As she had recalled, a pair of antlers sat in the corner. Not proof of anything, but Luba seemed jumpy and out of sorts.

'No one said you did.'

'Why are you here, my lady? Shouldn't you be with the Jaarl, seeing to his head wound, rather than imparting gossip to me?'

'Is there something wrong with your face, Luba? Why are you hiding it?'

Luba pushed the shawl further over her face. 'You ought to go now, Lady Cynehild. You've outstayed your welcome.'

'Show me your face first, Luba.'

Luba slowly and defiantly lowered her shawl. A purple bruise shone on her cheekbone.

'Who gave it to you? Your new son-in-law?'

'None of your business, Lady Cynehild. Leave everything to take its course. You should never have returned.'

'What happened to you wanting me to stay and marry Kal?'

'That was before.' Luba stuck out her chin. 'Before I knew the truth. About what he'd done and why he'd done it. What he'd taken and what he wanted from us.'

What *he'd* done. What Haddr had done. Haddr must have been the one to hit Kal, and somehow Luba had discovered something Haddr had taken. The antlers? Cynehild frowned. Not those—Luba could not know about them. It had to be the crossbow.

'Where did you find the crossbow, Luba? In the grain store, perhaps? Where had Haddr hidden it? I presume you found it after Kal and I went to the hall?'

Luba resembled a trout, opening and closing her mouth rapidly, with no sound emerging. 'How do you know I found a crossbow?'

'It wasn't hard to work it out, Luba.'

'I'd wondered why my daughter had recently become so insistent about going into the barn without me.' Luba tucked her head into her neck. 'Since she became pregnant, she's refused to go in there because she's frightened of the rats. Rats! I ask you. I followed her and confronted her as she was trying to move it. Haddr told her that he'd found it when he'd chased some outlaws away, but he was worried that someone would jump to the wrong conclusion.'

'Kal was hunting with a crossbow when he was hit. He had just picked up two magnificent antlers. I expect they are the ones in that corner...being stored until Haddr needs them.'

'I've no idea where he found them.'

'Does your daughter know?'

'Keep my daughter out of this—I beg you, my lady. She is pregnant. She carries his child. She didn't mean to be bad. She just couldn't keep her mouth shut about the gold that your Leofwine had buried in the church.'

Didn't mean to be bad. A cold shiver went down her back. Luba was speaking about something else entirely now.

'What has Haddr been doing, Luba?'

Luba wet her lips. 'It wasn't supposed to be like this, you see... I thought he would be good for the family. I agree with Jaarl Icebeard—they are here to stay now. We all have to get on together.'

'Haddr is Toka's stepson, isn't he?' Cynehild asked with sudden insight. That was why Kal had recognised the knife. And Kal knew. That was why he'd sent her away.

The woman blinked rapidly. 'Yes, he is.'

Cynehild put a hand to her face. Kal had gone with Haddr. Her lover was in extreme danger.

'I'm sorry, Luba, but you are going to have to come with me.'

'With you where?'

'To the hall.'

When Kal arrived back at the hall, his entire body ached from carrying Haddr's corpse. Once he was in the yard, he allowed the body to slide from his shoulder.

The scene in front of him swam and then righted itself. He couldn't be seeing double, but there were far too many retainers and horses in the yard. Toka stood there, pouring ale into horns, greeting them as if nothing was amiss. Alff was there as well—pale, but standing upright.

His heart sank when he spotted a figure in monk's robes.

'Icebeard, you are here at last. Where is Lady Cynehild?' Brother Palni asked. 'And who is that? Who have you murdered?'

'Toka!' Kal called, ignoring the monk. 'Your stepson attacked me, but sadly he lost the battle.'

Toka allowed the ale to flow onto the ground. 'Attacked you? Impossible. You are having delusions again.'

'We have company, Icebeard,' Alff said, hooking his fingers into his belt. 'I've explained about your black moods, sudden rages and loss of memory—and my fears for this woman of yours.'

'Answer the question, Deniscan,' said the monk. 'What have you done to Lady Cynehild?'

'Cyn is at the hut with her men. I sent her there for safety while I dealt with Haddr.'

'My sister isn't there.' A slender woman stepped forward and fitted an arrow to a bow. 'Where is she? What have you done with her? Your cousin says that you left earlier with her, and that he sent a man to inform you of our arrival. I presume the body you have just deposited is that man?'

Kal's mouth went dry. Cyn had to be there. He had told her to go there. She had to be safe. 'Send someone to fetch her. Then you will see.'

'You'd better pray that Lady Cynehild and her men are found alive,' Brother Palni said.

'Isn't it funny?' Toka remarked with a little smile playing on her lips. 'Sometimes things seem blackest before everything turns out well. I would recommend seizing Icebeard before he is able to harm anyone else.'

Kal raised Haddr's sword. 'Anyone who touches me before Lady Cynehild arrives will pay a heavy price.'

'You must slow down, my lady. I can't travel that fast.' Luba put her hands on her thighs and started panting. 'I can't go another step. I won't go.'

'Kal is in danger from your son-in-law.' Cynehild gestured to her men. 'Help her along, please.'

'I will do it, my lady. Just allow me to catch my breath.' The old woman evaded the men's hands. 'I will put things right.'

'Tell me the whole truth about the treasure. Why did Haddr think marrying your daughter might lead him to it?'

Luba shook her head. 'You've been gone a long time. We thought you were never coming back. That's when my husband decided to—'

She stopped, but Cynehild knew what she'd been going to say. 'Your husband dug up the gold, didn't he? He watched Leofwine bury it.'

'We had to survive somehow.' Luba moved to sit down. 'Lord Leofwine lost all rights to it when he left. Bad men were about. My husband became worried that we would need to hire warriors to protect these lands. He dug it up in the middle of the night and reburied it somewhere. Except he failed to tell me or my daughter where he'd hidden it before he died. I told that to Haddr and he gave me a beating. That is how I received this here bruising.'

Cynehild closed her eyes. Brother Palni had been right after all. It would not have mattered where she'd laid that sword. All her dreams about Wulfgar getting proper training had been for nothing. Although at least she would be able to tell him that his father had tried, and that was something. She would find another way to ensure Wulfgar was properly trained.

'Then it is truly lost.'

'I told you—you shouldn't have returned.'

'We will discuss this later.' Cynehild firmly grabbed the woman's arm and propelled her forward until they reached the yard at the hall. 'Saving Kal's life is far more important than debating who has a right to that gold or where your late husband might have hidden it.'

A tableau was laid out in front of her.

Kal standing with a sword lifted in the air, Haddr dead on the ground, Toka smirking and Cynehild's sisters, Elene and Ansithe, with avenging angel expressions on their faces.

Ansithe, ever the mild one, had an arrow fitted to a bow and appeared to be aiming it at Kal. Moir stood next to her. Elene had her arm about Wulfgar. Her heart skipped a beat at the sight of her sturdy son. Wulfgar must have grown two inches in the time they had been apart.

Cynehild clenched her fists. Brother Palni had obviously decided that she needed to be reminded of where her duty lay and had gone to fetch both her sisters and Wulfgar too. But her family had no right to interfere. Clearly someone needed to take charge before more people were hurt.

'Kal! I have Luba here. She has confessed. Toka and her stepson were behind it all.'

'I know.' Kal remained where he was standing. 'I am just having trouble convincing other people of it. They appear to consider that you are either dead or at the very least in mortal danger.'

'Put down your weapon, Ansithe,' she told her sister. 'No one is in any danger from Kal. It is totally unnecessary.'

Ansithe lowered her bow and watched her sister with curious eyes. 'That is not what Brother Palni said when he finally arrived. Seriously...that man could get lost in a farmyard.'

Brother Palni muttered that he had only become slightly lost, and had found his way to Baelle Heale first.

'You were not where you were supposed to be,' Ansithe said, glaring at Brother Palni. 'I feared the worst. My sister's life is worth more than anything.'

'No, it was I who was busy saving lives.' Cynehild pointed towards where Toka and Alff stood. 'If you wish to do something useful, secure them. My old maid is willing to testify against them and their plot to murder Kal, Jaarl Icebeard.'

In a calm, clear voice Cynehild explained about why they had left the hut to come to the hall. She skated over her intimate liaison with Kal, but left her sisters in no doubt of her debt to him.

When she reached the end of her narrative, Alff began to bleat that it had had nothing to do with him and that it had been all Toka's idea, while Toka blamed Haddr for everything. At Ansithe's signal, her men surrounded them and led them away.

'Brother Palni told you to remain at the hut, Cynehild,' Ansithe said.

Cynehild glanced between the man she loved and her

family. She needed to get these words right, because she knew she would not have a second chance. 'Do I have to do everything Brother Palni says? Or indeed what Kal says? I had to return. I had to fight.'

'Why? For your son's inheritance? We've already established it is long gone,' Kal said. 'You should have stayed safe, Cyn.'

'I came because I am never wrong in matters of my heart. I have made other mistakes, that is true, but the one thing I did right on this journey was to fall in love with you. And I needed to tell you that before I left. I wanted to see if we could reach another arrangement—one not based on peace-weaving but mutual respect.'

'Loving me is an impossibility, Cynehild. Everyone knows what I am like.'

His eyes begged her to say otherwise.

'Says who? Haddr, who hit you over your head, left you for dead and tried to steal your lands? Or maybe it was that witch who drove your first wife to despair and then married your cousin? Or your weak-willed cousin, who had to have known what was going on but chose to turn a blind eye to it? Their opinion is not worth the spit it takes to voice it. I love you. I consider you to be a good man and I don't care who knows it. I will be on your side and at your side.'

She waited. Both he and her sisters had to understand which side she was on. She did not want war in the family, but she would be staying with her warlord if he would have her.

She hadn't known until she spoke the words what a great part of her heart he occupied. Her heart still had space for her family, for her late husband and most especially for their son, but it had expanded because of this man who had done so many things for others. Right now he had to believe in himself and his ability to restore peace and prosperity to these lands. Otherwise his cousin and that witch had won and they were all lost.

'Your brother-in-law and your sisters want you to go with them. It is why they brought your son with them— so you can see your duty.'

'I will stay here—with you. I accept your offer of marriage.'

A distinct twinkle appeared in Kal's eyes. 'When did I offer that?'

'Earlier, when you tried to get me to go. Except you forgot to offer to train my son. That is my one condition—Wulfgar must remain with us.'

Kal slowly lowered his sword and Cynehild dared breathe again.

'Then I had best ensure we both survive, as I love you with my whole heart. And it would be a great honour to be entrusted with the training of your son.'

She gave him an uncertain smile back. For the first time since Moir and her sisters had arrived she felt they would manage to avoid bloodshed.

'It would indeed be best,' she said.

Kal walked over to where Wulfgar stood and knelt beside him. 'Are you Wulfgar, son of Leofwine and Cynehild?'

Wulfgar's eyes dwarfed his face. He gave an almost imperceptible nod as he shrank back into her sister Elene's skirts.

'Will you allow me to marry your mother? Will you allow me to serve as your protector and guardian? Will you allow me to train you to become a great warrior?'

'For Mercia?' Wulfgar asked.

'For whichever warlord you choose to serve.'

Wulfgar scrunched up his face. 'They say you are a great and terrible warrior.'

'Far be it from me to deny it... Except I'm trying to become a better man. Your mother is helping me with that. I know I need her with me to achieve it, though.'

'Do you really love my mother? With your whole heart?'

Cynehild's breath caught. 'You mustn't ask him that, Wulfgar. It is impolite.'

Kal rose and put a hand on Wulfgar's shoulder. 'I am happy to answer. Your mother makes my world a better place. She sees good in me and makes me want to show that good to the world. We are like the ply in the thread which she spins. Separately we can twist and break, but equally and together we create something which is far stronger. I love her more with every breath I take. I will love her until the day I die.'

Cynehild's heart swelled. Kal wanted an equal marriage in which they shared their life instead of having separate spheres.

Wulfgar looked very solemn. 'Then you may marry her.'

Kal held out his hand to her. 'Will you, Cynehild, marry me? Will you allow me to become your protector and your son's?'

She went over to him. 'With all my heart.'

All around them people cheered as he dipped his head and she tasted his lips.

Epilogue

Several months later

'Mother, see what Kal has shown me!'

Wulfgar raced to where Cynehild was putting the finishing touches to a new pattern she'd been weaving. The design was neither strictly Mercian nor Danish, but something in between.

'What has he shown you this time?'

In the months since their marriage, Wulfgar and Kal had grown close and their lives had settled.

Toka and Alff had been delivered to Kal's overlord, where they had faced trial for attempting to overthrow Kal. On the morning of the trial Alff had started to vomit blood and had known he was dying. With his final breaths he had confessed that he'd known his wife wanted Kal dead as revenge for her sister's death, but had not really believed she'd go through with it.

Faced with his deathbed denunciation, Toka had broken down and the entire story had emerged—how she'd married Alff because it would give her a chance to fulfil her vow to her dying sister and then, realising very quickly that Alff would not actively assist her, enlisted her stepson, promising him that he would inherit the lands provided he found the buried treasure.

Once Kal had gone missing, Haddr had insisted that she make good on his part of the bargain. So she had taken herbs from the infirmary and started poisoning Alff in earnest. She'd shown little remorse and a great deal of anger at what she'd called 'this unjust situation'.

After Cynehild's wedding, her sisters had returned to Ansithe and Moir's estate. Elene had strongly objected to their father's marriage machinations, but Cynehild had received word from Ansithe only this morning that Elene now seemed distracted and out of sorts, as she had heard that a Wessex warrior with whom she had thought she had an understanding was due to marry an heiress.

Ansithe was worried that Elene might do something rash, and had asked Cynehild for advice. Cynehild intended to have a long talk with Kal later, about how they might help, but right now she wanted to concentrate on Wulfgar.

'Go on—tell your mother,' Kal urged, coming to stand behind Wulfgar. 'Then show her like we practised.'

At first it had been hard for Wulfgar not to have her undivided attention, but Kal had shown infinite patience with her son, teaching him how to play *tafl*, how to hold a sword and a thousand other little things. She could not ask for a better warrior to train him or a kinder stepfather to nurture him.

Wulfgar lifted his sword. 'I have learned how to parry and block. Grandfather would never show me how. But that's not the best thing.'

'What's the best thing?' Cynehild asked, catching Kal's eye.

'Kal says that I can call him Father. He wants to claim me for his own.'

Kal came to stand behind the boy. 'With your permission, obviously. Not to replace his own father, you understand.'

'You are doing it out of love,' Cynehild whispered.

'Exactly—out of love. I want to make him my son in truth.'

Cynehild gathered both of them to her. Leofwine might have sent her to find treasure and secure their son's future, but she had discovered something far more valuable than gold—a good man who held her in high esteem and filled her life with promise and light.

'You wish to make Wulfgar your own?'

'Yes—if you are willing.' Kal gave a crooked smile. 'Some day he might even find Leofwine's hidden treasure, but for now he can learn how to manage this estate.'

'I've something of my own to share with you.' She put Kal's hand on her abdomen. 'Can you feel it? The quickening?'

His smile lit up his entire face. 'You are going to have a child? Truly?'

'Yes, we are.'

Kal put his arms about her and hugged her tight. 'Then our family will grow—but this young man will be the eldest, the child of my heart, just as you are the guardian of my heart.'

* * * * *

Author Note

The ninth-century Mercians can be hard to study. Far more time and effort has gone into preserving the history from a Wessex point of view rather than from a Mercian one.

The vast majority of what we can learn about them comes from various finds by metal detectorists, and these finds, along with the work that various archaeologists are doing, offers a different perspective on the primary written record source, which was compiled under Wessex rule.

In 2015 metal detectorists failed to declare a Viking hoard, including coins, which shed new light on this period. Their theft was discovered when they attempted to sell various coins, and they were duly convicted in November 2019. Unfortunately, a number of the coins remain missing, and it is thought that they were reburied in unknown locations.

Evidence from the recovered coins shows that Alfred was not above rewriting history to suit his own purposes. Several of the coins show that there was an alliance between Alfred the Great and Ceolwulf II of Mercia. In fact, Ceolwulf lists himself as ruler of London during a period when historians going from the written record had thought Alfred controlled it, as he made the claim.

Who knows what the truth is? But it is interesting to speculate.

A best guess is that the hoard was buried in approximately 879, shortly after the Battle of Edington, in Wiltshire, and that it also contained several items of Viking origin, including a dragon's head bracelet. Even though most of the hoard was Anglo-Saxon, because of the Viking objects the original owner is suspected to be a Viking who failed to retrieve it.

As ever, I have tried to be true to the time, and any mistakes are my own.

If you are interested in this historical period can I recommend the following books?

Adams, Max (2017) *Aelfred's Britain: War and Peace in the Viking Age.* Head of Zeus

Adams, Max (2016) *In the Land of Giants: Journeys through the Dark Ages.* Head of Zeus

Ferguson, Robert (2010) *The Hammer and the Cross: A New History of the Vikings.* Penguin Books

Jesch, Judith (2005) *Women in the Viking Age.* Boydell Press

Magnusson, Magnus KBE (2008) *The Vikings.* The History Press

Oliver, Neil (2013) *Vikings: A History.* Orion Books

Parker, Philip (2015) *The Northmen's Fury: A History of the Viking World.* Vintage

Williams, Gareth and Peter Pentz (2014) *Vikings: Life and Legend.* British Museum Press

Williams, Thomas (2017) *Viking Britain: An Exploration.* William Collins